P9-DKD-608

HOLDING HER HOSTAGE

Howdy ran with the rifle in one hand and belt gun in the other. Zigzagging, he made that dark, empty *portal*. Far back in the house a gun crashed behind a door, muffled, defiant. And behind the house revolvers barked in swift intermittent bursts, like yelps of a wolf pack with its quarry at bay. Howdy slipped into the house with a gun in each hand. Daggert's voice rang out ahead.

"Jones! We've got your daughter here in the hall! I'm holding her in front of me! Don't shoot through this door or you'll hit her!"

The guns out back fell silent. The tense hush of bloody drama filled that old adobe house. An oath whispered in Howdy's throat as he went forward. Daggert—hiding behind a helpless girl as he fought.

Juniper Jones's agonized bellow was audible. "If you hurt my girl, I'll take you to hell with my bare hands, Daggert!"

Sally cried out, "Don't let them in, Dad! They're going to kill you!"

"Shut up, you little fool!" Daggert snarled. "Jones! I'm coming through the door and she'll be in front of me."

Howdy stepped into the end of that narrow hall as Daggert finished speaking. . . .

Other *Leisure* books
by T. T. Flynn:

LONG JOURNEY TO DEEP CAÑON
NIGHT OF THE COMANCHE MOON

T. T. FLYNN

RAWHIDE

LEISURE BOOKS   NEW YORK CITY

A LEISURE BOOK®

June 2002

Published by special arrangement with Golden West Literary Agency.

Published by

Dorchester Publishing Co., Inc.
276 Fifth Avenue
New York, NY 10001

If you purchased this book without a cover you should be aware that this book is stolen property. It was reported as "unsold and destroyed" to the publisher and neither the author nor the publisher has received any payment for this "stripped book."

Copyright © 1996 by Thomas B. Flynn, M.D.
"Conquistador's Gold" first appeared under the title "Hell's Half-Acre" in *Star Western* (10/33). Copyright © 1933 by Popular Publications, Inc. Copyright © renewed 1961 by Thomas Theodore Flynn, Jr. Copyright © 1996 by Thomas B. Flynn, M.D., for restored material.
"The Rawhide Kid" first appeared in *Dime Western* (1/1/35). Copyright © 1934 by Popular Publications, Inc. Copyright © renewed 1962 by Thomas Theodore Flynn, Jr. Copyright © 1996 by Thomas B. Flynn, M.D., for restored material.
"Wild Wind, Brave Wind" first appeared under the title "Boothill for Sheepers!" in *Dime Western* (12/36). Copyright © 1936 by Popular Publications, Inc. Copyright © renewed 1964 by Thomas Theodore Flynn, Jr. Copyright © 1996 by Thomas B. Flynn, M.D., for restored material.
"Devil Brand" first appeared as "Walk Soft—Shoot Quick!" in *Dime Western* (2/50). Copyright © 1950 by Popular Publications, Inc. Copyright © renewed 1978 by Thomas Theodore Flynn, Jr. Copyright © 1996 by Thomas B. Flynn, M.D., for restored material.
"The Rawhide Kid Returns" first appeared in *Dime Western* (4/36). Copyright © 1936 by Popular Publications, Inc. Copyright © renewed 1964 by Thomas Theodore Flynn, Jr. Copyright © 1996 by Thomas B. Flynn, M.D., for restored material.

All rights reserved. No part of this book may be reproduced or transmitted in any form or by any electronic or mechanical means, including photocopying, recording or by any information storage and retrieval system, without the written permission of the publisher, except where permitted by law.

ISBN 0-8439-5072-2

The name "Leisure Books" and the stylized "L" with design are trademarks of Dorchester Publishing Co., Inc.

Printed in the United States of America.

Visit us on the web at www.dorchesterpub.com.

Contents

T. T. Flynn was already well known as a result of numerous detective, crime, railroad, and adventure stories he had written when *Dime Western* was launched by Popular Publications, Inc. Flynn was invited to write what would be his first Western story for that premier issue. *Dime Western* proved such an immediate success that Popular Publications followed it with another new Western magazine. "Conquistador's Gold" was written for the premier issue of what was called *Star Western*. In addition to Flynn, Rogers Terrill, editor of *Star Western*, commissioned stories by Walt Coburn and Eugene Cunningham, the "star" authors in Fiction House's *Lariat Story Magazine* and Ray Nafziger who enjoyed a similar status among readers of Clayton House's *Ace-High Magazine*. Yet, it was Flynn's story for that first issue more than any of the other stories that introduced the new tone that would define *Star Western* and would have a significant impact on how the Western story would be written over the next several decades. The protagonist is shown as a man forced into isolation by social and economic forces rampant within the community, and who has only superior courage and moral fortitude to break the cycle. Such a protagonist undoubtedly was an inspiration to readers who, flogged by the Great Depression, felt lonely and isolated and vulnerable. However, the theme of the nearness of death in all that we do and are that Flynn carried over into his Western stories from his crime fiction was more a personal hallmark of his own fictional odyssey. It was in part the consequence of the painful memory of his beloved second wife, Molly, who had expired in his arms on August 11, 1929, a victim of incurable tuberculosis. He brought her to life again in the character of Sally Jones in this story.

7

CONQUISTADOR'S GOLD

"HOLY JOE"

I

It was hot in Horse Springs. Hotter than any town had a right to be, even if it was only a cow siding less than a hundred miles from the border. The dun-colored adobe houses, the false-fronted stores and saloons along the sprawling, dusty main street stood quiet and deserted in the shimmering heat waves. Before the Longhorn Saloon a black pony, flanks sweat-caked with alkali, switched its tail at the droning flies. A Winchester butt, wiped carefully free from grit, rose from the saddle holster.

A lone rider, black Stetson aslant, lithe body erect and easy in the saddle, sloped from the railroad siding toward the Longhorn hitch rack. Halted there, the rider did not immediately dismount. Instead, his boyish, freckled face twisted into a frown, half of annoyance, half of surprise. He stared at the dust-caked cayuse, his gray eyes narrowing on the brand he saw there — a Ⓛ.

"Maybe we saved a trip . . . an' some trouble, Pink," the rider said, half aloud.

Pink snorted, jerked his head, and then stood still. They understood each other, this slender, determined young man with the dancing gray eyes and body of steel and whipcord, and the deep-chested roan who easily could have carried a man of twice the weight. A fine pair, man and beast, with the breath of the open and the joy of life in every movement of their bodies. But, for the moment, Howdy McFee was thinking neither of the roan nor of the long trip from Salinas in the confining railroad car which they had just made. His face was impassive as he dismounted and, flinging the reins over Pink's head, walked to the door.

Suddenly from inside, as if at a signal of his arrival, there came sounds of scuffing, shouts, and oaths. As the slender rider stepped into the doorway, a heavy object flew from the dimness of the interior straight at him. Howdy did not have time to dodge. Something thudded against his body and he took a precipitate backward step. He recovered himself, staring down at the thin, emaciated figure which lay at his feet. He saw a dried-up, shriveled old man whose wrinkled face with a straggling white mustache lay upturned upon the floor.

He was unconscious. Blood dripped from a wound on his bald head. Howdy stooped, the furrowed lines deepening on his forehead. Some old saddle tramp, most likely. But there was no call for a man to be treated like this! His fingers closed about the tattered calfskin vest.

The darkened room was deathly still. Howdy heard flies buzzing outside. And suddenly that silence was broken. A hoarse voice called, "Keep your hands off, fella! This fight's private . . . an' all took care of."

Howdy straightened. His hand edged toward his right

thigh, fingers curving. The speaker as yet was only a dim blob in the half light of the room. Trouble, menace, freighting the man's voice, his words innocent enough in themselves carried in their tone a challenge, a threat. And then Howdy remembered he was not packing a gun.

He stopped, and with a single movement lifted the tattered old fellow to his feet. The man's watery eyes blinked uncertainly. He spat blood from his mouth and shook himself.

"Gimme a . . . drink," he gasped.

Howdy turned toward the bar, and stopped. A thick-set man barred his way. Howdy saw the sullen, taunting grin play over the loose lips, saw the red, blood-shot eyes, and glimpsed the splayed hands dangling loosely near two tied-down holsters. He read something more in the man's opaque pupils — killer-lust.

The man laughed, coldly and without mirth, as he studied Howdy's face. He nodded, as if in confirmation; and there came a trace of bleak amusement to his small eyes. "This bar ain't servin' nosy kids, fella! I'm settling this old buzzard an' comin' back for you. Was I you an' wanted a whole skin, I'd fog *pronto*." His fingers thrust out, clutched the old man's collar, dragging him away from the wall where he had been leaning. "I'll teach you to mind your business, you ornery ol'. . . ." The old man's bald head banged once against the wall. The husky man's wrist was struck down by a blow that had come so fast he did not see it. His hand fell limply to his side. A look of surprise, then of anger, flooded the cowboy's face. He wheeled on Howdy, lips drawn back, eyes blazing, distended fingers hovering over gun butts.

"Damn you . . . go for. . . ."

He did not finish. Howdy knew that it was only the

11

lightning-like speed of his clenched fist that could save him from the guns of the 'puncher. Barely six inches that blow traveled before it smacked against the gunman's jaw. But six inches was enough. The man's knees slumped. He fell to the floor.

Howdy, frowning, puzzled, leaned over him. He took the man's weapons from their holsters, broke them, extracted the shells, and threw the brass cylinders out the door. He tossed the guns onto the bar.

The white-aproned bartender was just putting away the sawed-off scatter-gun he had grabbed from behind the damp pine counter. He shook his head. "He had a hate on, this mawnin'," he said briefly. "An' he'll likely be tough when he wakes up, mister. Better grab yourself a gun if you want to stick around."

The bartender came out and dragged the unconscious gunman into a rear room. A bottle stood on the bar. Howdy had himself a drink and passed it on to the old man.

"If that was a private fight, maybe I butted in," he said grinning.

The old man wiped his mouth with the back of his hand. He started to speak, then apparently thought better of it. His Adam's apple bobbed in his scrawny neck.

"The Lord's good to me terday, feller!" he said piously. "I never hunt no fight. But that Luke . . . that sidewinder jest didn't like my looks. An' I ain't waitin' 'round till he comes to, neither!"

The bartender nodded. "Good idee, Holy Joe! Say," — he fumbled behind the bar and produced a wadded slip of paper, tossed it to Howdy — "maybe you dropped that while you was puttin' the gent to sleep."

Howdy said, "Thanks." He unfolded the paper, turning

away from the bar, glanced at it. He stiffened, and re-read the scrawl:

Howard McFee — five foot nine, mebbe twenty, gray eyes, talks slow and quiet. Rodeo rider. Due at Salinas mornin' of the twelfth.

That was all. Who this gunman was, what he had wanted, beyond the opportunity of killing him, Howdy didn't know. But he was certainly interested in one Howdy McFee!

Howdy turned to the two men. "Know who he is?"

The barman shook his head.

Howdy said to the old man, "You started to tell his name. Guess he was lookin' for me."

The bald pate shook. "No . . . I . . . I never see him afore in my life!" the old man stuttered.

The lie was obvious. Howdy let it ride and scratched his head. He was remembering the gunman's flashing look of recognition when he had first spoken. Howdy and Holy Joe Andrews stepped outside.

"Know the Circle L near Las Palomas?" he questioned, watching the old man closely.

The old timer spat at a knot-hole, then turned his faded blue eyes on Howdy. "Reckon I owe you su'thin' fer what you did inside there," he said, "so I'll tell you. Yeah . . . I know that consarn country. It's so dry back there the lizards can't spit an' the horned toads has all packed up to look for a water hole. I was prospectin' north of there a while back."

Howdy built himself a quirly. "So . . . you don't know who this gunslinging gent is . . . a gent who's ridin' this Circle L pony, who's lookin' with both guns

13

out for Howdy McFee?"

The old man's eyes popped open. "Howdy McFee!" He whistled, then clamped his lips shut. Finally he said, "Nope. Never seen the feller afore!"

What was holding him back? Fear? Howdy guessed as much. And he knew it would be a hard task to make the old man talk. He turned toward his horse.

"Well . . . ," he said slowly, "I'll be movin' along."

Old Holy Joe spat and expertly nailed a wandering tumblebug in the dust. He seemed to be struggling within himself; his leathery, wrinkled face was screwed up as by some inner effort. He scuffed up to Howdy and leaned close to his ear.

"Has anyone told you," he asked in an undertone, "how old Jason McFee came to die so sudden? Do you know he was bushwhacked on his own range . . . in broad daylight?"

Howdy gave the old man a startled look. "Bushwhacked?" he repeated. "You're sure about that?"

"Sure."

Howdy pushed his sombrero back from his moist forehead and regarded the old man gravely. "Who did it?" he demanded slowly.

"The devil keeps his doin's under a ten-gallon hat," said Holy Joe Andrews in his cracked solemn voice. "An' I reckon he's still sittin' on the hat in this case. Leastways I ain't never heard they pinned Jason McFee's killin' on anyone." Holy Joe wagged his head and shoved the tattered brim of his worn sombrero with a horny palm. "They's queer doin's back in that country," he muttered. "An' you're goin' in Las Palomas district to find out who kilt your uncle?"

"I'm goin' in," Howdy McFee admitted. "This is the first

I've heard Uncle Jase went out that way. Haven't seen him since I was about ten years old when I spent a year on the Circle L." He grinned reminiscently, but there was a new grimness in his eyes.

"I reckon you don't know this Juniper Jones that's runnin' the Circle L now?" Holy Joe Andrews stated flatly.

"No," Howdy admitted. "He came after my time."

Holy Joe Andrews's eyes looked hopefully for a target, and then he spat on the bare ground with a trace of disappointment. "He's a danged leather-hided old tarantula," he stated bitterly, "an' that daughter of his is a wildcat. He's pizen an' onery an' tight as a fat rabbit in a prairie dog hole, an' Sally Jones is spitfire an' forked lightning. The Lord snatched away the milk of human kindness from this here Juniper Jones's belly an' the devil crawled in an' made hisself to home. An' the girl is a chip off the old block. Her old man's a low-down, no-account. . . ."

"Pull up!" Howdy broke in. "I didn't know a girl was made who could answer to all that."

"You've heard of one, son. They run me off Circle L land," said Holy Joe heatedly. "Juniper Jones reared back on that big black stallion that was the pride of Jason McFee's heart an' told me if I wanted to grub in the ground to take me up a homestead in the next state an' dryfarm beans. He said his was a cow ranch an', if I didn't hightail my outfit off Circle L land by the next day, he was personally gonna take his lass rope an' his six-gun an' rattle my old bones all the way to the Rio Grande." Holy Joe Andrews snatched off his tattered sombrero and slammed it down in the dust. "Furthermore," he said hotly, "this here Sally Jones told me to stop quotin' scripture or she'd git a prayer book an' make me read it aloud all the way to the Rio Grande. Juniper Jones is a sacrilegious, loud-cussin', old sinner who ain't got no respect for his betters, an' his girl takes after him. If they didn't bushwhack your uncle, it was because they didn't git there fust."

Howdy forced a grave expression on his face. "I can see that Juniper Jones didn't give you the right treatment," he agreed promptly, "but I guess he'll do what I tell him. Next time you're around the Circle L and want to do a little digging, it'll be all right."

Holy Joe Andrews's eyes brightened with satisfaction as he picked up his hat and slapped it against his leg. "You're a *caballero*, son," he said, mollified, "but watch your step. They ain't all as honest as Holy Joe Andrews in Las Palomas country."

Howdy McFee strapped a small war bag behind the saddle and rode out of Horse Springs, riding as one to the saddle born. As Pink ambled smartly along the rough track winding north into the sparse, dry Las Palomas country, Howdy's eyes narrowed with thought. A letter had found him at Salinas and brought him back to this vast dry land, a letter short, misspelled, cryptic.

Howdy McFee:
If you're the nephew of Jason McFee who owned the Circle L brand, he's ded and now you own part of the brand. I've been lookin all over for you and when I saw your name in the paper as a rodeo rider I took a chance and wrote this. Get here quick, but don't stop in Las Palomas or tell anybody who you are.

                    Respectfully yours,
                        JUNIPER J. JONES, foreman,
                        manager and part owner Circle L.

There was a mystery around that letter, and the conversation with Holy Joe Andrews had thickened it. In the first place it was news that anyone but Jason McFee had owned an interest in the Circle L. The letter said nothing about Jason McFee being bushwhacked. Why did Juniper Jones want him to come in secretly? And why had a busy cowman gone to such trouble to run a harmless old desert rat off his ranch? And was the gunman who rode a Circle L horse a grim welcoming committee from Juniper Jones?

As the hot dusty miles fell behind, Howdy McFee wondered what he was going to find ahead. He found himself thinking about Sally Jones, wildcat, spitfire, a chip off the old block — and the murder of Jason McFee.

II

"THROW DOWN!"

The small, back room office of lawyer Marcus Murphy in Las Palomas was like an oven. Glinting drops of perspiration stood out on Murphy's Buddha-like face as he scowled at the tall, spare man hunched in a chair opposite him.

"No sign of him yet," Murphy wheezed, "and it's crowding five o'clock. Your idea is a washout, Daggert."

Marcus Murphy's sleeves were rolled up and his soiled white shirt was open at the collar. His porcine bulk filled, overflowed the splint chair. His pendulous jowls were flabby, pasty, as if they seldom saw the clean fresh sunlight. His small eyes glinted shrewdly towards Daggert.

They were impatient, accusing.

Daggert was lean, leathery. A man would have been hard put to find any expression at all on his tanned, horsy features. A heavy, sandy mustache shaded the expression of his mouth. He chewed on the frayed cigar as his eyes wandered around the dusty office from the worn, leather-bound law books in a small, battered case to the cluttered desk behind Marcus Murphy.

"My idea is all right," Daggert said curtly. "He'll come. He wrote old man Jones he'd be here by the twelfth of the month. This is the twelfth."

"And he's not here!" Marcus Murphy affirmed irritably.

"The twelfth ain't over."

The chair creaked as Marcus Murphy leaned forward. "You sure this man of yours out at the Circle L knows what he's talking about?"

"Luke's sharp as they come," said Daggert comfortably. "And he knows which side of the fence it pays to be on."

"No mistake about this kid being dumb is there? What if he finds out what's up?" Marcus Murphy persisted. His beady little eyes bored at his visitor.

Daggert laughed shortly. "I keep tellin' you . . . he'll come by train to Horse Springs, an' ride from there to the Circle L. I've got everything set."

Marcus Murphy was still restless. "Maybe he'll get to talking in Horse Springs," he muttered.

"Maybe." Daggert shrugged.

"Then what?"

Daggert removed the frayed cigar from his mouth. He grinned unpleasantly. "Then," he said calmly, "Buck Briggs knows what to do."

Marcus Murphy stirred uneasily. His gray face seemed

to go grayer. "Not murder," he whispered unwillingly. "I . . . I don't like it!"

Daggert sneered openly as he stood up. "You like money a damned sight better, Murphy. I know you. Your own grandfather wouldn't be safe with a hundred dollar bill in his pocket. Don't go pious like that old fool, Holy Joe. It was your idea in the first place. I reckon you'll go through with it in spite of your squirming."

Marcus Murphy raked perspiration from his forehead with a crooked forefinger. "Maybe," he wheezed, "the kid won't come."

"He'll be here," said Daggert confidently. "And Buck Briggs is ready for him. So put ink in your pen an' oil up your tongue." Daggert paused, and his long teeth clenched on the cigar end. "If you fall down, I'll have to take a hand. An' that," he grunted as he turned to leave the office, "won't be soft for you, Murphy, nor soft for that McFee kid either."

III

"TRAPPED"

Two hours later, six miles out of Las Palomas on the Horse Springs road, Howdy McFee jogged easily along. He was whistling to himself when a big gray jackrabbit came dashing through the screen of *chamizo* bushes where the road curved around the bottom of a hill just ahead. The jack saw him, doubled sharply on a tangent back up the hill. Howdy stopped whistling.

"Something scared that jack," he observed aloud to Pink.

The words were hardly out of his mouth when a horseman rode from the brush-covered shoulder of the hill down into the road ahead. Fading crimson streaked the western sky and purple dusk was rolling in fast, but there was still light. Enough light to see the rifle in the leather saddle boot, the gun slung low on the hip, the square, stubbled face of the stranger. Howdy reined in.

"H'ya," he said politely.

The stranger who faced him was fifteen years older, forty pounds heavier. "Your name McFee?" he asked.

Howdy pursed his lips, whistled a disjointed bar before answering. "How come you ask that?" he questioned casually.

"I been lookin' for you."

"You got here in time then. They call me Howdy McFee. You from the ranch?"

"I been layin' out here by the road three days," said the stranger flatly. "An' gettin' damned tired of it too. My name's Buck Briggs. Friend of your uncle's."

"Glad to see any friend of my uncle's," Howdy admitted. "Jones sent you out to meet me, I guess."

Briggs spat. "Juniper Jones don't know it. That old cutthroat would probably have come hisself if he figured you would be met. Come with a rifle an' six-gun an' trouble on his mind."

Howdy said bluntly, "You talk one way and sound another. Do you mean Juniper Jones would come out to drygulch me?"

Briggs smiled crookedly. "You do much talkin' in Horse Springs?"

"Nope," said Howdy slowly. "I unloaded my hoss, saddled up, and rode this way. Want to make the ranch tonight."

Briggs pushed a hand out emphatically. "If you'd talked, you might 'a' heard things."

Here it was again — warning, innuendo. "Heard what?" Howdy asked curiously.

"This Juniper Jones is a smooth-tongued old scoundrel," Briggs told him. "An' that ain't all that's been talked around. That's why I been layin' out here to meet you. Friends of your uncle's figured it was the best thing to do. You ride into Las Palomas with me an' see Marcus Murphy before you go out to the Circle L."

"Never heard of him," Howdy said promptly. "Who is Marcus Murphy?"

"Friend of your uncle's. There's a lot you never heard of around here."

"Guess so," Howdy grinned. "Last time I was at the ranch I was only ten years old . . . that's twelve years back."

Howdy studied Briggs casually. This friendly talk did not match the face it came from. Briggs looked hard, determined. His request to see Marcus Murphy sounded more like an order. Howdy squinted at the darkening sky.

"Getting late," he decided. "It's out of my way to ride into Las Palomas. I'll come in tomorrow or next day and see this Murphy."

"Better come tonight," Briggs insisted.

"I got other business tonight," Howdy refused.

Briggs dropped a hand to his hip and Howdy looked into the muzzle of a gun.

"You're a stubborn young coyote, ain'tcha?" Briggs sneered. "I got a special kind of argument for bullheads

21

like you. Ride up in the brush ahead of me." The scant friendliness had changed to a surly, arrogant threat.

"I'm not toting a gun," Howdy pointed out.

Briggs rested his weapon on the pommel of his saddle. "You wouldn't know what to do with a cutter if you had one," he sneered. "Ride!"

Silently Howdy headed Pink off the road. The junipers, the savinas, the scrub piñon closed in behind, and Briggs rode close, watchfully.

Howdy was puzzled. He turned his head, asked: "You after money?"

"I'd take it if I wanted it," Briggs said shortly. "Ride on."

They breasted the crest of the hill and rode down into the shadows of a grassy hollow nestling beyond. Pink walked stiff-legged, rolling his eyes at the horse pacing at his withers. Pink had bared his teeth back in the road and had been quieted only by a stern pull on the reins. They crossed the hollow, mounted a steeper hill beyond, slipped and slid down a precipitous, rock-studded slope into a steep-walled, shadowy arroyo.

Briggs ordered shortly: "Climb down."

Howdy did so.

"Start walkin' down this arroyo," Briggs directed coldly. The six-gun was still in his hand.

Howdy tossed the reins over Pink's neck, stepped in front of Briggs's horse, and moved over the dry, yielding sand. Rocky walls rose, closed into a narrow defile ahead of him. It was almost dark in here, black, threatening. And the silent Briggs, tense in his saddle, was threatening too, ominous.

Howdy thought fast. It looked bad. He was trapped. Without looking around he raised two fingers to his mouth. A shrill whistle split the silence of that lonely spot. In the same instant Howdy dived down to one side. It was well he did so. The roar of a gunshot shattered the dusk.

A small geyser of sand erupted just beyond McFee. A close call. Briggs had shot to kill. But even as Howdy rolled over, came to a knee, and scrambled up with the shot still echoing, Briggs shouted with sudden alarm. The shrill scream of an angry horse rose loud. Pink came on, rearing with striking hoofs and tearing teeth at man and horse who blocked the way to his master's side.

Briggs was caught off guard. The roan tornado of bone and flesh, of sledge-hammer hoofs and wicked, gleaming teeth burst on him from behind. Briggs's horse reared, wheeled, tried to bolt into the precipitous bank before him. But it was too late. Pink struck him square, knocked him off balance, climbed his side, his neck.

Twisting in the saddle Briggs bawled with pain as a hoof smashed his leg. His gun whipped around. He fired wildly, and missed. His horse was already going down, with Pink tearing, trampling over the gunman and his mount. Sand scattered. Briggs screamed once, horribly, shrilly, as the full weight of his own horse crushed him. Pink stamped over them, nostrils quivering, and brought up by Howdy. Briggs's horse heaved up and bolted along the arroyo. A limp form that had one foot caught in the stirrup dragged after.

Briggs's gun had dropped as he went down. Howdy snatched it up, caught Pink's reins, swung into the saddle. Tight-lipped, he drove Pink up the arroyo after the runaway. It took half a mile, part of it up the rocky hillside, before Pink raced alongside. Then Howdy leaned over and caught the bit chains of the runaway. Briggs's body dangled limply by one leg. Howdy unfastened the saddle cinches and let the saddle fall with Briggs's body. The horse he drove off.

Leaving Briggs for the law to find and bury, Howdy rode back to the road, a little pale and shaken. He tucked Briggs's gun under his belt beneath his coat. Who — what was Briggs? The man had been no common bandit. He had not been after money or horse. Only luck had put Briggs's body back there under the brightening stars instead of his own. Juniper Jones of the Circle L should have been the only one aware that McFee would be along the road at this time. And yet — Briggs had known it. Apparently so had the mysterious gunslick at Horse Springs.

Howdy met no one as he rode toward Las Palomas. He had changed his plans. Las Palomas held a grim riddle, and Howdy McFee was hunting the answer.

He passed out of the junipers, the savinas, the stunted piñons, beyond gravelly hills where spiked *amole*, tenacious greasewood, scanty bunchgrass fought for subsistence. He followed the dry, dusty ruts into a bare open valley, and the lights of Las Palomas twinkled before him.

IV

"GIT A ROPE!"

Las Palomas — the doves. There were houses now, stores, saloons, for the ranches far back in that lonely country. There was a dance hall, too, where the gay, mad music of guitars and fiddles throbbed on the sultry heat-drenched night. There were horses, buggies, wagons, cowhands and dark-skinned Mexicans, for this was Saturday night.

Howdy stopped by a Mexican in the plaza, a fellow with a scar slashing over a cheekbone. "I want Marcus Murphy," he said.

"Sí," nodded the Mexican. "You find heem nex' Prieta Bar."

The Prieta Bar was just ahead. Howdy saw the false, wooden front painted black, the string of horses patient at the hitch rack, the lighted windows, and heard the buzz and hum of trade inside. Sandwiched between it and the next, larger place was a wooden-fronted building with a shed roof extending over the packed dirt walk. Peeling paint letters on the single front window said:

MARCUS MURPHY
LAWYER

Howdy found the lawyer in the grubby little rear room, oven-hot from the big brass kerosene lamp hanging from the ceiling. The splint chair creaked, swung about, and Marcus Murphy faced him.

Howdy eyed the flabby bulk filling the sagging splint chair, the pendulous, pasty jowls, the small shrewd eyes. "My name is McFee," he said. And waited.

Marcus Murphy heaved to his feet, thrust out a fat hand. "McFee!" he wheezed with a spreading smile. "Mighty glad to see you, young man! I've been waiting for you. Just get here?"

"Just," Howdy nodded.

Murphy's soft hand was moist, warm, unpleasant. Murphy's eyes searched past him into the front room. "You come alone?" Murphy asked him.

"Yes," said Howdy. "From California."

25

"I mean . . . uh . . . into Las Palomas. Didn't meet no one on the road?"

"You mean Briggs?" Howdy returned innocently.

"That's it, Buck Briggs! Buck was to meet you before you went out to the Circle L. You saw him then?" The small, glinting eyes searched Howdy's face.

"He met me," said Howdy mildly. "Had a little trouble with his horse. I rode in alone. I reckon Briggs won't be here for some time yet."

Murphy dismissed Briggs with a careless wave of his hand. "Don't matter. Didn't want him here anyway. Sit down, young man . . . we got a lot to talk over. As an old friend of your uncle's, I've been anxious about you."

"I'll stand, thanks," Howdy said. "I've been wondering how you knew I was coming and why you took the trouble to have me met."

Murphy dropped back into the splint chair. "Briggs isn't one of my men," he denied. "But he was a friend of your uncle's, too. He was glad to meet you."

"He seemed to be," Howdy sighed. "How come all my uncle's friends are rallying 'round? It reminds me of the prodigal son and the fatted calf. You people aren't going to kill the fatted calf, are you, Mister Murphy?"

Murphy gave him a startled look. Then meeting the mild grin which accompanied the words, he heaved with a deep chuckle that ran off in crinkles around his little deep set eyes, spread over his flabby face.

"That's a good one," he said. "I'd like to kill a fatted calf for any nephew of Jason McFee's. And we will, we will! But first there are other things to take up. You were sent for by a man named Jones who is running the ranch. He's been trying to find you."

"That's right," Howdy agreed. "You know a lot, Mister Murphy."

"It's my business to," Murphy nodded. "You know this man Jones is part owner of the Circle L?"

"His letter said so. First I'd heard of it."

Murphy reached around to the desk with a grunt and picked up the stub of a dead cigar. He scratched a match, held it to the cigar, puffed mightily, and flipped the match to the floor.

"Jason McFee had trouble," Murphy said. "Two dry years in a row. Cattle down and heavy losses when the grass burnt out and the water holes went dry. He had to borrow. Jones was working for him then as foreman. Jones inherited some money about that time. Bank money was hard to get. Jones used his inheritance to buy into the Circle L. From then on he was part owner."

Murphy puffed on the cigar and nodded. His fat, perspiring face glistened through the drifting veils of smoke without expression. Howdy watched him.

"That seems all right," he said slowly, "if both men were satisfied."

Murphy gestured with the cigar stump. "Both men weren't satisfied. Not by a hell of a lot," he grunted. "Your uncle fretted because he didn't own the Circle L clean any more. And this Juniper Jones, who had never done anything but take orders before, bought an oversize hat and began to give orders. He got ideas. He had part of a ranch . . . but it would be a danged sight better if he had the whole of it, he figured."

"My uncle knew that?"

"Yes," said Murphy forcibly. "And more than that, the hands saw it! Jones turned into a hard man, cold. He couldn't keep his ambition hidden." Murphy leaned forward. His voice became husky, sharp. "And then your uncle was killed. Shot in the back as he was riding out on the ranch."

"So," said Howdy softly, "murdered you mean?" He didn't show by word or expression that he had heard the news before this moment.

Murphy nodded. "Murdered," he repeated.

"Who did it?"

"Never was proven. The man who did it was too smart. He didn't leave evidence. But the bullet that did it was a forty-five. Juniper Jones carries a forty-five. Jones was not at the ranch house when it happened. He claimed he was riding out the other way alone. He made out to grieve at the inquest, and even went so far as to offer a reward for the man who did it." Murphy leaned forward, close to Howdy. "And then after the funeral Jones brought out a will that said he was to get the whole of the ranch in three years if Jason McFee's nephew didn't turn up. That will gave Jones the handling of the estate. He said, now and then, he was hunting you. But he never seemed to find you."

"My folks died. I was up in Canada for five years," Howdy said slowly. "Up there I started riding under another name. When I came back to the States, I used the same name for a while. Last fall I decided I had a good name and better use it. If you're trying to tell me Jones didn't want to find me . . . he wrote me a letter and said to come here!"

"One of Jones's hands saw your name in a paper as winner at the Salinas Roundup," Murphy grunted. "He showed the paper to Juniper Jones in front of others. Jones *had* to write you then!"

"And here I am," Howdy stated innocently. "That still

doesn't tell me why I was met out on the road and asked to come here."

Marcus Murphy smiled pityingly. "You've got lots to learn, young man. Didn't I just tell you your uncle was shot in the back? Jones *had* to send for you. But Jones wants that ranch . . . all of it. Your uncle was gotten out of the way. You're the only thing that prevents Jones from being cock-of-the-walk out there at the Circle L. If this Jones killed your uncle, what's to stop him from handing you the same thing?"

Howdy shrugged. "I hadn't thought of that."

"We did!" Murphy exclaimed. "Your uncle had a lot of friends. They got together and decided Jones couldn't get away with it. So we fixed to have you met and sent here."

"It touches me deeply," Howdy sighed. "I never knew I had friends like this before. It makes me want to do something back."

Murphy smiled broadly. "A chip off the old block!" he declared heartily. "That's the way I like to hear a young man talk! I can see you appreciate what your friends are trying to do for you. Now, I have the papers all fixed up. All you have to do is sign."

Howdy opened his eyes wide. "Sign? What papers?"

"Sale papers for your share of the Circle L," Murphy told him. "Ranches aren't worth much in these parts now, but your uncle's friends got together and chipped in a good price and turned it over to me. You sign. They take over your share of the ranch. And this Juniper Jones'll have a hard time freezing *them* out. You can take the money, go back to California, and know you won't get shot in the back."

"H-m." Howdy hesitated. But the lawyer could see the

flickering light that burned deeply in McFee's lidded eyes.

Marcus Murphy leaned forward confidentially. "You take my advice, son," he said paternally. "The advice of an older man who knows what he's talking about. Sign the papers, take the money, and get out of Las Palomas country. Ranches are losing money all the time these days. The cattle business is played out. These men who want to help you have got heavy stakes and can't pull out. A little more land won't matter. Maybe some day they'll get their stakes out."

"From Juniper Jones?"

"He hasn't got a spare dollar to his name. Couldn't buy or borrow. There's only one way he can get your share." Murphy stretched out a fat hand and slowly squeezed it into a tight fist. "Like your uncle went."

He dropped the fist on his knee.

Howdy nodded. "I see," he said slowly.

Murphy twisted around, picked up a sheet of paper from the litter on his desk. "Here it is. Sign, and I'll get a couple of witnesses to it. Your troubles will be over. I got a check all ready made out for you. Eighteen thousand dollars . . . and it's worth more than your share of the ranch, at that. You can't give cattle away these days. Read it just to see that everything is regular."

Murphy held out the paper.

Howdy's hands remained loosely at his sides. He shook his head. "I guess not. You-all are too open hearted. I'm near to tears. But I'll fight my own battles. If Juniper Jones figgers to plug me in the back, why I'll walk backward and fool him."

Marcus Murphy scowled. "You mean you won't listen to reason after everything I've told you?"

"Not tonight," said Howdy softly. "I don't like your looks, Murphy. If you were a friend of my uncle's, he showed mighty bad taste. But I don't think you were. He wasn't the kind to take up with a snake. And you're a snake, Murphy! Fat and greasy and two faced! If I wasn't in a hurry to get out to the Circle L and get the truth of this, I'd make you crawl and whine and tell me yourself. You look like the kind that would bleat all he knew when it got painful."

Murphy listened with dropping jaw. His pasty face flushed beet red with anger.

"Damn you!" he choked thickly. "You young fool! I give you a chance for your life and you act like this! *Sign this or. . . .*"

Marcus Murphy, lawyer, never finished the threat that bubbled on his lips. The hot dim room crashed with a single earsplitting reverberation. And the fat, gross figure in the splint chair straightened convulsively and pitched forward to the floor, the paper fluttering from his fingers.

So sudden and unexpected was that shot that Howdy acted instinctively, whirling in a crouch that brought him facing the rear of the room. There was a door in the corner, a window next to it with the shade a foot from the bottom. The window was open for ventilation, and a haze of powder smoke lazily drifted outside. No movement was visible there. Whoever had fired that shot had vanished instantly.

Marcus Murphy lay in a limp huddle, twitched once convulsively, and was still, face down, one arm doubled under him and one outstretched. Gun in hand Howdy stepped to him. Blood was welling from a red hole drilled above Murphy's right ear. The gunman had aimed carefully, coldly to kill. The lawyer was dead.

All this registered in brief seconds. Howdy snatched up the unsigned paper and lunged for the door. It was locked. He sidestepped to the window, snapped the shade up, and lunged through. Coming from light into darkness he was blinded for a moment. The buildings to right and left stretched on back, forming a narrow cul-de-sac for some twenty feet. The space was deserted. Howdy ran to the back, stopped, listened.

To right and left stretched a maze of rickety fences and open yards, looming building walls and lighted windows. No sound of flight was audible. But suddenly for an instant a flitting form was silhouetted against the light from a window two buildings away. A man was running there. Howdy vaulted a three-foot board fence before him and followed.

When he raced beyond the lighted window, he found darkness again, deserted quiet. Loud voices sounded back at Murphy's office. A man shouted, "He went this way!"

Howdy ignored the tumult behind and dodged into a narrow opening between two buildings. It led into Las Palomas' plaza. Howdy was on the packed dirt walk a moment later, gun still in hand. To the left men were erupting from doors and crowding before the office of Marcus Murphy. No one in sight looked suspicious. Shoving the gun back under his coat, Howdy joined the crowd.

There was growing excitement as the news of Murphy's death passed swiftly from lip to lip. Additional information was shouted from the men inside the little building to the milling crowd outside.

Howdy started to push through. Resentfully, men started to glare at him. One man said sharply, "Stranger, it's full inside! Wait your turn!"

Before Howdy could reply a loud voice rose above all others. "Thees man was in there. I don' see heem come out!" The dark-faced Mexican with the scarred cheek stood at arm's length, pointing at Howdy.

It was the spark needed to explode the excitement. In a breath Howdy found himself standing alone in a crowding circle of scowling men. He saw hands hovering over gun butts, saw the scowls on the faces of those nearest him. The crowd had sniffed gun smoke, and Howdy knew menace when he met it. Resistance would be folly. He faced them calmly.

"I was in there talking to Murphy when it happened," he admitted. "Somebody shot through the back window and killed Murphy. I went out the window looking for the man who did it. I saw him running. It looked like he came between those buildings back there into the plaza here. I didn't see him again. Maybe he's in the crowd here."

"Thees man ask me for Murphy's office," the Mexican stated loudly. "I see heem ride up here an' go in! He's still in there w'en I hear wan shot!"

"Search him!" someone called out.

The crowd surged in. Howdy's arms were pinioned. The gun under his coat was jerked out. A bowlegged cowman who held it sniffed the muzzle and spun the cylinder.

"There's fresh powder smell an' one shot has been fired!" he announced loudly.

A tall, lean leathery man with a sandy mustache shouted: "That's enough . . . he can't explain that away! Git a rope!"

Behind Howdy a voice bawled: "We oughta give him

33

a vote of thanks for smokin' down that fat carcass, Daggert! Murphy's been needin' that for years. Low-down skunk!"

But the sandy-mustached one called Daggert wheeled on the speaker angrily. "Murphy was all right! But it don't make any difference whether he was or not! Are we going to let strangers ride into town an' kill us off? His gun's all the evidence we need! String him up! Who's got a rope?"

V

"RENEGADE"

Daggert's angry passion swung the crowd with him. There were shouts of agreement. They closed in. Hands caught at Howdy, ripping, tearing his clothes. A fist struck his cheek, bringing blood. Another bruised the corner of his mouth. Pinioned, helpless, Howdy McFee bowed dizzily before that rising tide of blood madness. Only violence could appease them now.

But the man called Fisher refused to be silenced. He crowded around in front of the prisoner, a tall, slope-shouldered, wiry man whose mustache was black and close clipped. He had a powerful voice, an air of authority.

"Don't be fools, men!" he shouted, raising his hands for attention. "I ain't saying he didn't do it . . . maybe he did! That empty shell in his gun needs some explaining, but he's got a right to be heard! Hell . . . he's only a kid! Look at him! Take him inside an' let him tell his story! We've got all night to settle this!"

Cooler heads quickly backed the speaker. Before mob passion could swing into action again, Howdy was hustled through the crowd into the back room where Marcus Murphy still lay huddled on the floor. The door was still locked, the window still open. The hot room was packed. Disheveled, bruised, bleeding, Howdy faced them and knew he had never seen a harder, grimmer jury. No sheriff or deputy was in evidence.

The bowlegged cowpuncher who had the gun displayed it excitedly. A sudden wave of hostility swept through the men.

Daggert spoke hoarsely, excitedly: "He was in here with Murphy an' Peedro Gonzales saw him come in. He admits he went out the back window, an' we saw him trying to mingle with the crowd out in front. Look . . . he shot Murphy in the side of the head. There was only one shot. Murphy never carried a gun an' he didn't have a chance. There's real hangin' evidence, men! String him up!"

But Fisher said curtly, "Not so fast! Let's hear what the kid has to say."

Howdy shrugged and spoke. While ominous murmurs came from outside, the room was grimly quiet. He told them what he knew of the killing. When he had finished, a bearded man with a crooked nose and long ape-like arms looked up, holding Howdy's gun high. "What about this fresh fired shell, young feller?" he asked harshly.

Howdy hesitated. "That gun," he explained slowly, "belongs to a man named Buck Briggs. He fired that shot at me out on the Horse Springs road a little while ago."

Daggert was not the only man who greeted that statement with a startled look. Fisher, Howdy's champion, frowned. "Where is Briggs?" he queried.

"Dead," said Howdy. "His horse fell on him, and then dragged him." Even as he said it, he realized that the story sounded weak.

Daggert sneered. "It sounds purty, but it's a lie! Buck Briggs wasn't out on the Horse Springs road. An' Buck Briggs don't go around shootin' at strangers. That gun don't look like Buck's."

"Where was Briggs this evening then?" Howdy asked.

"Out to my ranch," Daggert answered promptly. "I saw him headed that way this afternoon. You can't save your neck by a yarn like that. Murphy must have told you Briggs wasn't in town before you killed him. I reckon that settles your meddling, don't it, Fisher?"

Fisher stammered something unintelligible. He appeared flustered. Howdy saw that even Fisher was beginning to believe that bullet from the empty shell had killed Murphy.

"I don't believe in hangings," Fisher declared stubbornly. "A court trial is the way to settle this."

"Bah!" Daggert sneered. "We don't want to waste time foolin' around with no court to settle this. Chances are he'd get away. A rope's the thing, an' by God they've got it waitin' outside."

"That's right," a man in the doorway burst out. "Bring him along!"

Howdy saw in that moment that the slender thread of hope Fisher had given him had snapped. There was going to be a hanging this night. He wondered for a moment if his name would stop them. And then decided not to try it. This mob did not want explanations. They wanted a hanging — and a quick one. The baying crowd out in front grew louder.

Strangely enough, no heads were visible at the back window. Men had poured out into the plaza at the sound of the shot, and they were all gathered out in front of the narrow wooden building. His captors had released him while he was being examined.

A man on Howdy's left side said, "Lemme see that gun."

The bearded one with the long arms reached in front of Howdy to give it to the speaker. At that precise instant, Howdy acted. His hand darted forward, snatched the gun from the loose gripping fingers. He ducked back against the wall and fired at the big brass lamp hanging from the ceiling.

The lamp swayed violently, crashed. Shattered glass cascaded down to the floor. In the sudden darkness a bright band of flame flared around the punctured side of the swaying lamp and then poured in a fiery stream on the men standing below. Shouting, swearing, they stampeded out from under that scattering rain of fire, beating at the searing drops which fell on heads, necks, shoulders. The space around Howdy was hastily vacated as he fired a second shot into the floor. In the eerie light of crackling oil men ducked, plunging to get out of the way of the rain of lead they expected to follow.

Some were not armed. Those that were could not shoot without hitting their companions. Howdy slid along the wall, losing himself in the confusion and panic that gripped the noisy room. He fired a third shot into the floor as he went and the shouting and curses grew louder. The room was packed by a mad, stampeded throng. Those that were not seared by the raining globules of flame left it to others to make the first move while they ducked to safety.

Howdy shouldered to the window where men were already tumbling out. One man could hardly tell another in that faint, treacherous light. Howdy went out with the rest of them. Darkness swallowed him. Men were still shouting and swearing in the office. Over the top of the building poured the rising wrath and excitement of the crowd in front.

On the other side of the cul-de-sac a man yelled: "Watch out he don't come out the window!"

He was answered from the window. "He's out back there! Don't let 'im get away!"

The door shivered and crashed outward. Men were still coming out the windows with the glow of the spreading fire following them. The lot of them would be out in back, fighting mad in short seconds. Howdy ducked against one of the adobe walls and ran along it. He collided with a man as he reached the end of the wall and dodged aside.

"Here he is!" the other yelled out of the darkness.

The livid roar of a gun shot crashed almost against Howdy's body. He felt the hot blast drive through his clothes, felt the tug of the bullet as it tore against his side. But it passed on — and he drove in and smashed hard with the barrel at the vague bulk of the figure before him. He felt the shock of the impact up his arm, heard the crunch of steel against bone. The vague figure wilted down to the ground.

Howdy paused long enough to tear the gun from nerveless fingers. He would need it. And then, with the rank bite of powder smoke in his nostrils, and the clamorous shouts in the darkness behind him, he fled along the line of buildings fronting the plaza. Even as he made that run, it seemed futile. A stranger in town, every man's hand against him, a scant few shots in the two guns, he had a small chance to get away. He ran looking for a way back into the plaza.

Behind him he heard a yell, *"He went this way."*

A back door opened ahead of him. A white-aproned bartender stepped out carrying a shotgun and stood directly in Howdy's path. Howdy shot without stopping. The door glass shattered loudly. The white-aproned man ducked back inside, slamming the door without using his shotgun.

The sound of the shot focused the pursuit. Guns began to bark. Lead screamed, whined viciously overhead, to the side. But they were shooting wild.

Panting, he came to a board fence and scaled it. He found himself in a deserted side street running into the end of the plaza. Howdy crossed it, made the end of the plaza. He could see the crowd milling, spreading out, from Murphy's office toward both ends of the block and pouring into the buildings to get back at the scene of action in the rear.

Howdy put his fingers to his lips and sent shrill whistle blasts ringing over the tumult that filled the plaza. He had scant hope that Pink would come. He had left Pink's reins looped on the saddle as he always did, but Pink had probably moved or been tied up.

Then, peering desperately, Howdy felt his throat tighten as he saw a familiar figure charging along the dusty street. Pink had heard. Pink was coming, head up, at full gallop, heedless of men and obstacles in the way. Men dodged aside, staring at the strange sight — the huge, charging, riderless horse that thundered past them.

Howdy whistled again and moved out into the center of the street. Men were tumbling over the board fence.

He was recognized as Pink brought up by him in a cloud of dust. Shots sounded from up the street. Howdy vaulted into the saddle, swung Pink's head around, and galloped across the end of the plaza.

Over his shoulder he saw men making for the horses at the hitch racks. Then he was out of the plaza, out of the light, with Pink's driving rush headed for the Horse Springs road. Four miles out of town the track cut off toward the Circle L.

If there was pursuit, it never got within sight. Behind the red glare of fire broke out against the sky. Two miles further out in the dry hills Howdy left the road and headed toward the Circle L. There was not enough light for any man to find and follow his trail.

Two hours later the still-bright stars vaulted the brush country as Howdy rode across the white sands of the Hondo Wash, only a mile from Circle L land. Far back in the piñon-studded hills the body of a man named Briggs lay unwatched and unguarded. In Las Palomas where the glare of flames had been visible for miles, Marcus Murphy lay dead and a posse hunted Howdy McFee as the killer. And men had said that Jason McFee had been shot in the back.

In the peaceful night through which Pink trotted it was hard to believe all that had happened. Short hours before in Horse Springs Howdy had been a joyous young man coming to claim unexpected good fortune. Now murder stalked Las Palomas country and men had spoken against the stranger, Juniper Jones, who owned a share of the Circle L. If part of what they said was right, it was not safe to show up at the Circle L. But the Circle L was the only refuge in all this barren Las Palomas country. And at the Circle L, danger or not, there was an answer to this web of mystery and danger and death the day had brought.

Howdy McFee left the ghostly white Hondo Wash and rode on to Circle L range. The ranch house was bare, brown adobe, sprawled close to the earth from which it had been puddled, with a long shady *portal* running across the front. There was a bunkhouse and a store shed, a windmill for the dry seasons, and the lazy crawl of Coyote Creek past the huge cottonwoods to the north of the house. Ringing that little patch of green fertile valley were the desolate, low-tumbled hills with their sparse, bare, stunted growth.

It was all there as Howdy remembered it through the years. There were still dogs that caught his scent and clamored loudly on the silent night as he rode up and dismounted before the *portal*.

He had thought at a distance there was a light at one of the *portal* windows, but now he saw that he had been mistaken. The windows were all dark. The house was deserted. Then, as he stepped toward the door, a clear sharp voice spoke ahead of him.

"Lift your hands and stop there!"

His heart leaped at the clear musical sound of it, like the middle strings of a harp struck gently. He stopped, laughing under his breath.

"Holy Joe Andrews said you were a wildcat and a spit-fire." Howdy said as his hands reached toward the *portal* roof, halted in his tracks. "But he didn't say whether you were pretty or not. Might I have the favor of seeing your face, Miss Sally Jones?"

VI

"SNAKETRACK"

"Keep a civil tongue in your head and your hands up high, or you'll have the favor of a bullet from this rifle I'm holding on you!" said the voice angrily. "If you've come from that old skulker, it's done you no good to say so. And if you have others out there, I can shoot fast and straight. What do you want at this hour of the night, and who are you?"

She was standing in the dark open doorway before him. He could see the faint white of her dress.

"My name is McFee," Howdy said. "I'm looking for Juniper Jones."

"McFee and Holy Joe Andrews don't go together. Stand still."

He saw her shadowy form bend down, and the next moment light shone from a lantern. Howdy laughed into the light with his hands high, and not until she spoke did he think of himself.

"Your clothes are ripped half off of you and there is blood on your face. If this is a trick, it won't work!"

Howdy said nothing. He was looking past the lantern at a face so young and lovely he caught his breath. In all the western country from Canada to the Mexican border there was no such girl as this. She was not more than eighteen, not more than a handful. Honest tan gave life and strength to her oval cheeks, and her hair was a wind-blown mass, black as the sable beauty of the sky above. Her nose was saucily tiptilted at the end, and there was a freckle on one side, plain in the lantern light. She stood so slender and straight and fearless that he thought of a mountain aspen defying the winter storms.

Then and there Howdy McFee was done with the advice of that old reprobate, Holy Joe Andrews. A man who could damn a girl like this was a man to be laughed at. Howdy laughed joyously at Sally Jones.

"To think," he said, "I've never come here and seen you."

"Your manners might be better if you had! Where did you come from?"

"Salinas and Horse Springs. In my pocket is the letter your father wrote me. I've come a long way and seen queer things this evening. Will you invite me in or must I sit down and wait for Juniper Jones to give me politeness?"

"Come in," said Sally Jones. "You look pretty tough, but you don't talk like a killer."

She closed the door behind him and led him into a big living room where age-darkened logs upheld the ceiling and rough rugs of Indian weave covered the floor.

"We've been needing a man," she said. "You got here just in time. What happened to you?"

The laughter faded from Howdy's face as he stood before her, sore and battered and disheveled, with a blood-caked crease along his side. He told her. Then: "Sally, who are Buck Briggs and Marcus Murphy?"

Even Howdy was not prepared for the black shadow of fear that sprang out of her blue eyes, from her swift exclamation of dismay. "Marcus Murphy! Dear Lord, has he been at you already?"

Before Howdy could say anything, a loud, rough voice called from another part of the house. "Sally . . . who's in there with you? Come here!"

"Come with me," said Sally, and led the way through a back door, along a little hall and into a bedroom. There a smaller lamp burned on a table beside a bed, and a great, gaunt, mustached figure lay propped against pillows glaring at them from feverish eyes.

"He is here," said Sally, and by the way she said it Howdy knew those two had been counting the days and the hours until he arrived.

"Lift the light," said Juniper Jones in a harsh voice. Sally lifted the lamp so that its rays shone fully on Howdy's face. Juniper Jones heaved himself to an elbow, leaned forward with a grunt of pain, while his feverish eyes gazed with such a terrible intensity that Howdy felt a chill creep down his back. They were the eyes of a desperate man near to madness, a man who had been close to the gates of hell — and was there still.

"You're young!" said Juniper Jones harshly. "Your face is soft . . . but there's McFee in you. Aye, there's McFee. I wonder how much."

Howdy stood straight and impassive, looking into the gaunt face of this man who was charged with killing Jason McFee from behind, this man whose mad, reckless ambition was said to desire all the Circle L range. Yet Jones's burning eyes were not those of a murderer, of a killer who would shoot a man in the back. There was nothing there that would betray a friend. But there was trouble here, beyond the broken leg that held Juniper Jones down.

"Enough McFee in me to do what has to be done,"

Howdy heard himself saying. "Enough to protect my rights."

Juniper Jones smiled as he sank back on the pillows. "I was hoping you'd say that, boy," he said with a sigh of relief. "I found you in time. Aye, just in time."

"Who killed Murphy?" Howdy asked after he had told Juniper Jones of his arrival in Las Palomas. "And why did Briggs try to kill me? For that was in his mind. And what about this Holy Joe Andrews? He seemed a harmless old coot."

Juniper Jones smiled bitterly. "If I knew who killed Marcus Murphy, the way would be easier, boy. You've told me the other answer out of your own mouth. Murphy sent Briggs to draw you into Las Palomas for Murphy to deal with. His tongue is noted all through this country. But if you would not come willingly, force would do Murphy no good. Briggs must have had his orders. If he failed to turn you off to Las Palomas, he was to make sure you never reached the Circle L to talk with me. You refused to go, so he drove you off the road to kill you, and only failed because you thought too quick. And when you went to Marcus Murphy, he thought Briggs had sent you.

"Murphy tried his best to swindle you," Juniper Jones continued. "The Circle L is worth a hundred thousand without the cattle. He tried to buy it from your uncle, and later from me. But he failed. Any other time I'd not know who killed him. Many men hated him. But the man who shot him was waiting outside that window while he talked to you. Maybe Murphy knew he was there. He waited until Murphy had failed and lost his head and started to threaten you . . . and then he stopped Murphy's mouth for good.

45

"If I knew who was outside that window, I'd know the man who gave Murphy orders. The man who wanted your share of the Circle L, or your life! Aye!" Juniper Jones exclaimed with a terrible bitterness, "I'd know the man who shot Jason McFee in the back while he rode unarmed. And I'd tear his black soul from his cowardly carcass and lay it on Jason McFee's grave to bring him peace!"

"You must have liked Jason McFee," said Howdy slowly.

"He was my friend," Juniper Jones said simply. "And this Holy Joe Andrews you met in Horse Springs is a psalm-shouting old skulker who was thick with Murphy. I ran him off the Circle L. It's been hell, boy, since your uncle died. Circle L cattle have been run off until, with the drought, I'm broke. Folks in town call the place 'Hell's Half Acre,' and they're almost right, at that. All the men but one left me, and my leg was broke with a bullet the other day. I've been sitting on a load of dynamite, fighting men who want this ranch . . . and Sally has taken the seat since my leg's been broke. Take it from her, boy."

At that moment Sally cried warningly, under her breath, "Dad! *The window!* Somebody's listening!"

Juniper Jones whirled, thrust an arm under the covers, and whipped a big revolver toward the window so fast it seemed one flash of movement. The crashing crescendo of three shots filled the room.

VII

"INTO THE NOOSE"

Glass shattered along the bottom of the window. Juniper Jones turned his head and bellowed, "Blow out that light!"

Sally was already at the lamp. As the room was plunged into pitch darkness, Juniper Jones rasped: "Boy, get out to the bunkhouse and bring me the man you find there . . . Luke Rowe. Watch him . . . drop him if he makes a move for a gun! But don't kill him. I want him to talk!"

"Dad . . . was it Luke?"

"Certainly!" Juniper Jones rapped out in the darkness. "The dogs weren't barking. Luke is the only man who could have been out there without rousing them. Hurry!"

Howdy was already making for the door, gun in hand. He felt a sudden interest in this Circle L puncher named Luke.

A light, firm hand fell on his arm. Sally Jones said, "I'll show you the back door." There was no fear in her voice, no hesitation as to the right thing to do. They went through a hall, a kitchen, and Sally opened a door and guided him under a small back *portal* into the cool open night.

"The bunkhouse is over there by the corrals," she whispered.

Howdy took the hand on his arm. It was warm and firm and steady. "Go back!" he told her.

"I'm not afraid, Howdy McFee! Don't you try to boss me!"

Howdy laughed softly. Boss her! Not a man lived who could do that. "Look under your father's window and see if he hit anything," he urged.

Sally went swiftly and lightly through the night to do that useless errand while Howdy made for the bunkhouse, looming nearby, dark and silent nearby. Dogs barked loudly. The door stood open.

Standing watchfully beside it Howdy called: "Luke Rowe! Are you in there?"

No answer came through the yawning door. But as he listened Howdy heard the dim, muffled pound of hoofs beyond the front of the house. He ran there, ignoring the clamoring dogs. The shod hoofs of a hard-pressed horse in the far distance echoed back to him. The skulker by the window had fled.

When Juniper Jones heard the news of Luke Rowe's flight, the lamp, relighted, showed his face grim and stern.

"I've been wondering how Murphy knew you were coming," he growled. "Rowe told him. He carried the mail when Sally was busy . . . and read it, I doubt not. If I could have gotten my hands on him before he left, he would have talked! Aye, he would have talked! And now, Howdy McFee, hear me out."

Juniper Jones laid the big revolver on the covers and turned his fierce gaze on the two who stood by the bed.

"Marcus Murphy offered your uncle more for this ranch than 'twas worth, with more cash down than Murphy could have raised himself. With all his sly tricks, he was only a seedy lawyer. When your uncle refused to sell, he was killed. Murphy was safe in his office in Las

48

Palomas at the time. But when he found I was part owner, he tried to buy from me, whispering you would probably never turn up to claim your share. I threw him out. And then, the trouble started. Cattle run off. Water holes poisoned. Fences cut. Murphy bought the mortgage notes on Circle L cattle and foreclosed. His man, Buck Briggs, shot two of our hands and claimed it was fair fight, and got away with it. Everywhere I turned, there was Murphy blocking me. The trouble I couldn't prove at his door I knew he was behind. And always while he was ruining me, he dangled the offer to buy."

Juniper Jones's big jaw thrust out stubbornly. "I wouldn't sell! Murphy was acting for someone who wanted this ranch so bad it wasn't reasonable. Wanted it so bad they were willing to kill an' forget the law to drive us off. When you find the answer, son, you'll have peace . . . and not until then. I've held your share of the place for you. Now it's up to you."

"If I'm not hung for murder first," Howdy said bleakly.

Juniper Jones leaned forward with a strange expression on his fierce old face. "Daggert!" he jerked out. "Henry Daggert! The man who tried so hard to put a rope around your neck in Las Palomas. That Mexican, Gonzales, works for him. Daggert is wealthy, owns three big ranches . . . an' his past is black. I wonder," said Juniper Jones harshly, "where Daggert was when Marcus Murphy was killed?"

"If we knew where your man Rowe rides, it might answer that," Howdy guessed.

"Son, you got a head on you. Look for the end of Rowe's trail an' you'll know."

Howdy cocked his sombrero at the old jaunty angle.

"I'll ride," he said.

But Sally Jones swung on him defiantly. "They'll put a rope around your neck and hang you, Howdy McFee! You're one against the whole town tonight! You sha'n't!"

"You're young to die," Juniper Jones said slowly. "But they've put death on us for no reason I can see. You're like your uncle, with a mind of your own. Take my rifle and plenty of shells."

"I'll ride with you, Howdy," Sally affirmed then with flashing eyes.

"You're mad and wild and too young to know what you're talking about," Howdy told her firmly. "You'll stay here with your father."

"I'm older now than you'll ever be," Sally retorted. "I'm a woman already, and there never was a man who got over being a foolish boy. No one wants to put a rope around *my* neck. I can ride and ask questions where they'll kill you on sight, Howdy McFee. I'm going. So save your breath and hurry!"

"Don't look at me, son," said Juniper Jones with helpless pride. "Maybe she's right at that. But don't come back without her."

VIII

"DAGGERT'S LAW"

The moon crept above the horizon, white and glowing, and the silvery light drove back the darkness and made the night a thing of glory. Sally Jones rode a great black horse Howdy had saddled. Her slender shoulders were cased in a leather coat. A small revolver was strapped around her waist. A rifle was thrust in a boot by her leg. Sally's mop of sable hair streamed back in the wind as she galloped by Howdy's side, reckless and brave.

Howdy knew suddenly he would rather have Sally riding there than any living person. Sally, no bigger than a breath, had taken his heart and trampled it. Howdy McFee, who had scorned girls all of his years, felt humble and meek, and fiercely joyous that it was so.

"We'll ride to Las Palomas, and I'll go into town while you stay outside," Sally called across to him. "There'll be news of Rowe in Las Palomas and when I've heard it I'll come out to you."

"Will you be safe?" Howdy asked. His jaw tightened at thought of anything happening to her.

Sally laughed in the moonlight. The saucy tiptilt of her nose lifted. She looked across at him. "There's not a man in Las Palomas who would dare lay a hand on me. I'm not the weak, helpless girl you think I am, Howdy McFee."

Howdy laughed in the pure joy and pride of that moment, as the drumming roll of their passing swept out through the silver night. What did a rope, a hanging, or a bullet in the back matter when there were moments like this?

They topped a rise and below them lay the dry white sands of the Hondo Wash, gleaming in the moonlight. Sally reined in abruptly. Howdy did the same when he saw the dark shapes on the bone-white sands. He jerked out the rifle Juniper Jones had given him.

"It's only one man with a pack horse!" Sally exclaimed.

Side by side they rode down the slope to meet the lone rider. Howdy chuckled with relief. The shrill quavering words of a Bible hymn were being rendered in a cracked solemn voice.

Howdy laughed. "There's only one man who could be singing like that tonight. Holy Joe Andrews!"

It was Holy Joe perched atop a big gray mule, with a fat pack on a second mule. The hymn died away as Andrews leaned forward and recognized them.

"Here I am, young fella," said Holy Joe Andrews. "And if that's Juniper Jones's gal, tell her what you told me."

"I said he could prospect on Circle L property," Howdy said unwillingly. For he sensed Sally's hostility, and what had seemed all right in Horse Springs, whether he liked it or not, was another thing now.

"That can wait," said Sally frostily. "Have you passed a man on this road?"

Holy Joe spat. "He come ridin' like the devil an' the damned was on his trail. It was one of your hands I've seen with Marcus Murphy. He asked me if I'd seen Murphy or Henry Daggert, an' when I told him, 'no,' he went on ridin' hell for leather."

"Daggert again!" Howdy blurted. He reined over and caught Holy Joe's arm. "What do you know about Marcus Murphy and Henry Daggert?"

In the moonlight Holy Joe's lips pressed tight and stubbornness came in his face. "Nothin'," he denied. "They're friends o' mine. They been good to me. Better," Holy Joe added tartly, "than some folks that might 'a' gained more by bein' open minded."

"What do you mean by that?"

"Nothin'," Holy Joe denied again. "I don't talk about my friends." It was plain that neither threats nor argument would move him.

"Listen!" said Sally suddenly.

Crickets cheeped in the stillness. Far in the distance the faint, thin howl of a coyote rose to the vaulting sky. But louder, closer, beating on the night with speeding rhythm, sounded the drum of pounding hoofs. Horses were coming toward them at a mad gallop.

"Sounds like a posse!" Howdy exclaimed. "And only one man could know where to lead them. The one who was outside Murphy's window! The one who shot him!"

"What's that?" Holy Joe demanded in a startled voice. "Marcus Murphy's shot?"

"Dead," said Howdy. "In his office while I was talking to him. Some one shot him through the back window. It was laid to me. I just got away from a noose. Ride off the road with us and let them pass."

"The Lord's doin's are strange!" Holy Joe wailed. "I'm an old man to have this brought on me. I been pious an' God-fearin' all my life, an' the sinners allus get the best of it. Git off the road quick before they find you here!" There was a sudden, feverish solicitude in Holy Joe's voice.

"Come with us!" Howdy threw at him.

"Not me! They ain't after me. I'll tell 'em I ain't seen you. I'll put 'em off the track. Get under cover! They're comin' fast!"

"I don't trust him," Sally said clearly.

"You'd better trust me!" Holy Joe shrilled. "This boy's showed me kindness! With Marcus Murphy gone he's the only one can help me. Git! Both of you. Quick!"

"He's out of his head," said Sally passionately. "He has no liking for the Circle L. Bring him along."

Howdy reined Pink around. Dangerously close to the Hondo Wash were the galloping hoofs. "We'll have to take him at his word," Howdy said.

Sally went without arguing. They had barely reached the screening growth off the road when the oncoming riders topped the rise beyond Hondo Wash and swept down.

Holy Joe Andrews waited in the road. Five horsemen pulled up around the old man. Howdy tensed as a familiar voice rang out.

"Why do you ride toward the Circle L tonight, Andrews?"

Holy Joe answered sharply: "Ain't a law against it, is they, Daggert? I ride where I durn please."

"There is law for you," Daggert said roughly. "My law! Turn back to Las Palomas and wait for me."

"I ain't takin orders from you, Daggert. I seen young McFee in Horse Springs today. He made me welcome on Circle L land."

Every word was plain and clear, ringing on the night like hammer blows.

"So Luke Rowe tells me," Daggert bit out. "Are you taking up with this McFee?"

"I'll do what I please," Holy Joe cried stubbornly. "Murphy's dead! I been tricked all around. I aim to look out for myself now."

"You're an old fool and you've been humored long enough," Daggert rasped. "I see you're ready to talk to the first man who pats your head. I've got a cure for that."

The sharp report of a revolver shot crashed out on the night. Horses stamped restlessly.

IX

"CONQUISTADOR'S GOLD"

Daggert's voice came calmly, decisively: "Let him lay there, boys. We'll plant him when we come back this way. Leave his mules here."

They galloped on.

Sally's small hand reached out to Howdy's arm. Her voice was unsteady. "They killed him in cold blood, Howdy."

Howdy caught her hand and found it cold. That small fact infuriated him. Fear Sally did not know, but treachery had unnerved her.

"That was no posse!" he said harshly. "Stay here. I'll see if there's anything I can do." But Sally rode back to the road with him.

The five riders were drumming off into the distance, out of sight. The mules stood by dumbly. At the right of the road lay Holy Joe Andrews, crumpled on his side. His battered hat had fallen off. His hair showed white and scanty as Howdy dismounted and leaned over him. His eyes were closed. He was breathing in painful gasps that racked his wizened form.

Suddenly Holy Joe began to swear. Never had Howdy heard such an outpouring. The prophets of old and the modern saints were dragged forth, larded with lusty range oaths culled during a lifetime of wandering. Lying there in the dust with his eyes closed and his thin chest heaving, Holy Joe backslid with a mighty rush.

Howdy put a hand on his shoulder and shook him. "Pull up," he begged. "Are you dying or coming back to life?"

Holy Joe opened one eye. Then the other. He turned his face up.

"I dunno," he choked. "My side's caved in and my breath's banged out. The Lord turneth His face away from His servant . . . an' that low down, no-account, whipsawed son of a pole cat shoved his gun in my belly an' shot me!"

Holy Joe groaned, swore again, and thrust a hand under his coat, under his shirt. He brought forth a heavy canvas sack, all ripped along one side. Chunks of light rock crossed with bands of color tumbled out and dropped into the dirt. He sat up with a mighty gasp, felt under his shirt, and then regarded the sack blankly.

"He shot into them ore samples. An' the rock turned the bullet alongside my ribs!" Holy Joe gulped. "Lemme stand up! Praise to glory I'm all here."

"Why did Daggert warn you away from the Circle L?" Howdy said, puzzled. "Why did he try to kill you?"

Holy Joe clutched the canvas sack in his two hands and held it out. "He's a Philistine!" he shrilled. "He's a low-down skunk. I been walkin' in a den of thieves and never knowed it! An' now I'll smite 'em hip an' thigh, like David did Goliath! It's gold, young feller. Gold on the Circle L! The old *Tres Compañeros* mine that's been lost fer two hundred years," Holy Joe babbled. "I been hearin' about it all my life, but nobody ever knowed where it was. The Spaniards worked it with Indians when they first came into this country. An' the Indians riz up an' wiped 'em out, an' the mine was never found again.

"I found gold float on that little crick that runs by your ranch house. I trailed it back into the hills. One day on a steep hill I found a whole heap of likely ore outside a badger hole. I dug in an' busted into a tunnel back of an old landslide. I made me a pine torch an' follered 'er back to the end." Holy Joe's voice cracked with emotion. "The vein's more'n five feet acrost! Solid, rotten with free gold! Fifty feet of it'd make a man rich fer life. They was skeletons in the tunnel, an' old tools. An' I found where one of them old miners had cut *Tres Compañeros* in the rock on one side. I knowed then what it was! The man who owned that tunnel was richer'n Midas. Praise glory!" Holy Joe's voice shook. "All my life I been lookin'," he said brokenly. "An' there it was! I picked these samples out that day. Been carryin' 'em ever since. Look! Wire gold all through 'em! You can see it even in the moonlight."

"Wait a minute," Howdy broke in. "Was that tunnel on Circle L land?"

Holy Joe nodded reluctantly. "All I did was find a fortune fer the Circle L owners. None of it was mine. The Circle L is part of an old Spanish grant owned outright. Only way a man could cash in was to buy the place."

"And you went to Murphy," Howdy guessed.

"Nope," said Holy Joe heavily. "I went to Las Palomas an' got drunk. I aimed to keep it secret till I figgered what to do. But the likker made me talk an' Murphy heered me fust. He sobered me up. He tried to make me tell where I got the ore. I had covered the hole up again an' I knew he'd never find it. I told him to buy the Circle L an' I'd talk turkey. He was like a crazy man after he seen that wire gold. He promised me half if I'd keep quiet. He said he'd get the Circle L."

Howdy grabbed Holy Joe's shoulder. "Was that before Jason McFee was drygulched?"

"Yep. I . . . I reckon so," Holy Joe stammered. "Murphy give me plenty of money to live on, an' said they was tryin' to buy the ranch. I prospected around a little bit an' stayed out at Daggert's most o' the time. Daggert an' Murphy was workin' together on it. But it took a long time." Holy Joe shook his head disconsolately. "I'd waited all my life . . . an' then had to keep on waitin', with the gold where I could put my hands on it. They said Juniper Jones was a hard man an' wanted too much money. They said it took time. I snuck over an' kept an eye on that hillside now and then, but Juniper Jones even run me away from there.

"I reckon," Holy Joe quavered, "I got to hatin' him as much as Murphy an' Daggert. But you was differ'nt today in Horse Springs, son. I got to thinkin', maybe you would treat me right. An' then when I heered Murphy was dead I knowed I'd have to deal with you. I didn't figger Daggert'd shoot me like that."

"You cantankerous, officious, bubble-headed old idiot!" Howdy exploded. "Jason McFee and Juniper Jones would have treated you right if you'd brought those samples to them. You fell in with thieves and the Circle L had been in trouble ever since. You cost Jason McFee his life and almost cost me mine. Murphy and Daggert were crazy . . . gold mad. When they couldn't buy, they were ready to kill until they got their hands on the Circle L. And as soon as they found where the mine was, your life wouldn't have been worth two hoots in hell! Sally!" Howdy whooped, swinging around, "there's the answer! That's why Murphy wanted to see me. That's why Rowe wanted to kill me in Horse Springs . . . and why they were all ready to drygulch me if I wouldn't deal before I saw your father. That's why Uncle Jase was killed and the ranch milked dry. They were trying to starve you out.

"When Murphy wasn't useful any more, Daggert got rid of him. He knew too much. He might have talked. He would have claimed his share of the gold. Rowe was Daggert's man, spying on the ranch. He must have tried to kill me of his own accord . . . beating Murphy out with Daggert. No wonder he made a break!"

"They've gone on to the ranch after you," Sally guessed practically.

Howdy struck his forehead with a clenched fist, crying, "I'm a fool! Why didn't I think of it? Your father's there. His life's worth no more than mine. Daggert has his own men or he'd never have shot Holy Joe in cold blood like he did."

Sally yanked on the reins until the great black horse reared high, pivoting on his hind feet and smashing down to the ground again.

"He's there in bed alone and helpless!" she cried out. "There's no one to help him!"

There was agony in her voice. She slashed hard with the *romal* ends. The big black leaped forward, scattering dirt over them, and rushed into the night with Sally bending low in the saddle.

"Sally! Wait here. I'll go!" Howdy shouted.

The drumming hoofs beat back his words. Howdy sprang for Pink.

"Watch yourself, Holy Joe, if you want to spend that gold!" he shouted as he swung on Pink. A moment later the big roan stallion snorted and bolted down the road as leather struck his side savagely.

Sally was already out of sight ahead. The dust of her

passing hung steadily in Howdy's face. Never was there a ride like that through the moon-drenched peace. Sally was ahead — always ahead. For once Pink had met his match. The black ran like a ghost from the lower world and Pink could not gain a foot. Leather and heels and bitter words did no good.

There were times when Sally was in sight far ahead. But mostly she was lost in the lonely night. And strength ran from Howdy like water from a broken vessel as he thought of what might happen to her. Sally Jones, so little, riding through the menacing night to save the life of her gaunt, helpless father.

Howdy was a full mile from the ranch house when he heard the first thin, staccato shots above the sound of Pink's mad rush. They continued, louder as he drew nearer. There was something cold and venomous about those sounds. They spoke of death without mercy. They spoke of greed and mad lust for gold. Lust willing to destroy everything in the way.

Half a mile from his goal Howdy turned Pink off the hard-packed track to softer ground. He checked Pink's pounding rush so their coming would not be heard ahead. He did that when instinct urged a reckless, plunging rush for Sally. A dead man would not save her or help Juniper Jones. And so he came to the rise which looked down on the Circle L buildings a hundred yards away. The shots were still blasting on the night. The dogs were cowed to silence. The low adobe buildings loomed dark and clear in the flooding moonlight.

Horses were grouped before it, and one lay prone, black, still on the ground. Sally's horse. Shot dead. Howdy groaned aloud as a clear, angry voice cried from the shadows under the *portal:*

"Let me go to him! You can't kill a helpless man like this!"

A hard, mocking voice replied. "Stand still! He ain't so helpless, or the boys'd have him now."

Sally, sobbing, cried out: "If I was only a man!"

Her captor demanded roughly: "Where's that McFee kid? We want him, too!" An oath of pain followed, the sharp sound of a slap. "Bite me, will you, you little hellcat!"

Sally spoke no more, but Howdy, already afoot with Juniper Jones's rifle, saw them stagger into the moonlight. Sally was fighting like a little wildcat. But she was jerked back into the shadows as Howdy raised the rifle. He could barely see her. She was being dragged into the house as he ran forward.

Sally's horse had been shot in full stride. Sally's rifle lay on the ground where it had fallen as she left the saddle. Shots came from behind the house in the direction of Juniper Jones's bedroom window. A gun barked hollowly inside.

Howdy, running with the rifle in one hand and belt gun in the other, felt his heart leap at thought of that grim old man, unable to walk — but still able to shoot. Zigzagging, he made that dark, empty *portal.* Far back in the house a gun crashed behind a door, muffled, defiant. And behind the house revolvers barked in swift intermittent bursts, like yelps of a wolf pack with its quarry at bay. Howdy slipped into the house with a gun in each hand. Daggert's voice rang out ahead.

"Jones! We've got your daughter here in the hall! I'm holding her in front of me! Don't shoot through this door or you'll hit her!"

The guns out back fell silent. The tense hush of bloody

drama filled that old adobe house. An oath whispered in Howdy's throat as he went forward. Daggert — hiding behind a helpless girl as he fought.

Juniper Jones's agonized bellow was audible. "If you hurt my girl, I'll take you to hell with my bare hands, Daggert!"

Sally cried out, "Don't let them in, Dad! They're going to kill you!"

"Shut up, you little fool!" Daggert snarled. "Jones! I'm coming through the door and she'll be in front of me."

Howdy stepped into the end of that narrow hall as Daggert finished speaking.

They had set a lamp on a chair. By its yellow light he saw a dead man huddled on the floor. And beyond, the tall, sandy-mustached Daggert held Sally from behind with both hands as he kicked open the bullet-riddled door. Standing behind Daggert was a stocky, bowlegged cowman with a gun in each hand.

Their intention was plain. Using Sally as a shield, and knowing no father would shoot at that target, they were going to march in and slaughter Juniper Jones.

In that moment Sally's courage broke. "Howdy!" she wailed. "Where are you, Howdy? Why aren't you here?"

"I'm here!" said Howdy. "Let her go, Daggert!"

X

"SALLY"

His words struck like the lash of a bullwhip. Daggert jumped back from the door, dragging Sally in front of him. The other man whirled, brought his guns up.

Howdy's two blasting shots shook the hall. Daggert's man shot once into the floor as he pitched forward. The guns flew from his limp fingers and skidded past the dead man toward Howdy as he struck the floor and lay still.

Cold sweat stood out on Howdy's face as he moved forward in a slow crouch, looking over his guns. Nothing but the hard grim certainty of death could have made him fire so close to Sally. Daggert backed away a step, still holding to Sally. Howdy realized why. Daggert had given his gun to his companion while he held Sally, and now it was on the floor out of reach.

"Howdy!" Juniper Jones called thickly from the back bedroom.

"I'm here," Howdy said again as he stepped past the dead man. He did not take his eyes off Daggert.

"Is Sally hurt?"

"She's all right," said Howdy, and he stepped past the door.

There was no exit for Daggert. The one window was small, set high. He dragged Sally back until the thick adobe wall stopped his retreat.

"Stop there, or I'll break her neck!" Daggert warned hoarsely.

Sally stood straight and slender and her eyes never left Howdy's advance. Her black, wind-blown hair cascaded about her pale face. Beautiful as she stood there so trustfully, waiting. Waiting for him.

Sally's little chin quivered as she begged: "Don't let them get Dad, Howdy!"

"They won't!" said Howdy briefly, and came on behind his guns, pistol in his right hand, rifle held at the ready in his left.

"Stand still!" Daggert shouted, with a rising note of fear in his voice. "You want her hurt?"

"Daggert," said Howdy softly, "you won't hurt her for I've got you cornered. This is the showdown. Hurt one hair and God Himself will turn away from what I'll do to you. I won't kill you clean, Daggert. I'll break you. I'll beat you. I'll tear you apart in little pieces until you beg for death. Let her go, Daggert!"

Daggert, who had been bold as a lion when he egged a mob to blood madness, wilted. He looked past those leveled guns into Howdy's face and cold sweat stood out on his graying face.

"Will you let me out of here?" he stammered.

"Let her go, Daggert!"

Daggert, with a rising note of hysterical fear in his voice, dropped his hands. "Take her! Rowe! Simpson! Come here! Quick!"

"I knew you'd come!" Sally choked to Howdy, and slipped past him into the bedroom.

Daggert cowered in the corner, breathing thickly, his eyes fastened on the gun muzzles less than an arm's length away. All that had happened in the span of a minute. Back of the house the guns had fallen silent. Howdy listened for the men Daggert had called.

Suddenly the heavy report of a rifle sounded out in front. A revolver answered with three fast shots. The rifle spoke again. And then the sound of a galloping horse faded quickly.

A wild, shrill whoop split the night out in front. "Howdy McFee! Where are you?"

Howdy fired once into the floor by way of reply. He grinned coldly as Daggert flinched.

Daggert gasped. "That sounds like . . . like. . . ."

"Holy Joe Andrews!" Howdy finished. "It is Holy Joe, Daggert. Come back from the dead, where you left him. Come back in time to rout those two men you left outside. Come to get *you*, Daggert! You're at the end of your rope. You've played your cards and your hand's no good. You spoke of law to Holy Joe, Daggert. *Your* law! Gun law! Speak up, Daggert, before you meet real gun law. Who killed Jason McFee? Who killed Marcus Murphy?"

Daggert went down on his knees. That tall, bold, mustached killer went down on his knees before the thing he saw in Howdy's face.

"My God! Don't look at me like that!" he babbled. "Don't shoot! I . . . I did. McFee laughed at me when I wanted to buy his ranch. And Murphy . . . he would have wrecked everything in the end. He was a liar, a cheat, and I couldn't trust him. He had it coming . . . he had it coming. . . ." His voice broke hysterically.

Holy Joe burst into the hall, lugging an old Sharps buffalo rifle. His battered hat was shoved on the back of his head. His wizened, wrinkled face was aflame with eagerness.

"I kilt one of them jaspers!" he yelled. "Glory be! I

plugged him in the moonlight like a buffler bull. An' winged the other'n as he made tracks hangin' on t' other side of his hoss. Holy Moses! What's come off in here?"

Holy Joe stopped short, staring at the dead men on the floor, at Daggert's cowering in the corner. "Daggert!" he shrilled, "Lemme at him!" Holy Joe raised the rifle.

Howdy stepped in front of Daggert. "Stop it, you fire-eater!" he ordered. "Daggert was just confessing his sins. Tell 'em over again to Holy Joe, Daggert."

Daggert, struggling slowly to his feet, repeated in a dull, dead voice his damning admissions.

Holy Joe spat recklessly and shoved his hat to the other side of his head. "I studied it as I kicked my old mule this way, an' figgered it about like that," he nodded. "You an' Marcus made a fool of me, Daggert, an' I hope they hang you higher'n Hamen. You're a skunk, an' if my side didn't hurt so bad I'd tell you more. What you gonna do with him, Howdy McFee?"

The swift murmur of Sally's voice had been coming from the bedroom. Now she called, "Howdy, help me get Dad back on the bed."

"Keep your eyes on Daggert," Howdy said. "We'll tie him up and keep him until the law comes and gets the whole story here at the house."

"I'll watch him," Holy Joe promised grimly. "An' if he wiggles a toe, I'll blow his gizzard out."

Howdy went into the bedroom. Sally had relighted the lamp. Juniper Jones was lying on a heap of pillows and bedclothes with his stiff splint-cased leg stretched out awkwardly. A Colt revolver and a pile of cartridges and empty shells lay beside him.

"Son," said Juniper Jones, "I reckon you just made it in time. Sally told me what it was all about an' I could wring that old psalm-singin' buzzard's neck for not comin' to us with the news of that mine. The way it is, I reckon I'll have to make Holy Joe rich along with the rest of us. But if he quotes Scripture at me all the time, I'll. . . ."

"Repent your sins, Juniper Jones, an' give thanks fer your good fortune." Holy Joe advised from the hall. "Glory be!"

"I was afraid of that," Juniper sighed. "I don't know whether the gold's worth it, or not. Son, I ain't gonna try and thank you. But I'm proud to call you pardner. You're a McFee down to your boots. An' I reckon tonight your uncle's restin' easier."

Juniper Jones swiped at his ragged mustache and coughed.

"That's for me," he said. "You're gonna be here some time, I reckon. Sally can thank you in her own way."

Howdy looked at Sally standing there by the lamp. A new Sally, a glorious Sally, all pink-cheeked and starry-eyed, and her smile was like the glory of the night through which they had ridden.

"She doesn't have to thank me," Howdy said severely. "Do you, Sally?"

Sally's smile faded to swift hurt. "Of course I do!" she cried. "I want to thank you. I . . . I. . . ."

"Then kiss me," Howdy said.

Neither of them minded Juniper Jones's snort and gratified chuckle. Or heard out in the hall the fervent, "Glory be!"

In 1934, according to his records, T. T. Flynn wrote 1,548 pages and every one of the twenty-seven stories he wrote that year was sold. Approximately half of these were Western stories. With the exception of "Rodeo's 'A' Man" which appeared in Doubleday, Doran's *West* (5/35), all of his Western stories were sold either to *Dime Western* or *Star Western* where they were always showcased on the covers and came in first position in the issues. Holy Joe Andrews in "Conquistador's Gold" was evidently a character that fascinated Flynn. He brought him back, although somewhat transformed, in a story he titled "Maverick Man." It was sold to Rogers Terrill at Popular Publications on October 16, 1934. Terrill changed the title to "The Rawhide Kid" for its appearance in *Dime Western* in the issue dated January 1, 1935. The story proved very popular with readers and Flynn was asked to write a sequel. Because Flynn titled the sequel "The Rawhide Kid Returns," Rogers Terrill's title for the first story has been retained although the text has been fully restored.

THE RAWHIDE KID

I

"LARAMIE"

How he got into Agua Fría no one ever quite knew. For seventy-odd miles in any direction a chuckwalla lizard would have starved and shriveled. Men rode through that desolation in the daytime with shoulders bowed under the sun blast and sombrero brims pulled low, counting the miles to Agua Fría and to the only water in those long harsh miles of dry, barren border waste.

It mattered little that the border lay fifteen miles to the north of Agua Fría. Men had drawn that line. A higher authority had put the great cool spring under the overhanging escarpment of rock, giving its cool waters an unending flow. Agua Fría *was* the border for all practical purposes. The border even under Mexican law — if law there was in that isolated little cluster of sun-baked adobe buildings.

Holy Joe Moran was the first to see him when Laramie Scott, staggering now and then as he plodded through the white, flour-like dust, came into Agua Fría that night. Laramie was limping. Half a dozen curs yapped at his heels. He ignored them and the occasional shadowy figure he passed. Head forward, shoulders bent, he plodded mechanically toward the long hitch rack and the lighted front of the Glory Hole Bar where life centered in Agua Fría after dark. But first Laramie came to the shabby *Cantina* Gonzalez where mescal, aguardiente, and low-grade whiskey were priced for peon pockets. The dregs of all that was lawless along the border passed through the *Cantina* Gonzalez. Dandy Gonzalez was known from Yuma to Brownsville for his hatred of the law, Yankee or Mexican.

The free lunch in the *Cantina* Gonzalez had just been replenished, and out of the open front drifted the hot spicy odors of fresh chili, *frijoles*, well-cooked meat. Laramie Scott stopped there as if a hand had caught him. Stopped, throwing up his head, sniffing ravenously.

In the band of yellow light he was small, thin, shabby. Not more than sixteen. Just a kid. Laughable. His Levi's were patched, ragged around the bottoms. His shoes split, and one sole flapped loosely. His neck was thin and his face thin and spattered with large brown freckles. An old hat, stained, misshapen, too large, lopped over toward one eye.

Young Laramie Scott was awkward, grotesque, as he stood there, head up, sniffing. But his manner held a tenseness akin to the wary alertness of the skulking dogs, lacking the threat of their snarls and bared white teeth. He swayed, staggering slightly, bracing himself against the side of the doorway.

Three Mexicans crowded out. The nearest gave him a quick look and brushed hard against him. Laramie staggered, almost went down. The man laughed.

"Damn you!" Laramie gasped thickly.

A second man spat: *"¡Gringo!"*

The old hatreds — greaser and *gringo* — lay always under the surface in Agua Fría. It boiled to a head now there in front of Dandy Gonzalez's dirty little *cantina*.

"*Borracho* . . . drunk," the third one sneered.

Dark-skinned peon stock, they were probably bandits from outside of Agua Fría. The law was no more strict out there than in town. Grinning, they hemmed Laramie against the adobe wall of the *cantina*. The third man said something under his breath — and suddenly jumped back with a startled oath as a spring-blade knife flicked open and menaced his middle.

Laramie Scott faced them, his freckled face drawn and haggard, his eyes feverish. The knife was unsteady in his lean hand. "If you want trouble," Laramie whispered thickly, "come an' get it!" He spoke with an effort, as if his throat were swollen and his jaws had not opened for a long time.

A brown hand snatched at his wrist, caught it, disarmed him with a dexterous twist. The three men closed in, smothering resistance.

Behind them a voice roared: "By the holy jumpin' Judas tree! What's comin' off here? *Vamos*, you onery hellions!" A shot blasted. Dust spurted at one man's heel.

They were armed, but the first man who looked over his shoulder yelped: "*¡Madre de Dios . . . el padre del diablo!*"

He scuttled into the darkness. The other two followed. Men had crowded into the doorway at the shot. They stopped there now, unwilling to come out into the open.

Laramie Scott leaned against the rough adobe, wiping the back of his hand over a smear of blood on his cheek. His knees were unsteady. He was breathing heavily. His freckled face was still without expression as he stared at the huge man who swung down from a long-legged bay horse and came forward, rumbling through a vast white beard.

"I thought I seen *gringo* skin afore they piled into you."

Holy Joe Moran would have made two of the trio he had routed. Topping six feet and a half the turned-up brim of his dusty black hat made him seem taller. Massive shoulders and long arms matched. And the clothes of Holy Joe Moran were hardly less worn and patched than those of the youth who stared at him. But the vast white beard, the fiercely hooked nose, the glinting eyes under bushy white brows gave dignity to Holy Joe Moran which patches could not lessen.

"How'd you come out of it, son?" he asked.

"All right, mister."

"Hell, what's the matter with your voice? Sounds like you swallowed the widow's cat."

Inside the *cantina* a man laughed. Laramie Scott turned his head, scowled, spoke with the same thick effort.

"I reckon my stomach'll take care of the cat. How come they called you father of the devil?"

"H-m, savvy Mex, huh? You're a sassy kid to be passin' questions to your elders. What's your name?"

"Laramie Scott, mister. An' I ain't a kid. I'm a man."

"Huh!" Holy Joe snorted. "Where you from?"

"I ain't from. I'm here."

"Sounds like you're a maverick. How long since you rode into Agua Fría?"

"Just come. I didn't ride . . . I walked."

"Hells bells an' salty saints! I'll turn you over my knee an' blister your britches ef you don't stop lyin' to me! I didn't run them greasers off to take sass from a freckled-faced dogie who ain't dry behind the ears yet. It's seventy miles to the next water. Where's your water bottle? Where's your grub?"

"I ain't got any grub an' I didn't have no water. I made it in all right . . . until I smelled that food in there. Git on about your business, mister, an' I'll take care of my britches. I'm a man an' a long ways from finished yet."

Laramie stooped to get his knife — and staggered and pitched forward onto his hands and knees. He reeled up, clutching the knife. "Soon as I get some water an' a bite to eat I'll be man-size!" he got out thickly, fiercely.

"My God Almighty! I figgered it was booze an' it's an empty belly. Gonzalez! You got a customer."

Holy Joe's powerful arm caught Laramie Scott erect, guided him into the *cantina*. The crowd fell back as Holy Joe made for the end of the bar and the free lunch.

Dandy Gonzalez met them, grinning welcome over the blazing diamond horseshoe in his collar. Tall, slender, fastidious personally, Dandy Gonzalez dressed better than any of his customers. He made capital out of shabbiness, vice, viciousness. Those who frequented the *Cantina* Gonzalez seemed to like it.

Gonzalez spoke good English. He cried, "Holy Joe Moran! They had you dead last spring. Welcome, my friend. Drinks are on the house. What'll it be?"

"Water," Holy Joe rumbled in his beard. "Never mind the drinks. I'll 'tend to my own dyin' an' celebratin'."

Dandy Gonzalez looked startled. "Water? You drink water?"

"You heard me!" Holy Joe roared. "Tell that squint-eyed barkeep to jump fast or I'll climb the bar an' shake some sense in him. My podner here is dry!" Holy Joe looked at the free lunch and dryly added: "He's hungry too."

75

Laramie Scott had braced himself before the free lunch, drawn a deep breath, snatched a slice of meat. He was wolfing it, having difficulty in swallowing. He had a glass of water, then he began to eat more carefully, but with a terrible intentness.

"Gimme tequila," Holy Joe said gruffly to the bartender. "Hell! Leave the bottle there! Who said anything about *one* drink?"

The crowd drifted back to the bar and tables. Two Mexicans began to strum a guitar over in one corner. Music, the hum of voices, filled the low-ceilinged room once more. A slender girl in a red silk dress drifted to Laramie Scott. Her hair was black, her creamy cheeks reddened. She was a little older than Laramie. Her hand caressed his arm. Laramie ignored her.

Holy Joe Moran snorted. "Tell your gals to stay away from the kid," he ordered Gonzalez. "He's in here fer grub an' water, *no más*. He ain't got any money. They're wastin' time on him."

Gonzalez jerked his head at the girl. She shrugged, departed.

"No money?" said Gonzalez softly. "No. He does not look it, eh? Or you my friend?"

Half the bottle of tequila was already gone. Holy Joe filled his glass again, tossed it off. "Don't waste your breath callin' me 'friend,' " he grunted. "I'm p'rticular. I got the money an' plenty more where it come from."

Gonzalez grinned warily. "I have heard talk like that before . . . but the money is hard to find."

Holy Joe shoved a big hand in his pocket, brought out a fistful of coins, slid one through his fingers to the damp bar top. "That make you feel any better, Gonzalez?"

Gold glinted yellow in the lamplight. Dandy Gonzalez

slowly picked up the coin and examined it. His glance slid to the bulging pocket from which it had come. Gonzalez waved an arm, grinning apologetically.

"My mistake, Señor Moran. Another bottle?"

Holy Joe pushed his dusty hat back and chuckled dryly. "Just like I figgered. Gold sets you droolin'. Keep your bottles. I aim to get drunk tonight. Plenty drunk. But not in your rat hole, Gonzalez. Kid, you got the wrinkles outa your belly?"

Laramie Scott wiped the blade of his knife on his trouser leg and closed it slowly with a dirty thumb. The ravenous look was gone. But his eyes were bloodshot and weary as he stifled a yawn. "All I could crowd in, mister. If there's anything I can do for you now, I'll be happy to oblige."

Holy Joe chuckled in his beard. "You're talkin' like a man, even if you ain't one. Nothin' you can do but stay outa my way tonight while I get lit up. Better go to sleep. You look beat out."

Gonzalez said: "I have beds in the back. . . ."

"I reckon it's as good as he can do," Holy Joe decided. "He ain't got any money to cause trouble. Look me up tomorrow, kid." And Holy Joe departed, clutching the *tequila* bottle in one big fist.

Laramie Scott stood there by the free lunch and watched Holy Joe duck out the low doorway. His freckled face was expressionless as he turned to Gonzalez. "Show me that bunk, mister."

Gonzalez smiled broadly. The diamond horseshoe in his collar glittered as he bowed with an air of sincerity. "This way, *señor*. The best we have for any friend of Holy Joe's. You know him long, no?"

"None of your business," Laramie said shortly.

II

"BONANZA LURE"

In all the border country no man could celebrate more freely than at the Glory Hole. Music, women, drinks, gambling, dancing were there. All trails for two hundred miles led to Agua Fria and water. Most men who rode them laughed at the law. No questions were asked at the Glory Hole. Hard cash was the only passport needed. The doors never closed.

Cinco MacDonald, Mexican-born enigma of a Scot father and a Mexican mother, was the owner. Holy Joe Moran was hardly less of an enigma. His patriarchal beard had earned him the title of Holy Joe. As far back as men could remember that beard had been in existence along the border, perhaps dropping out of sight for months, but as apt to reappear in the thick of trouble or a sporadic revolution as an honest mining development or cattle deal. Holy Joe's known prowess with guns, fists, drink had made him *el padre del diablo* among the Mexicans. But *gringo* or Mexican, after thirty-odd years, knew little about Holy Joe Moran.

Tonight the celebration of Holy Joe was an epic, an eighth wonder, a "bust" whose fame would travel far trails, to be told and retold by men who had witnessed it and been a part of it. Holy Joe Moran had gold tonight. Yellow gold, which rang clear and hard on the bar top, gleaming yellow under the bright lanterns which studded the beamed ceiling. And Holy Joe was spending riotously, lavishly. Drinks for all who cared to drink. More drinks. Music. Wild songs, led by Holy Joe Moran's deep bellow.

News of that wild evening spread throughout Agua Fria. Men flocked to the Glory Hole to join in. So wild and furious was the merriment that by midnight no one had stopped to wonder what the celebration was about. Holy Joe had not mentioned that.

Cinco MacDonald was cold sober, as always. Slightly hunchbacked, thin, taciturn, unsmiling, he moved about keeping his own council. But now and then Cinco went to the cash drawer, removed gold pieces which Holy Joe had passed over the bar, and carried them into his little cubby hole office behind. And each time he appeared again, his angular face was sharper, shrewder. If a man had cared to look closely he would have seen emotion flaming brighter, more fiercely in the deep-set eyes of Cinco MacDonald. And if he were a wise man, he would have known the reason why.

The ordinary hates and dislikes never touched Cinco MacDonald. He was a man without emotion. One thing, and one thing only, could make his eyes burn so brightly. Gold. Shining yellow gold!

Two cowmen from north of the border quarreled at one end of the bar. A gun roared. One of them weaved, dropped to the floor. Those around the spot crowded away. The second man put his back to the bar and looked warily around the room.

Gun fights were not new in the Glory Hole. A dead man, more or less, was not enough to stop an evening. A woman laughed shrilly. The quick tension began to relax. But in the quiet Holy Joe's voice boomed out.

"By Godfrey, this ain't no time to be cuttin' loose with a six-gun!"

Holy Joe pushed through the crowd. The turned-up brim of his hat was high above every other hat. He walked upright and steadily although he had been drinking hard for hours.

The cowman waved him back with the gun, uttered an oath. "This ain't any of your business, old man! He called me out an' I let him have it!"

Holy Joe advanced sternly. "You're bustin' up my party," he accused. "I don't aim to have any bowlegged cow chaser from up north spile my night. Gimme that gun."

"If you don't want lead in your belly, old man, get back an' shut up! I killed this jasper for being too open with his mouth. I ain't takin' any more from you."

"You're drunk," Holy Joe announced sorrowfully. "Gimme that gun, young feller, before you bust out with it again."

Cinco MacDonald never took part in trouble. He paid men to do that if needed. He had slipped out of his office a moment after the shot sounded, had stood hunched over at the end of the bar, listening.

Now as the gun whipped up and menaced Holy Joe, Cinco MacDonald reached under his coat, brought out a small two-barreled Derringer, and leveled it at the cowman's back. Before he could fire, Holy Joe's left hand chopped across and down in a movement faster than the eye could follow. It knocked the cowman's six-gun over against the bar, and an instant later a massive fist smashed into the cowman's face. The force of that mighty blow drove the man half over the bar. He lay there on his back inertly.

Holy Joe ran fingers through his beard and viewed the result benignly. "I don't aim to have my night spoiled by no such goings-on," he announced mildly. "He's yours, Cinco. Throw him out or kill him, but keep him outa my way."

"Anything you say," Cinco agreed obligingly, the Derringer out of sight again. "I guess the drinks are on the house." He raised his voice. "Everybody up to the bar!"

Holy Joe boomed: "You're a man, Cinco!"

Cinco MacDonald did not answer. But his bright eyes were speculative as he watched Holy Joe Moran breast the bar again and reach for a bottle.

III

"PANCHITA"

Laramie Scott slept like one dead. The room to which Dandy Gonzalez had conducted him was more like a cell — small, bare, whitewashed, containing a cot and chair. The door stood ajar, but the occasional steps outside did not disturb him. He had been asleep before Dandy Gonzalez had disappeared. Five hours he lay there, face down in his clothes without moving. At the end of that time he came awake as suddenly as he had gone to sleep.

Silently he rolled off the cot and stood up, looking, listening. Then yawned, stretched, rubbed his eyes, moved to the door. He stepped out on a narrow *portal* which faced the patio.

The night was dark. Across the patio several curtained windows glowed dimly. A phonograph was playing in one of the rooms. Otherwise everything was quiet. Laramie moved toward the front, the loose shoe sole slapping softly despite his efforts to walk quietly. He stopped after a moment, drew the big knife, sliced off the sole. It bared the bottom of his foot, but thereafter he moved silently. Two doors were at the head of the patio, the left-hand one leading into the *cantina*, the right-hand one into a narrow passage to the street. Laramie tried the right-hand door. It was locked.

He stood considering, ignoring the *cantina* door which stood slightly ajar, giving out the sound of voices.

A low voice spoke almost at his elbow, in Spanish: "You leave early, *señor*."

Laramie jumped, turned as he recognized the voice of the *cantina* girl whom Holy Joe Moran had sent away. She was standing there in the blackness beside the door. He could barely make her out. He answered gruffly: "What're you doing here?"

She laughed softly. "*Pobrecito* . . . poor little man . . . I have been watching you. So tired. So lonesome. Such a little boy. I think you miss your mother . . . no?"

Her hand touched his arm. Laramie pushed it away.

"Stop it," he said gruffly. "I'm broke an' I don't fool with girls, anyway. Hunt you another man."

She laughed again. "Man?" she said. "If I was looking for a man I would not be here with you, boy. A man, when he has no money, needs a woman. A boy needs a mother. Tonight, little one, I will be this mother you need."

"Damn it!" said Laramie disgustedly. "You been listening to old Holy Joe."

"And why not? He is your friend, no? He should know about you."

82

"He doesn't know anything about me, lady. And I don't know anything about him."

She said quickly, "That is good. He will bring you trouble. You must not see him again."

"Bad *hombre*, eh?"

"You must not see him again."

The *cantina* door opened. A band of light struck out onto the patio around the elegant figure of Dandy Gonzalez who came through the doorway. Gonzalez saw them, stopped short, peering.

"Panchita," he said sharply in Spanish, "what are you doing here?" Gonzalez shifted into English, turned to Laramie. "Did she wake you up?"

"No," Laramie denied. "I woke up an' walked out. Met her here on my way out."

"Get in the *cantina*," Gonzalez ordered the girl curtly. And when he was alone with Laramie, he spoke politely. "You did not sleep well? Something was wrong?"

"Nothing, mister. I'm moving on."

"You were tired. You have been here only a few hours."

"I had all the sleep I want, mister. Can I get out past the bar in there?"

Gonzalez chuckled. "There is no hurry. The old man will not want to see you until tomorrow. He is drunk now. Where, my friend, did you come from with Holy Joe? A long way I am thinking, since you were so tired."

Laramie was silent for a moment, then agreed cautiously. "Maybe."

"Allow me, a cigarette?" Gonzalez offered him one, struck a match. The flare showed his dark face was smiling, friendly. "Where did you and Holy Joe come from?" he questioned.

"You're askin' a lot of questions," Laramie said coolly,

exhaling tobacco smoke.

"Holy Joe is my friend," Gonzalez replied airily. "As a friend I am pleased to hear all he has been doing."

"Ask him, then."

"I have been wondering how it is that Holy Joe's pockets are full of gold tonight. Never have I heard of him so rich."

"I guess," said Laramie slowly, "it's time you were hearing something new then. You say he's drunk?"

"Drinking hard and throwing his money away. By morning there will be none left. And I suppose," said Dandy Gonzalez carefully, "he brought all the gold he has, eh?"

Laramie said vaguely, "You better ask him that, mister. It's his gold."

"But tomorrow you will both be broke again, my young friend."

"I been broke before. Thanks for the smoke. I got to be going."

"First, a drink in the *cantina*, on the house."

"No," said Laramie, "I don't drink."

He moved past Gonzalez toward the *cantina* door. Gonzalez caught his arm, whirled him back roughly. "Not so quick, boy! I have questions for you to answer with more respect. I have listened to you strut like a young cock until I am sick in the stomach. You understand me? Stand there and talk."

"I'll bet," said Laramie Scott, "you think you're the first man who's tried that on me. But you ain't, mister. Get outa my way."

Laramie staggered from a blow in the face. "A whip would do you more good!" Gonzalez said through his teeth. "Keep quiet before I get a whip and cut your back in strips. Answer my questions."

Laramie stood still. "I'm listening, mister."

"Where did Holy Joe get that gold? How much more of it has he got?"

"That's all of it, I reckon."

The second blow was harder. "Don't lie to me! There is more of it! Much more! Where is it?"

"Listen, mister, if I tell you, what then?"

Dandy Gonzalez chuckled in sudden good humor. "Then," he said, "you will get your share of it too, instead of waiting around with empty pockets like a young dog."

"What'll happen to Holy Joe, mister?"

"What do you care? Where is the rest of Moran's gold?"

"Bend over, mister, so you can get it. That's right. Don't want anyone else to hear this. Stand still!"

Laramie's hand came out of his trouser's pocket. The blade of his knife flicked open in the darkness. The point pricked hard into the stomach beside him. Gonzalez swore, jumped back. The knife followed him.

Laramie said: "Stand still! The last man I stuck this into had to hold hisself in with both hands when I got through."

Gonzalez froze there in the darkness. The keen knife point was in his skin. A wrong move on his part, or a push on the knife, would send the blade deep in his body. Breath whistled through his teeth.

"I oughta kill you, mister," said Laramie. " 'Cause I reckon next time we meet you'll be all set to even this up. But I guess I ain't man enough to do that while you ain't got a chance. But I savvy you now an' I'll be lookin' for trouble next time. See how quick you can frog it across the patio."

Dandy Gonzalez felt no shame in diving through the

darkness when the pressure of that sharp knife blade came off his stomach. Perspiration was cold on his face. Fear made him weak for the moment.

Not until he was safe beyond all possible reach of the knife did he stop and shout in Spanish: *"Gregorio . . . Max . . . Felipe . . . stop him!"*

A moment later the voice of the bull-necked Gregorio who kept order in the *cantina* came anxiously: "Here, *patrón*. What is it?"

"Stop him! Don't let him get away. Is he there?"

Gregorio's voice came through the darkness in anxious apology. *"Sí, patrón.* But who is this man I must stop?"

"Fool! Son of a burro! The one who came with Holy Joe Moran. Where is he?"

Gregorio's voice showed relief. "Only the boy, *patrón?* But a moment ago he went out, walking slowly through the *cantina.* He was sleepy. Even I, Gregorio, felt sorry for him. A nice *gringo,* eh, *patrón?* Shall I go after him and say you wish to see him?"

Gregorio was unable after that to understand why a storm of abuse burst about his head.

IV

"HOLY JOE'S TRAIL"

The dead cattleman had been removed from the Glory Hole. His killer had been dragged out unconscious into the open night for better or worse. More gold from the seemingly inexhaustible pockets of Holy Joe Moran was passing over the bar.

The night was in full blast again when Laramie Scott appeared in the front doorway. The youngster stood there a moment surveying the room. He looked thinner, shabbier, more laughable, if possible. His thin, freckled face was serious. The old hat, canted toward one eye, looked larger than ever on his head. He spotted Holy Joe at the bar surrounded by a noisy throng and pushed through until he came to Holy Joe's side.

Big Tom Wade, a cattleman who was staying south of the border for reasons known best to himself, looked down as Laramie edged in front of him.

Wade yelled: "Where'd this half-pint come from? Room at the bar, boys! We got a customer fer a glass of milk!"

Red faced, perspiring, hat clutched in one hand, Laramie let himself be pushed to the bar. Laughter burst out about him.

"Milk!" another man yelled. "Who's got a can?"

Laramie rested an elbow on the bar. "Gimme the milk," he said to the barkeep. "I like it."

It was doubtful if such a request had ever been made across the Glory Hole bar. The barkeep looked indignant. "Ain't got any," he replied sourly.

"Gimme beer then, mister."

Holy Joe turned, looked down, saw who was standing at his side. "Great snakes!" he exploded. "I put you to bed once tonight, kid. Git back to your blankets."

"I'm slept out," Laramie said.

"Git on back, anyway. This ain't no place for you."

"I like it," Laramie said. "How long you going to stay here?"

"Hell's fire, what business is it of yours, kid? As long as I can stay on my feet, I reckon. Git on back to Gonzalez's place, I tell you."

Holy Joe swayed slightly, gripped the bar edge with one hand. His eyes, keen and certain when he had left the *Cantina* Gonzalez, were now bleary, cloudy.

Laramie reached for the glass of beer which the barkeep had pushed to him. "I ain't a kid," he said. "I'm staying."

Cinco MacDonald, standing hunched behind the bar, frowned at the answer. "Run along," he said curtly. "Holy Joe's buying the house. His word's law tonight."

Laramie set the beer glass down with a thump. His eyes were on Cinco MacDonald's left hand resting on the bar top. "Mister," he said, and every man standing around heard him, "where'd you get that ring?"

Cinco MacDonald jerked the hand off the bar, then put it back carefully. The ring on his lean finger stood out clearly under the light. Gold, thick and heavy, it was set with a wedge-shaped piece of rough rainbow quartz which glowed under the light with all the hues of the rainbow.

Cinco smiled — and many men said afterward that they had never seen a smile on Cinco's face before. It did not matter that the smile had no humor in it. Or that Cinco's eyes had narrowed, hardened.

"I bought it," Cinco said. "Fellow drifted through here about six months ago. He was broke and wanted some grub and a bottle of whiskey. He sold me the ring for ten pesos, gold."

"What was his name?"

Cinco shrugged.

Laramie slipped a hand in his trouser's pocket. His eyes were riveted on Cinco MacDonald's face, and on his own thin, freckled face there was something which caused Cinco MacDonald to step back from the bar.

"Mister," Laramie Scott said, "you're lying. You never

88

bought that ring. It belonged to my brother. His dead wife gave it to him. He'd 'a' starved before he'd 'a' sold it. An' he never drank, let alone traded his ring for a bottle of whiskey. I'm lookin' for him. Long Bob Scott, they called him. What happened to him, mister?"

Cinco said: "I don't know." His voice had an ugly rasp. He pulled the ring from his finger, tossed it on the bar. "You can have the ring if it means anything to you," he said.

Laramie's fist closed over it. "I ain't thankin' you, because I think you stole it. What about Bob? He had plenty of money when he came over the border."

Cinco shrugged again. "How do I know? I can't keep track of every man who stops here at the bar. We don't ask questions in Agua Fría, youngster."

"Maybe," Laramie said, "it might be a good thing if someone started to ask . . . an' found some answers!"

"Help yourself." Cinco turned away. "The next is on the house, men! Line up and take a long one to Holy Joe."

The rush to the bar was quick and enthusiastic. Holy Joe bent his head.

"Kid," he advised from the corner of his mouth, "drift outa town an' keep going. It ain't healthy to cross Cinco here in Agua Fría. You called him out in public in a way he won't ferget. Here's a stake." Holy Joe put three gold pieces into Laramie's hand, pushed him back from the bar.

Edging through the crowd, Laramie walked out of the Glory Hole. No one was loitering outside at the moment. He moved around to one of the side windows and removed his hat. By standing on his toes he could look into the barroom.

At the end of the bar Cinco MacDonald was just jerking his head to a short, thick-set Mexican. The man followed the hunched figure back into the office at the rear of the bar.

The second window farther back opened into the office. It was up from the bottom. The two men were talking Spanish — old Mexico Spanish, different from that spoken north of the border.

"You saw this young *gringo?*" Cinco MacDonald asked.

"*Sí, señor.*"

"I don't want him around."

"A small matter, *señor.*"

"Or anyone else to know what happened to him."

A moment's hesitation. "That is another matter," the Mexican said. "It will be worth more."

Cinco swore in English. "Damn you, Martínez! Who said anything about what it would cost? You heard what I wanted."

Martínez agreed hastily: "*Sí, señor.* It shall be done. Is that all?"

"Yes. Find Salazar and send him here."

The Mexican went out. Steps padded back and forth across the room for a few moments, stopped. The clink of coins on wood came out the window. Laramie looked in.

A double arm's length away Cinco MacDonald bent over an old desk intently examining a handful of gold coins. His manner was almost hypnotic as he picked up first one, then another, holding each one close and turning it over in his fingers.

A knock on the door caused him to open a drawer hastily and sweep the coins clinkingly into it. Laramie

dodged back out of sight and heard: "Come in, Salazar."
The door closed.

Cinco MacDonald said curtly: "I'm going out of town
tomorrow. I want several good men along who can keep
their mouths shut. The horses must be good travelers."

"Where we go, *señor?*"

"Damn you, don't ask questions. We go. That's
enough."

The man agreed hastily: "*Sí.* What time we leave?"

"I don't know yet. I'll tell you tomorrow."

"*Sí, señor. No mas* . . . no more?"

Cinco MacDonald hesitated. "Yes," he said. "If Martínez
needs any help from you, give it to him. Anything he
asks. That's all."

In the dark Laramie grinned faintly, and then flattened
himself against the adobe wall as Salazar emerged from
the Glory Hole and walked into sight past the end of
the hitch rack, and on across the street.

The other Mexican had vanished out into the night.
Cinco MacDonald left his office a few moments later,
strolled back behind the bar again. Laramie walked off
into the darkness and vanished.

Fifteen minutes later he stopped in the moonlight a
half mile beyond the last straggling adobe hut. A tangled
mesquite thicket loomed darkly just beyond. Behind him
scattered lights and the occasional barking of a dog were
the only signs of life. No one had followed him.

Laramie entered the mesquite, found a flat, sandy spot,
swept it clear of mesquite thorns with his old hat, and
lay down. The earth was still warm with the heat of
the preceding day. He was asleep in a few moments.

The rising sun was driving back the early morning
chill when he awoke. Presently, when the outer fringes

of Agua Fría were stirring to life, he arose, brushed the clinging sand from his clothes, and walked into town.

The escarpment of rock spawning the swiftly-flowing spring of water which never went dry lay at the base of dry, gravelly, dun-colored hills. North and south those Agua Fría hills stretched, and to east and west of them the land was a dry waste for a hard day's ride.

Agua Fría sprawled in a small huddle of sun-baked adobe buildings below the spring. Small irrigating *acequias* threaded to meager garden plots. Scattered trees raised welcome greenery. Horse and cattle corrals were scattered about. The population was mostly Mexican.

The first Mexicans Laramie encountered paid him scant attention. He drank from the cool, clear water of a little *acequia,* washed face and hands, and then wandered about the edge of town, stopping at the corrals, talking to those Mexicans he met. Within two hours he owned a roan horse. A good horse, worth more than the few dollars he had paid for it. With reasonable certainty some legitimate owner north of the border had mourned its loss. But with that owner impossible to find at the moment, Laramie took his place cheerfully. The horse, a battered saddle, a bit and bridle took one of the gold pieces, and breakfast had been thrown in by the seller.

Laramie rode back to the short main street, entered the dim interior of a little general store. The stock was scanty, the prices high. But after an hour of bargaining with the close-lipped Mexican proprietor, Laramie owned an old rifle with a split stock bound with copper wire, a handful of cartridges, a large canteen, and a canvas sack full of grub.

He filled the canteen, tied the grub sack to the saddle horn, and rode north out of town. Beyond sight of anyone in town he turned off the road to a clump of mesquite and dismounted, hidden from the road. There he waited.

Scant traffic passed along the road. In the early afternoon a lone rider and a pack horse came out of Agua Fría. Holy Joe Moran's white beard was visible at a distance. Holy Joe was heading north also, the way he had come into town.

When Holy Joe was almost out of sight, Laramie followed, keeping off the road. The two horses ahead turned east off the road, began a great circle which carried them back past Agua Fría, well out of sight of the town. Riding without haste, Laramie made that circle too, following the tracks in the soft dry earth. Now and then he grinned and sang under his breath.

The mesquite grew thicker as they rode south. But presently they were on the narrow, dusty road again, well south of Agua Fría. Holy Joe Moran was out of sight. The fresh tracks of his two horses showed plainly in the road dust. Miles further on they turned right toward the barren Agua Fría hills.

Holy Joe was following an old trail, unmarked by wheels, seldom used by horses. By nightfall the trail was leading into a frowning cañon which cut back into the hills.

Two hours later while they were deep in the cañon, gaining altitude, the moon came up behind them. No fire had glowed against the night ahead. When the moonlight was bright enough, Laramie dismounted, struck a match, held it low over the narrow trail. The twin tracks were still there. Holy Joe evidently was traveling on through the night.

An owl hooted mournfully overhead. The high, eerie yapping of a coyote drifted ghost-like up the cañon.

Just before daybreak the trail came out on a desert-like mesa. Laramie stopped, drank sparingly from the canteen, hooked the reins over one arm, and lay down on the ground for half an hour. He was whistling softly through his teeth as he rode on with the gray, cool dawn coming up behind him.

In all that long night's ride there had been no sign of human habitation. Daylight showed none. The mesquite had been left in the lower lands. Greasewood and cactus stretched as far as the eye could see. The serrated crusts of the hills through which he had come during the night were sharp against the golden dawn behind. The land was sharply rolling, cut by dry arroyos. The trail grew fainter, still stretching into the west. And Holy Joe Moran still traveled ahead.

Fatigue lay heavily on Laramie Scott. Dark circles grew under his eyes as he followed the double set of tracks which seemed to have no ending. Gradually through the morning another chain of hills took shape in the distance ahead, hills lower, greener than the ones by Agua Fría. At noon Laramie turned off the trail, rode north a full mile, turned up the dry bed of an arroyo.

Dismounting by a shady outcropping of rock, Laramie opened a can of tomatoes with his knife, ate the contents; and then with loaded rifle by his side and the reins hooked around his arm, he lay down against the outcropping rock, pulled the ancient hat over his face, and went to sleep.

Through the late afternoon the sun dropped over the

spot and brought a measure of coolness. For four hours Laramie slept like one dead. And then he came awake abruptly, sitting up, staring about, warned by an instant, inner alarm.

V

"GHOST TOWN"

A moment later Laramie knew what it was. The roan horse was standing with head upflung, ears pricked forward. It whinnied now, as it must have whinnied a moment before. Yanking on the reins, Laramie came to his feet, catching up the rifle.

Then down the arroyo a horse whinnied. The roan answered before Laramie's hand clamped over its nostrils.

"Damn your stubborn hide," Laramie said through his teeth. "You're too blamed sociable. Just got to let anyone around know we're here, don't you?"

The next moment from the crest of the arroyo bank behind a voice snapped in Spanish: *"¡Arriba, tonto!"*

The accent was old Mexico. Laramie looked over his shoulder, saw the speaker silhouetted on the bank crest above. The rifle was covering him.

"¡Buenos tardes, señor! Where did you come from?" Laramie asked.

The man descended the bank, pebbles and small rocks cascading ahead of his feet. His rifle was a short-barreled carbine. His eyes were intent, ready and, as he came to the jutting rock, he spoke sharply.

"What you do here?"

Laramie had seen before this stocky fellow with mahogany-colored skin, broad nose, and coarse Indian features. Cinco MacDonald had spoken to him the night before. This was Martínez. Now the man wore a high-crowned straw sombrero, close-fitting trousers, a short jacket with silver buttons. A gun hung on one hip and a bandoleer of cartridges for the carbine was slung over his shoulder.

Martínez scowled. "What you do here?" he asked again.

Laramie replied politely in north-of-the-border Spanish: "I was sleeping, *señor*. Do you live around here?"

"Fool. Only lizards and snakes live around here. Why you sleep so far off the trail?"

"Is it far? I did not know. I was sleeping in the saddle."

Down the arroyo the horse nickered again. The roan answered, moved restlessly.

Only Martínez had appeared. Only the one horse was nickering down there out of sight. What had happened was plain enough. Martínez had followed the tracks off the trail and up the arroyo. He had heard the roan or sighted it, had dismounted, circled on foot.

"Why do you ride this way, boy? Where do you go?" he asked.

"*¿Quien sabe?*" Laramie answered with a shrug.

Teeth showed in an unpleasant smile as Martínez asked: "Why you follow Holy Joe Moran?"

Laramie shrugged again. "There is a trail, *señor*. I do not care who goes ahead." He was as tall as Martínez but thinner, slighter, so that he looked smaller. The old rifle was still in his hand, the reins still looped around his other arm.

The carbine covered him as Martínez eyed the roan appraisingly. "Give me your gun, boy," Martínez ordered.

Laramie surrendered the rifle silently.

"And the horse."

"Señor," Laramie said, "if you take my horse, I die. I cannot walk to water."

Martínez grinned. *"Dios,"* he said, "that is bad, no? But we will not worry, boy. Vamos down into the arroyo."

Laramie spoke slowly. "I bet you're fixing to put a bullet in my back."

"Si," Martínez agreed.

"Why?"

"Because," said Martínez, "it is time for you to die."

"I don't want to."

"Dios . . . who does? But we all must die. I will give you a chance to run."

Laramie was pale. Slowly his jaw set. "I reckon you mean it," he said.

He put a hand in his pocket, looked about. There was no cover. He might get the roan between him and the carbine. But that would be good only for a moment. If he ran, he would be shot down in a few steps. Laramie patted the roan's muzzle and drew his other hand from the trouser's pocket. A long keen blade flicked out from it, glittering as the hand snapped forward.

Martínez cried out as the streak of steel gashed his gun hand. His finger pressed the trigger as he dropped the carbine; the bullet thudded into the sandy earth and the roan snorted, bolted from the spot. Martínez's hand hung limply, spurting blood. Martínez plucked the blade from his hand and stooped, his good hand groping for the fallen gun. Then Laramie was upon him.

Swift, hard-driven blows rained upon the Mexican killer. Laramie grunted as his fists flailed, buried themselves in Martínez's fat paunch, sending the air whistling from the swarthy man's lungs in painful gasps. Bending over to cover up, Martínez exposed the back of his neck and Laramie Scott put everything he had into a hard chop with the edge of his right hand on that nerve center. Martínez collapsed without a word, face down in the sand. He shook once, convulsively, and then lay still.

Laramie stood there, for a moment, breathing hard. "God knows I ought to kill you, but . . . but . . . ," he shrugged, moved quickly, retrieved his knife from where Martínez had thrown it and then got the Mexican's rifle. He kicked his own rifle out of reach.

Apparently no one else had heard the shot. White faced, shaking a little, Laramie removed the gun belt and blood-stained bandoleer from Martínez's unconscious form. He'd be out for fifteen minutes more, anyhow, left without a gun and horse out here. . . . He caught up the grub sack and hurried down the arroyo watchfully.

The caution was needless. Beyond the first turn he found a fine bay horse tied to a big *cholla* cactus. It stood quietly when Laramie came up. The saddle was good; the bridle mounted with silver. Two canteens were slung from the saddle horn. A folded blanket and full saddle bags showed that Martínez had set out from Agua Fría on a long ride. Laramie hung his grub sack to the saddle horn, untied the reins, climbed into the saddle.

The roan had gone. Left alone it would probably make its way to water with sure instinct. The sun was sliding swiftly down toward those greener hills in the west as Laramie back tracked down the arroyo.

No other riders were in sight as he rode cautiously to the trail. There he reined in, staring at the ground. Many horses had passed this way since noon, proceeding leisurely. The story was plain there in the white alkali dust. They had seen his tracks turning off, had sent Martinez to investigate while the others had gone on. Cinco MacDonald had evidently not changed his mind about the trip out of Agua Fría.

The party was gone from sight now, would probably stay that way unless another man was sent back to see why Martinez did not catch up. And that was not likely.

As the long night hours fell behind, he came into the heart of the green hills. Scrub trees and runty bushes grew here. He rode down a steep slope in a narrow little valley where a six-foot stream of water brawled over stones.

Splashing into the water, the bay buried its nose deeply. Laramie filled the canteens, bathed face and arms, went on. The trail looked different beyond. He got down and found that Holy Joe had not come this way.

Riding back, he saw where Holy Joe had ridden down into the water and had not emerged from it. For some reason Holy Joe had ridden up or down the narrow stream bed. After a few moments' reconnoiter, Laramie set off upstream.

The rhythmic splashes of the bay's hoofs in the shallow water, the clash of shoes against the rocks, were the only sounds that broke the silence. Black shadows crept over the valley as the moon went down.

Then the first gray of dawn touched the sky. The valley had narrowed to a bottleneck. Laramie rode through that bottleneck into a bowl-shaped depression among the hills. Scattered trees grew on the slopes, cactus and low bushes among them. Grass was thicker along the stream banks. Riding up on the left bank, Laramie reined up shortly, alert and watchful.

A small village lay just ahead, a strange village — a silent, spectral cluster of low stone houses. No smoke curled up into the chill air. No animals were about. Not even a dog barked. Staring hard, Laramie saw that most of the houses were roofless, doorways and windows gaping empty, walls sagging.

He rode forward and the desolation of the place reached out and enveloped him. It seemed to Laramie that the ghosts of those who had built and lived here long ago still lurked about. Perhaps a hundred huts were standing. More of adobe had long since crumpled to earthen heaps. Ranged roughly in a square, the village had a small plaza in the center and in the plaza Laramie found Holy Joe's two horses, hobbled and grazing. Holy Joe was not in sight.

On the left side of the plaza was a somewhat larger stone building. It once had been a church, indicated by the stone cross set in the arch of the gaping doorway. Unexpectedly, Holy Joe Moran appeared in that doorway with a rifle at his shoulder.

"Climb down offen that hoss!"

Holy Joe's voice was harsh, hard in the ghostly silence. He stood alertly in the doorway where he could step backward to cover instantly.

VI

"KILLERS' BRANDING FIRE"

Laramie dismounted, walked forward with the carbine. He was pale, haggard, more so now than when he had stumbled into Agua Fría afoot. He said: "Good thing you didn't ride much farther, mister. Don't know if I could've made it or not."

"My God Almighty!" Holy Joe swore, staring. "It's the kid!" His astonishment turned to quick suspicion. "What're you doing here?"

Laramie grounded the carbine, stock down, and leaned on the barrel. Holy Joe looked as saintly as he had back in Agua Fría, but somehow dangerous now, out here alone in the mountains. He seemed, with that ragged white beard, a part of the ruins, the ghostly silence and desolation. Laramie's grin was uncertain. He knew it, but it was the best he could do.

"I came lookin' for trouble," he said.

"You found it," Holy Joe replied shortly. "Who's with you?"

"No one."

"Huh! Lemme see that rifle. Hold it up."

Holy Joe squinted, frowned. "Thought so," he said. "Belongs to Cinco MacDonald. So does the rest of the arsenal you're packing. So you trailed me for Cinco?"

"Nope. Just trailed you, mister. MacDonald's back aways with some men."

"An' you came on ahead to tell me?"

"Sorta," Laramie agreed. "Got any more of that gold hid around, mister?"

"What's it to a maverick like you?" Holy Joe grunted.

"Nothing. But it seems to be to a lot of others. Gonzalez was interested a heap. I saw MacDonald studying over what you spent with him an' heard him give orders for horses ready to leave next day. You stirred up a heap of interest with that gold, mister."

From his pocket Laramie took the last of the three coins Holy Joe had given him.

"I been wondering myself," he said. "This one's got 'Maximilian . . . 1866' stamped on it. I've heard that just before the Emperor Maximilian was shot down here in Mexico he started a heap of gold up north toward the border where it'd be safe . . . and then they shot him and no one ever heard about the gold again."

Holy Joe fingered his beard. "For a maverick kid you're mighty smart," he said. His voice hardened. "You read that, or have it told you in Agua Fría?" He shook his head. "They wouldn't tell you," he muttered. "Hell's fire an' damnation! I had a feeling I'd get into trouble headin' into Agua Fría an' tossin' that gold around. But I needed grub an' a good drink quick. Son, what're you doing here? Took a lot to bring you in at my heels. Not many men could have made it."

"I'm a man, mister. You filled my belly there in Agua Fría and staked me when you thought I was in trouble. While you was making a big night of it with that gold, I saw you were headin' for trouble yourself. Gonzalez and Cinco MacDonald were actin' like coyotes down wind from a dead steer."

"H-m," said Holy Joe. "Why didn't you tip me off before I left Agua Fría?"

"Maybe you wouldn't have listened to me, mister. And I knew you were all right there in town. Long as they didn't know for sure if there was more gold, they weren't going to stop you from heading back to where it might be."

"An' so," said Holy Joe skeptically, "you mighty nigh killed yourself riding out here to see what was going to happen. An' you show up loaded with Cinco Mac-Donald's outfit."

"I pulled off the trail to sleep, an' a man named Martínez tracked me there an' fixed to put a bullet in me," Laramie explained patiently. "I pitched my knife into him, left him on the desert, and took these off him."

"Pitched your *what?*"

"My knife, mister."

The knife was in Laramie's hand an instant later. His thumb flicked the blade open. A short length of rotting wood lay on the ground half a dozen paces away. His arm jerked — the keen blade flashed through the air and was buried deeply in the wood.

"Like that," said Laramie simply, stepping over and pulling the knife out with an effort. "I been practicing throwing since I was a kid." He sighed as he closed the knife and put it in his pocket. "I came over the border looking for my brother. Took me a couple of months to track him to Agua Fría. He's dead now, I guess, or he'd have had his ring. I couldn't do much in the Glory Hole. Too many men around for MacDonald to call on. He sent a couple of Mexes after me soon as he found who I was. But when I figured he'd follow you, I came on, too. I can handle him better, out here away from Agua Fría."

"My great aunt's half sister!" Holy Joe Moran said dazedly. "You look like a raggedy, drought-starved maverick, an' you're actin' like a range bull. Damned if I don't believe you'll back it up!"

"Not much use in a man talkin' if he can't back it up," Laramie said mildly.

Holy Joe laughed shortly. "There'll be plenty of backin' to do if Cinco MacDonald is heading this way. Cinco'd cut off his grandmother's ears if she had *centavos* sewed inside. He's three parts snake an' one part wolf for all his crooked back an' close mouth. An' the gold's here, kid. A load of it. Them rumors about Maximilian's gold were right. I been hearing them along the border since long before you was born. Smoke always means some fire. The gold that started north never was heard of again. Hard to tell what happened. Maybe it was ambushed. Indians or bandits. Anyway, some of it wound up here. Nobody's lived here for over a hundred years. Soledad, it was called . . . The Lonely Place. Smallpox wiped out the last livin' soul. The Indians still tell about it. They won't even enter the place. They say it's cursed."

"Looks kind of spooky," Laramie agreed, looking about.

Holy Joe stroked his beard. "I've been in worse," he said. "Anyway, somebody drifted in with a pack of gold who wasn't worried about the curse. Must 'a figured it was just what was needed. Gave a private place to hide the gold. I camped here last week and got to pokin' around. My grub was low an' my pockets empty. I was hoping I could turn up a little silver in one of the houses. When a place like this gets wiped out, there's always things hidden away which are never found. . . . I rooted out enough for a grub stake. Then I tried the old church here. Have a look."

Holy Joe led the way back into the church. Laramie followed.

The roof had fallen in. The interior, open to the sky, was cluttered with debris, in which weeds, bushes, and one stunted tree had long been growing. Holy Joe climbed over the rubbish to the back, where the stone altar base still stood. A two-foot square slab of stone had been pried out of the altar side.

"Look in there," Holy Joe said. "I just opened 'er up again."

In a dim hollow under the altar two rotting leather sacks had been crammed. The weight of the contents had burst them; gold coins had streamed out, as bright and yellow and tempting as the day they had been minted. Holy Joe's voice shook.

"For over thirty years I been looking for easy money in these parts . . . an' I found it. First thing I had to do was throw a bust to celebrate. Agua Fría was nearest. I had my bust an' tracked back here fast with a pack hoss to get this gold over the border an' bank it safe. I'm going to take it easy from now on. I'm too old to be on the move much longer."

He was silent for a moment, then his deep voice boomed again, as his knotted fist lifted slowly. "An' if Cinco MacDonald or any other dirty crook is counting on cutting me out of that, they'll find they've tackled hell an' all the devils!"

Outside in the plaza a horse nickered loudly. Laramie turned quickly.

"Some one near!" he said.

"Help me get this in place," Holy Joe grunted, heaving on the stone.

Laramie put down the carbine — and, as he stepped

to the old man's side, a mocking voice spoke behind him.

"Never mind, *amigos!*"

With an oath Holy Joe caught up his rifle and turned — to meet the blast of a shot which seemed twice as loud inside those bare stone walls. The rifle clattered from Holy Joe's hand. He grabbed his forearm where blood welled into sight.

Cinco MacDonald had fired the shot. Two small windows gaped breast high in the side walls back by the altar. Cinco had pushed a gun through the window on their side. A grinning Mexican whom Laramie recognized as Salazar had done the same through the other window. As Holy Joe stood there with blood seeping around the gnarled fingers holding his arm, two more Mexicans rushed in from the front, scrambled over the rubbish heaps, disarmed them.

Cinco MacDonald looked tired but jubilant as he leaned on the window sill. "For an old man you travel fast," he said to Holy Joe. "But others can travel fast, too, my friend. You were speaking about hell and the devils. Did I hear my name mentioned, too?"

"You did if I was speakin' about hell!" Holy Joe snapped. "Never mind showing what a smart tongue you've got, Cinco. You played in smooth luck . . . so now what?"

"First, we'll see what eggs you've got in that little nest," Cinco said. He shifted into Spanish, speaking to the two men who had rushed into the church. "Watch them closely, *hombres*. Salazar, if one of them moves, shoot him. Martinez did not . . . and Martinez is gone. But see . . . his guns and belt are here."

Salazar scowled over his rifle. "For that," he promised, "I will be ready."

Salazar in the window and the two men inside watched them closely while Cinco MacDonald searched. He peered under the altar, thrust in a hand, brought it out full of coins. In that moment mockery and jubilation left Cinco MacDonald's face. It hardened, blazed with an ugly inner fire. Teeth showed white as his lips drew back and his faster breathing was audible as he bent and thrust a hand deeply through a split in the nearest sack.

In English, under his breath, his words jerked out. "No wonder you tossed that gold around like it was nothing the other night, Joe! My God, a man couldn't spend all this in a year!"

"Not in ten years, the way you hang onto a peso," Holy Joe replied sourly.

Cinco straightened. "Is this all?"

Holy Joe laughed harshly. "Like to know, wouldn't you? Mebbe there's a heap more. After you put a slug through my head, see how long it takes you to find it, Cinco."

"Ah . . . so there *is* more?"

"Mebbe."

Cinco MacDonald breathed sharply through his teeth, stepped closer, and yanked Holy Joe's head around by the beard. His eyes were blazing as he shoved his face up at the old man.

"Where is it?"

Holy Joe's great fists knotted. His shoulders swelled tense, hard under his ragged coat. His eyes rolled at the two Mexicans who were covering him with their rifles and grinning at the sight. His voice was calm with a terrible threat.

"If I get the chance, I'll kill you fer this, Cinco!" he promised. "You'll never know how much more of it there is . . . an' I hope you go crazy lookin' for it. Soledad was cursed a hundred years ago an' you won't escape it, Cinco. For," said Holy Joe, "you'll never die happy wondering how much more gold there is here . . . an' you'll never find it!"

Cinco MacDonald glared up at him. And from the white beard which he still held, a great bellowing laugh rolled down at him.

"The joke's on you, Cinco," Holy Joe roared. "You'd 'a' been happier if you'd stayed behind your bar an' kept on cuttin' throats for a fistful of pesos."

For a moment Cinco MacDonald went mad, yanking on the beard, striking up at Holy Joe's face.

"Throw him down and beat it out of him!" he yelled. "No . . . light a fire and heat a rifle barrel! I know how to make a man talk! He'll beg me to let him tell the truth before I'm through!"

Holy Joe's bellowing laughter rolled through the desolation of the ruined old church. He stood there with his legs braced apart, a helpless giant mocking a raging pigmy.

"Heat your rifle barrels, Cinco," Holy Joe invited. "Heat a dozen of 'em an' see what it gets you! I'm ready to cash in anyway . . . an' I'll go laughin' at what I'm leavin' behind."

Salazar had run in and joined them. He stood watchfully, rifle in one hand, short gun in the other, while the two Mexicans tripped Holy Joe and threw him on the debris underfoot.

Rotting chunks of roof beams lay about. One of the men quickly gathered a pile of them, applied a match to a sliver of wood, and on his knees began to coax the fire alight. While he was doing that, Cinco MacDonald caught Laramie by the arm. A wolfish look was on his face.

"What do you know about it?" he demanded.

Laramie said: "Nothing, mister. What happened to my brother, Bob?"

Cinco struck him in the face. "Damn your brother! I'll send you after him! He's dead! Salazar put a knife in his back!"

"Patrón!" Salazar protested uneasily.

"Shut up!" Cinco raged at him. "It doesn't matter what this young fool knows. I'm going to make him talk."

From the ground Holy Joe said: "Let the kid alone, Cinco. He don't know more'n you do. He rode in just ahead of you an' I showed him the little cache under the altar there. It didn't matter whether he knew about that or not." Once more Holy Joe's big laugh echoed up to the cloud-flecked blue sky above him.

Laramie gave Salazar a long, speculative look. The man's black eyes glared back at him. Neither spoke — and yet the threat was plain enough in Salazar. He would kill the instant he got a chance. But that chance had to wait a little.

Cinco MacDonald was raging: "You're lying! Both of you are lying! He wouldn't know part of it without knowing all. He was here before. You two came to Agua Fría together. He covered your trail when you came back here, and pushed on ahead to tell you we were coming. I heard him warning you."

"You're always hearing something, Cinco," Holy Joe said. "Only there's one thing you won't ever hear. Maybe there's wagon loads of it hid around here, Cinco . . . an' you won't ever find it."

The fire blazed up. Smoke eddied about them. The

man tending the fire picked up the carbine Laramie had dropped, methodically unloaded it, and thrust the end of the barrel in the flames.

"Hot . . . *red hot!*" Cinco urged thickly.

"*Sí, señor.*"

An instant later a single rifle shot nearby echoed across the little valley. Cinco MacDonald and his men went tense and rigid at the sound.

VII

"BULLETS FOR GOLD"

Salazar said, "Pablo. It must be Pablo!"

Cinco licked his lips. "What could he be shooting at? We left him alone with the horses. There's no one else here with these men."

"Perhaps Martínez comes," Salazar suggested.

"Burro! Martínez is dead! His guns would not be here if he were not! And he could not have walked from where we left him. Tefoyo, run and see what that fool shot at!"

Tefoyo exchanged the hot carbine for his own rifle and hurried out. Cinco MacDonald moved nervously about for a moment, then with a muttered oath followed. He was barely outside when Tefoyo's shout was audible.

"*Patrón* . . . Pablo is dead and the horses are gone!"

Cinco MacDonald stood outside the doorway like one stunned. Salazar licked his lips, looked uneasily about. And Holy Joe's shout of delight rang about them.

"I told you the place was haunted, Cinco! You come

fer gold an' you're getting hell! You ain't got a chance now!"

Uneasily Salazar asked: "What do you mean, old man?"

"You know damn well what I mean, Salazar. You ain't lived in Agua Fría all your life an' not heard about the ghosts of Soledad. You can't fool with ghosts, Salazar."

Salazar licked his lips. "Ghosts do not fire shots, old man."

"No? You heard one then, didn't you? Where's your hosses?"

But as Tefoyo joined his master out in front, Salazar turned and moved uncertainly a short distance in that direction. He could still see but not hear them. Holy Joe lifted his head, screwed his face up inquiringly at Laramie. Holy Joe was as much in the dark as the rest of them.

Laramie was in a thoughtful study. A grin suddenly came over his face. "I bet this is one ghost that Mac-Donald won't like to see," he said under his breath to Holy Joe.

"You know something, kid," Holy Joe whispered hoarsely. "What is it?"

"I got an idea."

"Unhobble it quick! If these jaspers get rattled, they'll shoot us first an' start thinkin' later. I don't hanker fer a red hot rifle barrel down my guzzle or a bullet in the head any more'n you do. An' we're sittin' right on top of both."

Cinco called: "Salazar, come here!"

"These two, *señor.* . . ."

"They don't matter now! Tefoyo will kill them when I call. This is important."

Salazar waited until Tefoyo came back and then, telling

111

him to watch sharply, he stumbled hurriedly over the rest of the piled debris toward the front door. Cinco MacDonald led him out of sight.

The man who had been silently standing guard at some distance spoke uncertainly under his breath to Tefoyo. "*Compadre*, what is it?"

Tefoyo crossed himself hurriedly. His dark-cast face was nervous, uneasy. "The Holy Virgin knows," he said in a loud voice. "I look . . . I see Pablo on his back, dead . . . and the horses gone. All was silent. This place *is* cursed. All my life I have heard it. Now I know."

In Spanish Holy Joe said mournfully: "You two *hombres* should have known better than to follow Cinco here. He is mad . . . mad over gold. There is a curse on the gold, a curse on Soledad, a curse on you both for coming here. Have you wives and children you hope to see again, *amigos?*"

Tefoyo's companion shivered slightly.

Laramie stood there dejectedly, listening to them talk. His hand was carelessly in his trouser's pocket. His eyes were on the two men. Tefoyo now stood an arm's length from Holy Joe who was half raised on an elbow.

Tefoyo was gripping his rifle with both hands, holding it ready for instant action. Tefoyo's companion was now standing two paces away, his rifle held more carelessly because Laramie, unarmed and dejected, seemed to be worth little notice.

In a moment when neither man seemed to be looking at them Laramie rolled his eyes at Holy Joe and winked. Holy Joe winked back, nodded assent.

He had barely done that when a second shot cracked sharply across the plaza. A voice which sounded like Salazar's yelled in pain. Other shots followed in a ragged burst. Cinco MacDonald's shout followed it. "Tefoyo, shoot them and come here!"

"All right!" Laramie declared.

His right hand flicked out of his pocket as he spoke, and once more from his short arm snap the keen bright blade flashed through the air. At the same time, from the corner of his eye, Laramie saw Holy Joe's big hand grab up at the rifle muzzle above his body.

Laramie's target was swinging around as the knife started. Lunging after the knife, Laramie heard Tefoyo's rifle blast at Holy Joe.

He could not look. His knife was striking the man before him, the rifle was swinging to meet him, one brown hand convulsing about the trigger guard.

This man would not be helpless, after all. He was going to shoot — and there was the knife quivering deeply in the shoulder, the man flinching as his hand pulled the trigger.

Laramie's left breast took the impact of the shot; hot gasses and powder driving through to his skin, the cold, numb feeling of the bullet striking his side. He knew fleetingly that he was hit; and then the gun muzzle was sliding under his arm, his rush was knocking it aside, and his fist was smashing into the brown, contorted face behind the gun. And then they were both down, rolling in the rubbish on the floor.

A hand beat frantically at him. Feet kicked. Fingers clawed for his eyes — and Laramie's hand closed about the familiar handle of his knife. He glimpsed a revolver coming out of a holster as he moved to strike with the knife.

Laramie's next action was instinctive. He meant to strike with the knife. And he found himself pressing the sharp blade against the jerking brown throat, gasping in Spanish:

"Quiet, or I'll kill you!"

The man went rigid, quivering. Air whistled through his lips. His bulging eyes stared into Laramie's face. His hand released the revolver, crooked up in the air, fingers spread in futile, convulsive tension. With death pressing in a fine hairline of steel at his throat, his brown skin drained to the dirty gray of stark terror.

As those few mad seconds of action stalled abruptly, a squeal of fright came out of a furious scuffle behind them. The dull, sodden impact of a heavy blow followed. Holy Joe Moran's voice said with harsh satisfaction: "If they have hot rifle barrels in hell, I hope you meet one goin' in!"

Laramie came to his knees, reached over, grabbed the revolver and stood up. Over him Holy Joe snorted: "You mean to say you didn't cut his throat while you had the chance?"

The man was cowering on the ground, watching them. Laramie cocked the revolver, grinned apologetically. "I guess I ain't a good killer," he admitted. "I stopped him without it, an' that was good enough. He ain't the one who knifed Bob."

"You'll get your own gizzard sliced open by actin' like a milk-fed yearling," Holy Joe grumbled as he buckled a gun belt around his middle and snatched up Tefoyo's rifle. "Shoot him an' make a good Mex outa him. Your side's bleedin'. How bad you hit?"

The place was beginning to smart and hurt. Fresh blood oozed warm and wet against the skin. Laramie ran his fingers over the spot while he looked at the man Holy Joe had fought. Tefoyo's body blocked the opening

114

in the side of the altar. The man's head was canted at an unreal, grotesque angle. Blood oozed from his open mouth. His eyes were wide and staring.

"My side got creased," Laramie said. "What about that man?"

"I hit him. Neck's broke," Holy Joe grunted. Blood was still seeping down over his hand. He ignored it as he stood there with head cocked and white beard bristling pugnaciously.

And then Laramie realized that the gunfire across the plaza had stopped.

Cinco MacDonald's wrathful shout rang on the ominous quiet: "Tefoyo! Are you coming?"

"Funny things happening around here," Holy Joe grumbled. "I wonder who cut loose with them shots. Step back a minute while I put a bullet in this fellow's head. He's bad luck long as he's around us. An' we ain't fixed to handle bad luck right now. Got enough as it is."

"Give him a chance, mister. A mad dog's about the only thing I wouldn't give a chance."

Holy Joe had thumbed back the hammer of a big .45. He let the hammer down slowly. "All right, son," he said. "He's your man. I was young an' foolish once, too. Look the other way."

Laramie looked. He heard a faint dull blow. When he looked around, the man was limp on the ground and Holy Joe was straightened up.

"That'll hobble him for a while," said Holy Joe. "But he'll be all right when he comes out of it."

"Tefoyo!" Cinco MacDonald yelled again.

A rifle shot snapped at the sound, and a shout rolled across the plaza. "That was close, Cinco, my old friend!

Better luck next time. Call that no-good Tefoyo out! We'll cure his laziness!"

Laramie grinned faintly. "I kind of thought so," he said. "*Gonzalez!* He was interested a heap in your gold. He must 'a' tracked after MacDonald an' his men."

"I'll be derned an' be damned!" Holy Joe said. He scratched the white tangle of hair wild, flying. "I didn't pay much attention when you mentioned Dandy Gonzalez," he said. "Didn't think what little I saw of him that night counted fer much. I mighta knowed it would. Dandy's got a fox's nose for money. Wonder how many men he brought along."

"Two or three or more cut loose with their guns a while ago."

"Uh-huh. He wouldn't 'a' come out with less'n that. In one way it's pretty good," Holy Joe said with sardonic satisfaction. "Dandy Gonzalez killin' off Cinco an' his men. An' in another it's more bad luck, because we got Dandy an' his men on our hands now. They're worse'n Cinco, if it's possible. They'll kill us just as quick, or quicker.

"We ain't got a chance of gettin' out of here, even with empty pockets, while any of them are out there. They're all gold-mad. They won't let us go until they get the gold . . . an' they kill us quick if they do get it, so that we won't be able to notify the Mex government which would have that gold in two shakes. We're damned if they do an' damned if they don't," concluded Holy Joe.

He spat deliberately, hitched at the gun belt, then said cheerfully: "Hell! We might as well make some fur fly, ourselves . . . unless you want to skin out that window an' make a run for it, son. Might be you could get a hoss an' ride off."

"How about you, mister?"

"Me? I'm too old to rabbit around that away."

Laramie drew a deep breath. His face was a dusty, drawn mask of fatigue, but he grinned. "I came here to have it out with Cinco MacDonald," he said. "It's Salazar now . . . an' MacDonald, too. I guess he's just as guilty. An' you need some help in getting the gold up over the border. I'll do what I can."

Holy Joe chuckled. "I'm glad *I* didn't stick a knife in your brother's back. Don't seem to be a healthy pastime. All right, son . . . there's a pack of wolves out there an' we're cornered in here. Let's move up front an' see if we can put a little lead where it'll do the most good."

Laramie picked up his old hat and moved to the window behind him. He pushed the hat cautiously out the window with his gun barrel. Nothing happened.

"We're cornered in here," Laramie said. "I'll feel better outside."

He wriggled nimbly through the window, dropped lightly to the ground outside — and the next instant a rifle snapped across the plaza and lead struck a stone beside the window, ricocheting into space with a savage whine.

"So long," Laramie yelled as he scrambled toward the back of the church.

Another shot threw lead whining past the window but, when Holy Joe thrust his head out, Laramie Scott had vanished. Holy Joe drew his head back in hastily, spat, swore aloud vigorously. His comment to the staring, stiffening Tefoyo echoed hollowly through the ruined shell of stone about them.

"Damned freckle-faced pyuriatin' kid!" Holy Joe jerked out. "He'll get hisself killed sure!"

117

VIII

"KILLERS — BACK TO BACK!"

Chips of stone had stung Laramie's face as he straightened outside the window. A bullet whined back of his shoulders as he ducked around behind the church. No bullets sought him there. The church screened him from the other side of the plaza where Dandy Gonzalez and his men all seemed to be.

In the roofless stone buildings on the north side of the church Cinco MacDonald and Salazar had taken shelter. A twenty-foot space on the south separated the church from the adjoining house. Laramie sprinted across that space safely and then slipped, crouching, toward the south edge of the settlement. Dandy Gonzalez was evidently keeping his men together. No shots searched Laramie out.

Cinco MacDonald's horses had been left at the south edge of the settlement. But now the smooth stretch of short dry grass was empty. Fifty yards out from the nearest house a huddled figure lay motionless in the grass. The bright new sun overhead gleamed dully on a rifle barrel beside one outstretched hand.

Dandy Gonzalez and his men, riding warily through the bottleneck into the valley, must have spotted horses and watcher before they were seen, and stalked the man and killed him from ambush, and quickly run the horses off.

They could not be far. Gonzalez and his men had appeared too quickly across the plaza after that first rifle shot. To the west, clear to the sparsely wooded valley slope, no horses were visible. Or to the south where the slope was steep, rocky, without much cover.

The stream lay to the east. Beyond it, the valley lay flat for a long quarter of a mile, screened now, for the most part, by the intervening houses. Laramie began a crouching advance through the ruins toward that eastern side, the slight noise he made muffled by the scattering shots across the plaza. Every man in the valley, Laramie knew, was exhausted by the grueling ride from Agua Fría. The long day lay ahead of them. They might last it out; they might not. The lids over his own reddened eyes felt leaden. Fatigue held his body in a tightening grip which could not be held off much longer. Yet to sleep meant disaster. The hand of every man there was against Holy Joe and himself. Dandy Gonzalez would be no safer company than Cinco MacDonald.

He came to the last houses, looked over the grassy level beyond, and saw five saddle horses scattered along the bottom of the hill slope. Those would be the ones MacDonald and his men had ridden in.

Going down on his stomach, Laramie looked cautiously to the left along the straggling outer fringe of stone walls. A short distance away stood the four horses which had brought Dandy Gonzalez and his party. Three men had come with Gonzalez, and one was holding the horses in against a stone house wall, where they were safe from the guns across the plaza.

Rifle ready, cigarette in the corner of his mouth, the Mexican holding the horses was casting watchful glances about. A shot at his back would have dropped him —

and warned Gonzalez and his men. Laramie dodged back out of sight as the man turned his head.

For some minutes Laramie hid himself in the ruins, a creeping, shifting shadow which moved up abreast of the little group of horses, edging in until only the corner of a stone wall hid him. There he picked up a rock, threw it high in the air over the house so that it would fall beyond the horses. He heard its dull impact against the ground, lunged around the corner, the .45 in his hand.

The Mexican was staring at the spot where the stone had landed. Two lucky gunshots filled the air with sound while Laramie's rush carried him to the man's back before his steps were audible. Then the man heard him, whirled, and Laramie smashed the heavy gun barrel under the broad sombrero brim with all his weight behind the blow. He shoved the man's hand gun in his belt, tossed the rifle over the house wall out of sight, clapped the sombrero on his head. Then he stepped in among the uneasy horses and walked them toward the house where Gonzalez and his men had taken cover.

As he came near, Gonzalez was shouting across the plaza: "A little more, Cinco, my friend, and Gonzalez will be the *jefe* of Agua Fría! How is that?"

Cinco MacDonald's silence had the appearance of sullenness and desperation. Gonzalez was light hearted, sure of himself but, as the horses trampled to the rear of the house, Gonzalez appeared in the doorway, venting his anger heatedly.

"Back with those horses, *cabrón!* I said to keep them away!"

Half hidden by the horses, only the top of Laramie's

sombrero was visible to a quick look as he swung the four animals around. Gonzalez disappeared inside and Laramie dropped the four sets of reins and made for the doorway, drawing the two hand guns.

IX

"TASTE OF BLOOD"

He hadn't been sure all three men were in the house. He saw them now. They were firing through two front windows. All Mexicans.

"Put 'em up!" Laramie yelled. His voice warned them. The first man who whirled came with gun up, thumbing back the hammer as he dodged to one side. Laramie shot him. The man went to the floor, dropping his gun, groaning.

Dandy Gonzalez pushed his hands up. The third man did the same and stood still. Gonzalez recognized the sober face under the sombrero. His jaw dropped. "Where is Max?" he stammered.

"Max went to sleep, mister," said Laramie. "Tell that peon to drop his gun before I ventilate his liver. You, too!"

They both did.

Laramie fired at the groaning man on the floor. Dirt flew up beside a hand which had been stealthily reaching for the gun. The hand jerked back.

"Next time, *hombre,* I'll kill you," Laramie said — and to Gonzalez: "You miss out on the gold, mister. All you get is trouble, and a heap of that."

Gonzalez moistened his lips. His smile was painful.

"Give us," he said, "our horses and keep our guns and we will ride away. Or, better still, my young friend, give us our guns and we will settle Cinco MacDonald and his men. I will find my gold in Agua Fría with Cinco out of the way."

"You talk almost as well as you dress, mister," Laramie said. "I reckon it does mean a heap for you to down Cinco MacDonald. I'm going to take you up on that. You're going over there an' meet Cinco."

"Smart, my young friend," Gonzalez applauded. "When this is over, we will have a little drink and a big laugh at Cinco, eh?"

He bent to pick up his gun, and stumbled back as Laramie put a bullet by it.

"Don't hurry, mister. Who said anything about you takin' a gun? You're walking across the plaza with your hands in the air and, the first time you stop or step out of line, you get a bullet in your back!"

Dandy Gonzalez stood with bulging eyes. "Without a gun?" he choked. "MacDonald will shoot us down! You, too!"

"Maybe," said Laramie. "Maybe not. I'll be the last one, anyway. You come looking for trouble an' you're getting a dose of it you'll remember till the day you die . . . if you live long enough to get across the plaza."

"Cinco will kill us, I tell you!"

"Maybe," said Laramie, "you can make your peace with him while you're walkin' across the plaza. You two ought to understand each other. Get going."

"And if we don't?"

"Then I'll kill you here," Laramie said.

Perspiration glinted on Dandy Gonzalez's face. He bit

his lower lip hard, groaned to his companion: "Felipe, the man is mad!"

Felipe answered stolidly, "Sí, señor, mad . . . but what will you? He has the gun. I think he will kill us here. Perhaps Cinco MacDonald . . . ?"

Felipe broke off, shrugged silently with characteristic fatalism, and turned to the doorway.

"Fall in, Gonzalez," Laramie said.

For some minutes no shots had come from across the plaza. The bright sun was drenching the plaza with golden warmth and light as Laramie herded his two captives into the open.

Holy Joe was the first to appear, stepping cautiously from the doorway of the church. Rifle in hand, Holy Joe stood, eyes bulging, mouth agape, as if unable to believe what he saw.

Laramie threw his sombrero on the ground. "Here they come, mister," he called. "All that's left over here."

A rifle barrel appeared in the window of the second house north of the church. Cinco MacDonald's jubilant cry rang across the plaza.

"If it's a trick, Gonzalez, it'll be your last. I've got you now. Got you where I've wanted you for a long time! Who will be *jefe* in Agua Fría now?"

Dandy Gonzalez faltered.

Laramie jabbed him in the back with a gun.

Gonzalez went on, crying: "Don't shoot, Cinco! It is no trick! By the Virgin, I swear it!"

The bullet which answered knocked the hat from Gonzalez's head. They were half way across the little plaza now. Holy Joe had vanished back into the church. Cinco MacDonald, growing bolder, appeared in the house doorway, his hunched figure looking evil and malevolent as he stood there.

Dandy Gonzalez stammered: "Look behind me, Cinco! It's no trick! You'll be next!"

Salazar came out also. The jeering smile on MacDonald's face was visible.

"So the kid tricked you, Dandy?" he taunted. "You had it coming. After I drop you, we'll take care of him."

Cinco MacDonald fired again. Gonzalez cried out, whirled half around, went to his knees. Laramie left him. Ignoring the stolid Felipe, he began a crouching rush, shooting as he went.

Bullets smashed about the doorway. Salazar ducked. Cinco MacDonald fired wildly, missed. Salazar snap shot hastily as he retreated through the doorway. Laramie heard the shrill whine of lead past his ear, and plunged on, still firing.

Cinco MacDonald staggered, reeled back inside. Salazar had already vanished ahead of him.

Laramie reached the front of the house. His guns were empty. No time to reload now. Holy Joe had vanished. No, not vanished for, as Laramie hurled the useless guns aside and reached in his pocket, Holy Joe's bellow came out of the doorway to meet him.

"Put 'em up, you two!"

Holy Joe was inside the house. Laramie saw him as he went through the doorway with the knife blade flicking open. Holy Joe was just thrusting head and shoulders through a side window, shoving a six-shooter ahead of him.

And inside the doorway Salazar spun on his heel and lifted the revolver he had drawn. His shot crashed with Holy Joe's shot. Stone chipped out of the side of the doorway as Holy Joe missed. But Salazar's shot hit. In the window Holy Joe jerked suddenly, and then for a moment his great shoulders and white beard were framed there as if carved from rock. In the calm poise there was an awesome threat. Holy Joe's big hand held the six-gun steady. Then — it crashed and Salazar pitched down on his face.

It all happened in the space of two breaths. Laramie blinked in the gloom.

A snarl came from the corner. Cinco MacDonald weaved at him, a hunched, desperate figure that swung up a rifle barrel. Laramie threw the knife. The rifle spoke over his head and he heard the bullet strike the opposite stone wall.

He dove forward. The rifle barrel came down hard on his shoulder, and he fell to the floor on top of Cinco MacDonald. The knife had missed for the first time that day. MacDonald fought like a cornered animal, kicking, biting, striking wildly. Laramie got him by the throat, ducked his head, and hung on doggedly.

He heard the man gasping desperately for breath, felt his struggles growing weaker. A crimson wave danced before Laramie's vision. Blindly, madly, he dug his fingers deeper, clung on with a deadly grip. And then he felt strong hands grasp him from behind, jerk him loose from the man he was set to kill.

Holy Joe flung him away, and dimly Laramie was aware of the old man's rifle barrel crashing down on Cinco MacDonald's head. Then Holy Joe turned to him, as the kid struggled to his feet.

"You'd 'a' killed him sure, son," Holy Joe said. "There's been enough killin' here to last all concerned for a while . . . and particularly you. You said back there in the church that you guessed you wasn't a natural killer.

Me, I know you ain't. But with that fightin' energy of yours, you're mighty close to it. Listen to me, young feller. If you ain't killed a man, it's too late to start in now. Once you git a taste for blood, you never git over it. It means the gallows in most cases . . . or, at best, a wasted life. Nameless an' hunted you'll ride without ever knowin' a minute's peace or rest from the law, from vengeance-hungry partners of the man you done in. I know that, son . . . know it too well! An' you ain't goin' to be a killer . . . not if I can help it."

Laramie, his face grimy, bloody, his lungs gasping from his efforts, said, "Shore, I'd've killed him, mister. Didn't you kill Salazar back there?"

"Just one of the reasons why I wasted my own life bein' a border jumper, son. Until I found this cache. But the good things of my life is over now. Money, shore . . . more'n I could spend or know what to do with. But what good's money when you're as old as I am? Never makes the things worth livin' for . . . at most a drunk in some border town an' a headache next day. That's all."

The edge of Holy Joe's white beard was stained red. He brushed at the spot, leaned heavily against the wall. Laramie's eyes were thoughtful. But he said, "You're hurt, mister. Lemme help you."

"It's nothin'," the old man grumbled. "Nipped through the meat. Be all right soon's I can plug the hole an' stop the bleedin'. You able to travel, son?"

"Reckon so, mister."

"Help me make a pack an' load that gold, then. She'll be yours, pretty quick. We . . . we need each other, son. You're young, strong. You pack dynamite like I'd've never believed if I hadn't seen it. You've earned every penny of what's comin' to you . . . in there." His big hand swept toward the abandoned church. "An' you need me, too. Someone to harness that hell fire that's in you, an' show you how to use it where it'll do the most good. . . ."

"Salazar," breathed Laramie. "He's the one I could've killed. Could have. . . ."

"Salazar's dead," interrupted Holy Joe gruffly. "What difference whether you or me salted him down. Your brother's score's all settled, an' Cinco's got a lesson he'll never forget. So have the others." Holy Joe grinned. "Now, you maverick kid. . . ."

"Mister," Laramie said, "I ain't a kid. I'm a man."

Holy Joe spat. "By my great aunt's britches," he said, "you're right, an' I'm proud to say so . . . partner!"

Laramie swallowed. A widening grin was on his face as he went over and picked up his knife.

"All right, partner," he said. "Let's start."

T. T. Flynn was scrupulous about his research in writing Western stories. In 1934 he married Helen Brown, a doctor's daughter from Halls, Tennessee, whom he had met in New Orleans. The couple had two children, Thomas B. Flynn who would become a physician and Richard M. Flynn who would become an Episcopal priest. His son Richard remembered how one time his father took great pains to discover the year blue-checked (as opposed to red-checked) table cloths were introduced on the frontier. "No matter what you write or how much general knowledge you have," he confided to his younger son, "there is some reader who's an expert on some aspect of your story and who will delight in catching you in an error; and your editor or publisher will NOT be happy." Around the time he wrote the story that follows, he acquired a large Chrysler Airstream trailer and was traveling extensively. He assembled an impressive research library and, when on the road, would spend hours upon hours in public libraries wherever he happened to be while a story was in progress, trying always to get it exactly right. He completed "Wild Wind, Brave Wind" on March 18, 1936 and it was bought by *Dime Western* where Rogers Terrill changed the title to "Boothill for Sheepers!" Flynn's original title provides a much better suggestion of the actual subject of this story since, increasingly, he was paralleling human emotions in their extremities with the stunningly abrupt changes in mood of which nature was capable.

Wild Wind, Brave Wind

The government man said coldly, "Lanyard, this is the hardest thing I've ever had to do. But I've got my orders. There's your damned permit to graze the sheep. And I wish a bullet went with it!"

Searles, the grizzled government man, had been raised a cowman. So had Tom Lanyard. They understood each other perfectly.

Lanyard's face was expressionless as he took the paper. "I'd almost be minded to throw the bullet myself," he said.

Searles stood up. He was a graying man with a short, bristly mustache and reflective depths of experience in his lined face. His eyes, puckered at the corners, were keen and probing as he eyed the younger man.

"You sounded like you meant that, Lanyard."

"I don't talk when I don't mean it."

"Then . . . why in God's name are you throwing in with a woolly outfit?"

"No explanations to make," Lanyard replied shortly. "I could wish you felt different, Searles."

"Your wish is wasted, Lanyard!"

A faint, cold smile touched the corners of Lanyard's mouth. "You're honest anyway, Searles. There'll be more to this. I'm expectin' you to be fair."

"I'm one man against a range," Searles warned brusquely. "I'll not try more than my bare duty. Think it over before it's too late."

The same wintry smile was on Searles's face as Lanyard moved toward the door. Before he went out, he turned, saying: "I've thought it over. I'll ride the whirlwind through."

"God help you then, Lanyard. You'll find it a wild wind. Too wild for one man."

A shadow passed over Lanyard's face. "I wonder," he said slowly.

A stranger on the walk outside, seeing Lanyard leave the office, would have thought, "cowman." And would probably have followed with, "busted."

The look was there. His riding boots were old and worn; his Levi's had been patched, and patched again. The leather vest, once brave and bright, was snagged, worn, and shabby. The battered sombrero was poor for even a busted cowman. Only the gun in the scarred old holster at Lanyard's side was bright with care and attention.

The same stranger, noting the quick look Lanyard cast up and down the street, would also have guessed, "Heeled for trouble."

At twenty-six, Lanyard looked older. Spare flesh had been worked off his stocky frame. His jaw had a gaunt, hungry line. His face was bleak and strained, the look of a man who walked with matters of the spirit as well as the flesh.

Along the street Lanyard occasionally nodded and spoke to men he passed. More often he met an unfriendly stare and passed on without expression. He was aware he inspired low-voiced comments on both sides of the wide, dusty street.

A mahogany-skinned Mexican in overalls had been left in charge of the livery stable.

Lanyard said briefly, "I'll want my horse in an hour," and walked on along the street to the Palo Verde Hotel, and stopped at the desk and paid his bill.

The young, sandy-haired clerk casually inquired, "Riding back across the mountains, Mister Lanyard?" His nonchalance was elaborate.

Lanyard smiled faintly. "You'd make a bad poker player, son," he said, and turned away without giving satisfaction.

The Palo Verde Hotel, massively built of adobe, was two stories high. The bar to the left of the front patio was the center of the heart — the friendly heart of the friendly San Pedro range. But Lanyard, eating in the noisy clatter of the dining room, was conscious there was no friendliness here for him.

Worse, there was a vague tension in the air, a furtive gathering of hidden strain, like the black storm clouds gathering over Los Hermanos peaks.

Unhurriedly Lanyard finished eating and from the table walked though a gauntlet of unfriendly eyes into the lobby. He was aware of chairs scraping back and men drifting after him.

There near the desk other men waited, cowmen, booted, spurred, dusty, rough. Many were armed. Lanyard's mouth tightened as he moved through them without expression.

"Lanyard!"

The speaker was Buck Loring of the Rafter T, one of the larger spreads to the south. Flanked by a dozen men, Loring stood hard and uncompromising as Lanyard turned a level look.

"I hear you've got a grazing permit for the Hanley sheep, Lanyard."

"That's right, Loring."

"You're fixing to bring those damn woollies over on our grass?"

"It's free grass, Loring. Free to anyone who holds a permit."

Buck Loring spat on the floor. He was a big man, broad and solid, weathered to the color of jerky. Anger was gathering in a slow, dark surge on his face.

"Don't hold me off with fancy words, Lanyard. You were raised on this range. You were a cowman until you got wiped out. You know what it means to bring sheep over on this slope."

"Hanley applied for a legal permit."

Loring spat again. "To hell with your damn' permit! You're a skunk, Lanyard! But as long as you keep your stink over on the sheep range, it's your business. When you come after our summer grass, it's *my* business, an' every cowman's!"

"I won't say it's not, Loring."

"Are the sheep coming over?"

"I guess they are."

"You *guess?*" Loring blazed with rising anger. "They are if you say so! You're in charge! *You*, who usta be one of us! *You* . . . a damned sheepman now for the Hanleys! An' the first tight you get into, you think of the grass your old man scratched to keep. It's worse than if you'd been raised a sheepman. They don't know no better. Are you going through with this?"

"I don't start what I don't aim to finish, Loring."

Lanyard saw it coming and tried to dodge. He failed. Buck Loring's hard palm cracked like a bull whip against his face. "Pull your gun, you two-faced wolf!" The older man's hand hovered near his gun. He was rigid, red with fury.

"It won't work, Loring," Lanyard said quietly. "I don't aim to be forced into a draw so the lot of you can pot me."

Buck Loring's voice rasped with cold scorn. "You wouldn't have taken that before you went into sheep. Sam Lanyard would turn in his grave on that hill by Clear Creek if he could see you now. Sam was a man. A cowman!"

"Leave the dead alone," Lanyard said in a stifled voice. "I've said my say."

He felt the hate of his old friends, old neighbors, boring into his back as he walked to the stairs. Some of these gray and grizzled men had opened up the San Pedro range with that mighty cowman, Sam Lanyard, and held it with guns and hardship for their sons and their sons' children. Held it for the grazing cattle that moved year after year off the friendly grass to the shipping pens.

He was at the stairs when an oath rang out.

"Are you gonna let him walk off an' laugh at us? I'm not! I've gunned wolves before!"

Lanyard whirled before that threat, drawing his gun. So fast was his flow of motion his crashing gun met the shot he faced.

Plunging out of the line of fire, those who had guns were drawing them. Chunky, black-browed Nueces Kennedy, for ten years a truculent partner in the Circle K, stumbled back with a crippled shoulder.

Kennedy's bullet had missed its dodging target and dug into the trapping wall behind. With the same fast flow of motion, Lanyard hurled himself at the stairs, up behind the false shelter of the close-spaced banisters. The bitter blast of gunfire leaped after him. Splinters from the wooden banister flew against his face. He felt the tug of lead through his weathered sombrero crown as he gained the landing.

Breathing hard, Lanyard bolted into his room. He threw up the window and slid over the sill. His feet found the *viga* ends below, the outer tree trunk tips two feet long of round *viga* beams which supported the second floor.

Hanging at arm's length from a *viga* tip, Lanyard heard the tumult reach his door. He dropped, lit hard, came up easily, and ran outward into the night.

Panting, he reached the pungent dimness of the lantern-lit livery stable. His saddled roan, short-coupled and wiry, stood waiting. It was fed, watered, rested and sleek. So swiftly did Lanyard mount and leave, he almost rode down the staring Mexican by the doorway.

Midnight found the dry, dirt road steeply lifting. The high air of the upper mountains was cool and resin-laden. On the steep slopes the pines stood stark and dark. The distant, dismal howls of a wolf echoed off the high peaks.

Hunched in the saddle, Lanyard heard their call. He thought: "Loafer wolves, have to trap 'em out. They'll be hell on the sheep." Then with only the moon and pines to witness, he muttered, "the *sheep*," and spat.

Dawn waited in the pass. The air was chill. Ahead the cloudless sky was a purple dome touched with gold and scarlet against the lower rim. The road dropped steeply toward the living dawn, the harsh, parched plain lay yellow and softened by incredible distance.

Lanyard twisted in the saddle and looked back, and down, across the long night's ride to the far San Pedro range. His stubble-crusted face was weary as he headed down the eastern slope and, presently in the full glory of the risen sun he met the first sheep. Hanley sheep.

Across a wide-gashed rift in the mountain he saw them on the far slope, a slow-moving, restless river of white, grazing inexorably upward. Their never-ceasing blatting, *baaaing* chorus was like the far sound of destroying water. Lanyard turned his face away and rode down into the sheep country and toward Hanley's.

The Hanley house faced south, where the warm sun flooded the long front *portal*. There on the *portal*, where he lived these days from sunup to sundown, old Rack Hanley's querulous voice cut through the rising heat. "Did you get the permit, Tom?"

Walking stiffly onto the *portal*, Lanyard said, "I got it." He nodded shortly to the younger man who stood by Rack Hanley's chair.

Cliff Davis was about thirty. His round, handsome face was shrewd and alert. Today, Lanyard noticed with swift distaste, Cliff was wearing a new gray suit and a bright tie, and his trousers were tucked neatly into expensive, soft-leather riding boots. Lanyard realized that on these days, Cliff Davis always dressed up when he rode over to visit.

No reason why he shouldn't be well dressed, Lanyard grudgingly conceded. Cliff Davis looked what he was — a prosperous sheepman. But the signs were not hard to read. He lifted smooth, thick eyebrows.

"Going to try and use that permit, Lanyard?"

"I got it, didn't I?"

Rack Hanley moved feebly. As usual, Lanyard was stirred by sight of the shrunken, withered figure. Years ago, Rack Hanley had been a big man. He'd been confident and masterful in his strength. The blight of paralysis had been doubly cruel. Rack's spirit had broken, too. The shrunken shell in that blanketed chair was not the Rack Hanley who had come West with young Sam Lanyard, when the range on both sides of Los Hermanos peaks was lush and virgin.

Rack's voice was fretful. "Everything's all right now, ain't it, Tom?"

Lanyard's face softened. "It's all right, Rack. Leave it to me."

Cliff Davis's lips raised to uncover strong, white teeth. "You've turned quite a sheepman, haven't you, Lanyard?"

Lanyard eyed him coldly. "I'll never be a sheepman."

In the silence which followed, all three looked at the door. It was opening.

Rack called, "Kay, we c'n celebrate! Tom got the permit! Tell mother!"

Kay was dark haired, with a wary pride behind the free, soft comeliness of the early twenties. A new eagerness crept into Lanyard's face; he was smiling when a graying, motherly little woman came out a moment later and lost her worried look at the news.

"I declare, I'm so relieved," Ma Hanley confessed thankfully. "Tom, I don't know what we'd do without you."

Cliff Davis laughed. He put in gallantly, "*I'm* always around, Mother Hanley."

"It does seem so," Lanyard agreed gently. Lanyard never raised his voice.

Cliff Davis looked annoyed.

Hastily, Kay said, "Tom, you look worn out. You rode all night, didn't you?"

"I'm fresh as spring rain," Tom Lanyard said.

"Coffee, something to eat, and bed for you, my boy,"

Kay said firmly. She turned to the older woman. "Never mind, Mother, I'll do it."

In the kitchen as she measured coffee, Kay said, "You weren't very nice to Cliff."

"Want me to be tender and gentle with him, Kay?"

"Idiot!" Kay said, flushing. "You know what I mean. Cliff tries to be nice. He came over this morning to offer father a loan. Cliff's been a sheepman all his life. He knows how things are."

"You mean I don't?"

"Are we going to argue again?" Kay said with exasperation. "We couldn't have gone on without you, Tom. You know that perfectly well. But you've always been a cowman. Cliff and father are sheepmen. They see eye to eye."

Lanyard said, "Well . . . ?"

Kay turned suddenly and picked up the battered sombrero. She put her finger in the bullet hole. "Trouble, Tom?"

"Nothing to speak of."

"The permit makes everything all right, doesn't it?"

Lanyard grinned reassuringly. "Oh, sure, leave it to me. I'll bring the sheep through, until we get rain."

"Will it *ever* rain again?" Kay burst out. "The range is ruined anyway!"

"It's as dry on the San Pedro side as it is where we're grazin'. But they still have grass."

"Here, drink your coffee . . . *cowman!*" Kay flashed with quick annoyance. Immediately she was apologetic. "I'm an ill-tempered wench." Then, changing her mood suddenly, "Tom . . . you look so tired."

But the thing was always there ready to flare up, Lanyard reflected glumly. Sheepman — cowman, always antagonistic. What hopes could two people build on so unstable a foundation?

Then, a little later, in bed, Lanyard thought dreamily that solicitude was even better than a good meal and a soft bed. It soothed, comforted, and brought strength for the future. It even helped a gent endure a constant visitor, like Cliff Davis.

Eight days later Searles, the government man, saw Lanyard. He spoke angrily from his saddle: "It will mean murder. And fourteen hired gunmen won't stop it! Every cowman on the San Pedro range is ready to fight!"

Lanyard was gaunt, unshaven, and unmoved. "Then I'll hire more gunmen, Searles."

Two thousand feet above them, thunder rolled over Little Hermano Peak. But the black clouds were scattering to the west. Five thousand feet below, the sheep country scorched in glaring sunlight.

In sudden passion Lanyard shook his fist at the retreating clouds. Then he gestured violently at the dry, close-grazed meadow, the blatting sheep which seemed everywhere, and the cook wagon at the lower end of the meadow where the hired guards lounged.

"There's no pasture left below us, Searles!" Lanyard bit out. "There'll be no more growth until we get rain . . . and the rain don't come! Hanley's sheep have got to have grass or they'll be dying off before the summer's over, let alone making out through the winter. I've ridden five horses under in the last eight days hiring guards and getting the sheep headed toward Echo Cañon for the tally into government land. Hanley's sheep are going to live, if I can ride and fight!"

Searles's voice was heavy. "A range war is a terrible thing, Lanyard. You're young, but you should know.

140

Recklessness can't explain your stubbornness."

"I'll not order the first shot fired," Lanyard said woodenly.

Searles's reply was a flare of temper. "I warned you it was too wild a thing for one man, Lanyard. It's coming. Make no mistake. You're a fool to cause it . . . a criminal fool!" The grizzled little man angrily spurred away.

Lanyard stared after him for a full minute, and then sighed and rode down to the cook wagon. His manner was grim when he pulled up by the lounging men. They were not a pretty lot, but they would fight — for a price.

"We'll start the sheep into Echo Cañon tomorrow," Lanyard told them. "And whenever they're past the tally point, you can look for trouble."

"How much trouble, Lanyard?"

"That's up to you men. That's what you're paid for."

A second man spoke. "I'll risk my neck for cash . . . but not for sheeper glory," he grunted, looking around for approval. "A man'd be a fool to look at it any other way."

Lanyard was smiling. But there was no mirth in his voice as he picked up the reins. "You may be right, Dawson. Who knows?"

And that was the last time Lanyard smiled that day.

There was hard riding to be done to check the bands of sheep slowly converging toward Echo Cañon. Lanyard tried to drown the turmoil in his mind and the sharp pain, in furious activity. When he rode wearily back past the bands of bedding sheep and sighted the cook fire through the deepening dusk, his face was set and expressionless again. Then he was in his bedroll, asleep, fifteen minutes after eating.

By nine o'clock next morning, meaningless thunder

was rolling over Little Hermano Peak again, and the sheep were approaching Echo Cañon. Lanyard drew rein in the cañon mouth while eight of his hired gunmen rode briskly on toward the tally fence, two miles farther.

Half a mile down the mountain the first rivulet of sheep was crawling into sight. In his imagination the rivulet became a white, devouring flood that by noon would be spilling down the western slope. And then what he found at the tally fence across the cañon head banished all other thoughts.

Searles and two tally men were waiting beyond the fence. The eight hired sheep guards sat their horses in an uncertain, restless group. Between Lanyard's eight riders and the tally fence, across the narrow cañon, was an advance barrier of armed riders. Lanyard counted them rapidly as he rode up. Seventeen. All were armed.

Buck Loring, solid and grim, was there. So was scowling Nueces Kennedy with one arm in a sling, and old Shadwell Jones and his son, Dan, from the SJO ranch. There were other neighbors: Peter Starling, Boston Beames, usually as droll as his name but now hard and watchful, and others, all waiting in grim silence.

Dawson jerked his head with a surly expression. "Didja aim for us to tackle all them, Lanyard?"

Lanyard rode between the groups without reply and politely addressed the waiting line.

"Maybe it ain't known that I'm bringing Hanley sheep through here this morning."

Nueces Kennedy started to speak violently, but old Shadwell Jones beat him to it.

"We heerd somethin' like that, Tom. Too bad we got here fustest to study the scenery. Purty, ain't it?" Shadwell cocked one eye aloft at the gathering clouds.

142

The tense quiet had a living quality, gathering, tightening.

Lanyard nodded gravely. "I admire the beauty in your soul, Shadwell. And I know where you can see a heap more scenery easier."

"Wouldn't think of troublin' you. We like it here," Shadwell refused. His hand crept nearer his holstered gun. Lanyard raised his voice. "Searles, it's your duty to admit my sheep past that fence!"

"I'm waitin' here to tally 'em in," the government man replied indifferently. "My authority stops at this fence line."

Thunder rolled again in the distance. Nueces Kennedy challenged softly: "Try an' get 'em to the fence!"

"Never mind. Keep watchin' the scenery, Nueces," Shadwell Jones reproved.

The murmur of the advancing sheep was louder. A galloping horse drummed through the sound. Lanyard looked. His throat contracted as he saw Kay Hanley approaching. Her face was anxious and troubled as she stopped her sorrel mare abreast of him.

"You're having trouble, Tom?"

"Not much. You mind riding out of the cañon and waiting for me, Kay?"

Wide eyed and uncertain, Kay looked about. She read the signs. "They're not going to turn our sheep back to . . . to die, Tom?"

Lanyard smiled reassuringly, "Didn't I tell you I'd get 'em to grass? As soon as this little argument is over, we'll tally them through."

Warmed by the gratitude Kay mutely gave him, Lanyard looked past her. "Those aren't my men coming. Isn't that Cliff Davis in front?"

143

Kay nodded with a strained smile of relief. "I rode on ahead of them. It's Cliff, with sixteen men to help you, Tom. He suggested bringing them up now, instead of later with his own sheep. He had an idea," Kay said with a defiant look at the grim line of men, "that they might be needed."

Lanyard's voice sounded strained, choked. "Later . . . with *his* sheep? What do you mean?"

"Mean? Tom, you sound strange! You . . . you look strange. Here's Cliff. He'll tell you."

Davis took in the situation as he rode up. "We seem to have gotten here just in time, eh, Lanyard?"

"Kay said something about *your* sheep." Lanyard had never realized how much he disliked that white-toothed smile.

"That's right. After you and Hanley got a permit, I managed to get one, too. I'm bringing part of my sheep over after yours. We'll work together on this."

Lanyard turned toward the government man. "Searles, you didn't tell me Davis got a permit, too."

"I thought you knew it," Searles bit back. "A dozen others are fighting for permits, too. Hanley broke the ice. After you got a permit, they mean to follow."

"Do they now?" Lanyard heard himself saying in a choked voice. "Here's my permit, Searles!" He tore the permit, and dropped the pieces. Then he called, "Dawson! Take your men, an' turn those sheep back!"

Kay cried sharply, "Tom! Are you crazy?"

"Just gettin sane, Kay!"

Cliff Davis flung angrily: "So you lost your nerve, eh? Well, I haven't! Let those sheep come on. I'll see them through."

Lanyard drew his six-shooter. "Dawson, you heard me!"

144

"Tom!" Kay cried fiercely. "If you're afraid, let Cliff handle this."

"Keep out of this, Kay. Dawson, damn you, move!"

Dawson hunched uncomfortably. "You hired us, Lanyard. Your dinero talks. I guess your orders go. Come on, boys."

They galloped off.

Cliff Davis opened his mouth, then closed it silently. He looked at Kay, pale, dismayed, biting her lips. Kay's sorrel danced nervously as she lifted the reins.

In a shaking voice, Kay said, "Come on, Cliff. Let's get away from these . . . cowmen."

The frightened sheep were eddying up the cañon sides, crowding back before the riders and barking dogs. Slowly the tide began to ebb down the cañon, Cliff Davis, his men, and Kay following.

Behind Lanyard, Shadwell Jones spoke gently. "I've got a place on my ranch . . . for a *cowman*. Any time."

Lanyard rode off without looking back. He rode down the cañon after the ebbing tide of sheep which this year would not roll down on the San Pedro grass. Inside he felt dead. Thunder peeled overhead, and its mocking promise held no meaning to him.

"It's over," he thought. "She'll marry him now."

Then from his slow-walking horse he saw Kay waiting at the cañon mouth, alone. A faint hope stirred within him and died as he rode near and saw her stony face. Stopping beside the sorrel mare, Lanyard said all he could say. It was only, "I'm sorry, Kay."

Kay smiled scornfully. "So you're sorry, Tom? Sorry your promises were lies? You're sorry you wiped us out?" Kay's voice shook. "Well, I'm sorry, too! Sorry I ever listened. Sorry we ever knew you."

"Kay . . . please!"

"But I'm glad, too," Kay said coldly. "Glad there'll be no more lies, no more promises to be broken, no more of you around . . . *ever!* If I were a man, I'd quirt you, you miserable cowardly *cowman.*"

"Wait!" Lanyard called roughly as her mare danced around to leave.

Kay said coldly, "Well?"

"I was busted when Rack sent word he needed me," Lanyard said. "His helplessness was the only thing that could have made me run sheep. Rack and Dad were always close. Rack helped us out in a couple of tight spots. So I took his sheep, an' did the best I could without pay."

"If you want back wages now. . . ."

"Shut up!" Lanyard said furiously. "Look at the sheep country below us. It's grazed out! The sheep were forced into the high pasture before the snow was off. That's gone now, because the rains held off. It's just as dry on the other side, but there's grass. That's why the San Pedro ranchers never let a sheep get on their side of these mountains."

"I've heard that story all my life!" Kay flung back bitterly.

"You heard it because the sheep range was going and the cow range wasn't. That government grass on the other side is what carries the valley cattle through the summer grazing. They count on it."

"Sheep have as much right to it. A few sheep won't hurt it."

"A *few* sheep. That's what I tried to tell myself. Rack's sheep . . . just this one summer. But I knew it was a lie, an' I went ahead anyway. I turned against everything

146

I was raised to believe, because you Hanleys needed me. I turned against my friends, got myself despised, threatened, shot at. I was all set to start a range war, to see my friends killed. All because of your damned sheep!"

"They had no right to stop us!" Kay said angrily.

"No *right?*" Lanyard shouted. "Hell, they had all the right! Everything they were afraid of happened. Every sheepman on this side of the mountains jumped for my coat tails and fixed to ride through to the San Pedro grass on what I was doing. I sold out my friends and my convictions, and that wasn't bad enough. But you and Rack and Cliff Davis sold *me* out! You took what I was doing for Rack an' gave it to every greedy sheepman on this range. And then you called *me* coward when I stood against it.

"I was fool enough to think I was in love with you," Lanyard continued passionately. "But not now! Marry your fancy sheepman an' see eye to eye with him the rest of your life. If you get rain, your sheep'll pull through. If you try to bring 'em over on the other side, God help you! Good bye."

A louder peal of thunder drowned the last word as Lanyard yanked his horse around and galloped back into the cañon. Thunder was rolling again when Kay's sorrel mare caught up with him and crowded him to a stop. Kay was crying.

"Tom! How could you ever think I'd marry Cliff Davis? You're brave, you're fine! How could I know how it all looked to you? I . . . I've never been a cowman."

Lanyard swept her over to his saddle and held her close.

It was some moments before Kay could speak again,

this time against his old leather vest. "Tom, are *you* crying, too?"

Lanyard held his hand into the first wild blast of wind off the peaks, and chuckled. "That was a raindrop. The rain's coming. We'd better get to cover."

Kay sighed without interest. "Just as you say . . . cowman!"

Lanyard kissed her. "Say it again," he begged. " 'Cowman!' I like it . . . that way."

"Devil Brand" was one of the last stories T.T. Flynn wrote for the magazine market. It appeared in the February, 1950 issue of *Dime Western* where Flynn had been a regular contributor now for nearly two decades. For some years already Mike Tilden had replaced Rogers Terrill as the editor and, the name notwithstanding, *Dime Western* now cost 15¢. Tilden had a penchant for even more garish story titles than Terrill had and retitled this one "Walk Soft — Shoot Quick!" It is a title totally irrelevant to anything that happens in the story. The contributors to *Dime Western* had also changed over the years. While this Flynn story was showcased on the magazine's cover and put in the prestigious first position in the table of contents, the same issue also had stories by Louis L'Amour, Dee Linford, George C. Appell, and Peter B. Germano under his Barry Cord byline. Ted Flynn had only been living in New Mexico for a few years when he wrote his first Western story. By the time "Devil Brand" appeared, he had traveled extensively in the West, as well as continuing to live part of every year in New Mexico. He had absorbed the Mexican culture and the Spanish language by osmosis, and it showed. His preoccupation with mortality, if anything, had grown more abiding. Death was seen to affect his protagonists more devastatingly as, through it, they were able to touch so intimately the most delicate membranes of meaning in life.

DEVIL BRAND

I

"DEATH COMES TO BLACK WATER SPRING"

Any man could make a bad mistake. Some men could make two bad mistakes. Three in a row were dangerous. In this part of the border country, men died from that. Matt Davison made the third mistake, too.

Purple twilight deepened over Black Water Spring, at the mouth of Lost Man Cañon, two days north of the border. Davison and Carlos Sedillo had covered the distance easily, not pushing their horses.

South lay gray-green rolls of mesquite country. Some miles up the cañon the first tall pines lifted, so Carlos said. Black Water Spring seeped over its limestone overhang, pooling darkly, wandering down the slight slope to oblivion in the sand of the cañon bed.

Carlos Sedillo had a frying-pan fire of tiny dry sticks crackling between two smoke-blackened rocks. His teeth flashed in the firelight as he smiled and spoke in Spanish. "At this place my grandfather's father was scalped by Apaches. Perhaps here, where we burn the fire to his memory, eh?"

Davison chuckled where he sat on the ground a few feet away, cigarette drooping from his lips. *"Acaso,"* Matt agreed in Spanish. He turned slightly, listening. "They are bringing his scalp back now?" Matt asked.

Carlos turned his head, too. With a quick reach he put the frying pan over the fire, cutting off most of the light. It wasn't much of a fire anyway. Their two hobbled horses had lifted heads and pricked ears.

Up the cañon horseshoe metal chinked against rock. Shadows were thick that way where the cañon made a quick bend. Carlos stepped farther from the fire, with the caution that had become habitual with them both in long months together across the border. Almost a year, in fact, since trail luck had thrown them together one explosive night.

Matt Davison sat where he was, unmoving. Sun and wind had made his face as dark as Carlos's. Each wore greasy leather trail pants and jackets of Mexican cut, and high-crowned Mexican sombreros.

South of the border they had passed for natives. Not *ricos*, the well-to-do, either. They'd been wandering *vaqueros*, down on their luck, with little attention paid to them. Only their horses were exceptional, and anyone could understand a *vaquero* with a fine horse.

Matt's big coal-black horse would have been the pride of any hacienda. Had been, as a matter of fact. Matt said softly now, "Three," and watched to see what manner of men rode from the cañon.

They came onto the cañon sands at an easy trot and turned up the small slope toward the fire. Matt stood up. He wasn't a big man, but tall enough, hard-flanked, tight-waisted, balancing with the springy ease of smooth muscles, if one cared to notice closely. He spoke as a Mexican *vaquero*.

"*Buenos noches, señores.*"

Two of the newcomers were Spanish-American like Carlos. The third was a big man with light yellow hair, gray Stetson, wool riding pants, expensive bold-stitched boots, and a gray wool shirt. All three were armed with side and saddle guns.

They pulled up watchfully, estimating the camp. The big one swung down. "Just you two here? Talk American, dammit."

"*Sí, señor,*" Matt said politely. He'd dropped the cigarette end and was rolling another with lean brown fingers. He watched the big one look around and then step toward their hobbled horses.

"That black ain't a bad one. How much for him?"

"No sell, *señor,*" Matt said. He twisted the cigarette end and lit it.

"Hell! Everything's for sale! What brand's he carryin'?" The big one had a thick neck set solidly on broad shoulders. His cheekbones were high and features heavy. The rowels of silver-inlaid Chihuahua spurs clinked as he stepped to the black horse. He whistled audibly. "Broad Arrow an' Big Cross! That's General Salazar's Hacienda of the Moon, down Chihuahua way."

Matt said nothing.

The big man swung toward him. "Border jumpers, huh?"

Matt shrugged.

Carlos was in the background, watching silently.

"Two damned horse thieves!" the big man said. He had a heavy voice, slurring a little. "Come across on the jump,

I bet, with Salazar's men on your tails."

"No, *señor*," Matt said. He drew smoke and let it out slowly.

The two other riders had stayed on their horses. They were grinning now.

"Don't lie to me!" the big man said. "Hoss thieves get shot quicker this side of the border than south of it. I'll take your word you bought that black one. I'll buy him off you. My hoss an' fifty dollars for a bill-of-sale. Let's get at it!"

"No, *señor*," Matt said.

"Don't stand there tellin' me no like a damn' Guadeloupe parrot! I made you a fair offer."

The big stranger was working himself into a rage. Most of it was pretense, Matt guessed.

He said mildly, "No, *señor*."

"Then we'll trade like you damn' border thieves deserve. Cover 'em, boys!"

There'd been no way to head it off without giving up the black horse. From his first sight of the horse, the big stranger's purpose had been set. And six-gun lead would probably have paid them for a bill-of-sale.

Carlos had known it, too. He fired the first shot.

Matt's shot piled into the racket. A plunging horse knocked him to one side. The rider was sliding off and more gunfire crashed behind Matt. But he'd seen the big stranger's gun arm go limp before he got off his first shot.

The plunging horse came between them. Its falling rider hit the ground hard, tumbled over and lay still.

The big stranger was still hidden by the frightened horse. Matt swung in a lurching crouch. The second rider was reining savagely at him, revolver lining up.

Matt dodged. Twice he fired, fast, aiming for the rider instead of the horse.

The second bullet struck under the man's chin strap, ranging up and seeming to tear out the whole front of his face. Then that second horse went by with the faceless rider still balanced in the saddle.

The big stranger became visible again. He had caught the first horse, swung up, was spurring away, still partly protected by the second horse and the toppling dead man. A long shot might have knocked him out of the saddle. Matt held the shot. Two dead ones were enough.

He watched the man head for the darkening mesquite thickets. The wounded arm dangled and flopped. It would be a long time before that arm pulled a gun on another stranger.

Matt remembered Carlos, and turned. Driving hoofs had kicked the frying pan away and scattered tiny embers. Carlos Sedillo lay on the ground.

He lived, but not by much. Gun in hand, Matt dropped to a knee beside Carlos. He marked the thin line of bubbling red on Carlos's lips. He'd been shot through the chest.

The tally was plain. Here by Black Water Spring, where the father of his grandfather had been scalped by Apaches, Carlos too would die.

Carlos knew it. He blew out froth, gasped and spoke weakly. "*Compadre*, go not to my home now. There will be danger. He and more of his blood are of that range. The yellow hairs we call them."

Carlos was speaking Spanish, although his English was good. "The Hobbs family is how they call themselves. They will hunt you now, because one got away. We should have killed three." Then, in English: "Ees bad. For you, ees bad. Me, I go." Carlos groaned. "*¡Aie!* No breath!" He choked.

Matt used his neck cloth to wipe Carlos's mouth. "I'll look after everything," he promised.

Carlos was past caring. He muttered, "My oncle. Is not too far, no?"

"I'll take you," Matt promised again.

"*¡Compadre!*" Carlos gasped. His hand groped across his chest.

Matt reached for the hand. He was on one knee like that, holding the slender fingers, when Carlos died, perhaps near the spot where his grandfather's father had died.

The gray-black night was marching in, but there was still some light. Their horses, hobbled front leg to back, had retreated a short way from the gun fight. Matt brought them back. There would be no camp at Black Water Spring tonight.

He saddled both horses, dropped the heavy saddlebags on, and tied their single blanket rolls in place. They'd been traveling light and fast.

All that took but a few minutes. He made one last change. He untied Carlos's blanket and wrapped Carlos in it against the night chill sliding down off the mountains. The act gave him a small measure of satisfaction. Carlos had been only twenty. He'd been a faithful friend.

The other two dead stayed where they'd dropped. The coyotes and bears, tomorrow the buzzards, could have them for all Matt cared.

He used both their ropes to lash Carlos across the saddle. The horse didn't want to carry death but Matt used a hard rein on him. When he rode away from Black Water Spring, he took the down slope toward the mesquite country, where the yellow-haired stranger had headed.

He had no intention of trailing the man. He knew where he was going, and it was an all night ride, perhaps longer. Carlos had spoken of it today as they came from the south. Some forty miles off their trail was the settlement of Palomas.

There was a church in Palomas, with consecrated ground for the dead. The old priest who served Palomas and other *placitas* was some relation to Carlos. Not uncle, as Carlos had called him, but of the Sedillo name. He would do what had to be done.

II

"THE MAN WITH THE YELLOW HAIR"

Palomas was an irregular cluster of flat-roofed adobe houses on fertile flats skirting a small stream which headed back into the mountains. Matt rode off the higher land into town as the sun came up.

There was a chance the yellow-haired Hobbs had headed this way with his shattered arm. Matt's bloodshot, sleep-heavy eyes scanned houses, people, horses as he brought his lashed, blanket-wrapped burden to the church.

He called to a boy, asking for Father Sedillo. The boy pointed and ran ahead to a small adobe house beside the church. The priest came out as Matt dismounted stiffly. He was a small, white-haired old man.

"Father Sedillo?" Matt inquired.

The priest nodded, evidently familiar enough with death brought to his door. Matt indicated the lead horse. "Carlos Sedillo," he said in Spanish. "Son of Ramos Sedillo, west of the Rio Chamorro. Carlos asked me to bring him to you." Matt added, "I'm hungry and need sleep and feed for my horses."

"With me, my son," the old priest told him quickly, "everything will be done." He made a Sign of the Cross toward the lashed body.

Matt glanced at the curious crowd gathering. He asked the priest in Spanish, "Has a yellow-haired man with a wounded arm ridden this way?"

The padre asked all within earshot. None of them had seen such a man.

A little later a stooped and wrinkled old housekeeper, wearing a black mantilla over her head, fed Matt at the padre's table. He wolfed down chili beans and goat meat with thick wheat flour tortillas. There was a bottle of red wine and strong black coffee. After eating, he slept in a small, cell-like room, cool and quiet, his saddlebags under the narrow bed and holstered gun on a wooden chair alongside.

Late afternoon sun slanted through the small high window when Matt came awake instantly, as was his habit. The belt gun was cocked in his hand as he sat up, so fast had he moved. A creaking hinge on the opening door had awakened him.

The padre, in the doorway, looked at the gun muzzle. He smiled and said, "Peace."

Matt lowered the gun almost sheepishly and sat on

the edge of the narrow shuck-filled pallet.

"I wake up fast, Father," he said.

"We have buried Carlos Sedillo," the priest said. He had not asked how Carlos had died. "A young woman . . . a *Yanqui* woman . . . has stopped in Palomas and wishes to speak with you. A *Señorita* Brenda Scott."

Matt shook his head. "Friend of yours?"

"I have not seen her before," the priest said.

"Her business?"

"She did not say. She has walked back to admire your horse."

That was where Matt found her, out back at the adobe shed where the padre's good roan horse stayed. She saw Matt come out of the house, sombrero in hand, and she came to greet him.

He hadn't shaved for two days. With the greasy leather pants, Mexican jacket and black-burnt, unshaven face, he looked more than ever like a border jumper.

The first American girl he'd seen in months, this Brenda Scott had features almost startlingly fair. She was slender, and walked with an easy stride. She had a pleasant mouth and level gray eyes, he noted. Her riding skirt and jacket were of the same matching brown woolen stuff.

She wore a cream-colored sombrero. Her hair was fine and tawny, almost yellow. Matt really saw her hair first — *yellow hair*. Or close enough to be classed that way.

In Spanish, ducking his head, Matt asked, "*Señorita*, you wish to see me?"

She studied him calmly. Then, slowly: "Do you speak English?"

Matt grinned. "Leetle bit, *señorita*."

"I'm Brenda Scott," the girl said. "They say you rode

in this morning with a dead man tied on his horse."

"*Sí.*"

"They say you asked about a yellow-haired man with a wounded arm."

"*Sí.*"

"The dead man was Carlos Sedillo."

"*Sí,*" Matt agreed.

"Then you're from across the border," Brenda Scott said.

Matt shrugged.

"The black horse," she said, "is from across the border."

Matt shrugged again, watching her as she was watching him. He'd come out liking the idea of talking to an American girl. A little curious, too, as to why she would want to speak with him. But he hadn't expected this.

She said, "This man with the yellow hair . . . do you know who he is?"

Matt stared at her stupidly.

She was getting annoyed. "What happened?" she asked. "And where did it happen?"

"Thees," said Matt politely, "ees business of Carlos Sedillo. Me no sabe."

Temper began to edge into Brenda's cheeks. He waited for it to flare, barely suppressing a grim smile. She knew better than to ask questions like that about a dead man. He heard booted feet coming around the padre's house, and turned and backed off a little to keep the newcomer in sight.

The gray, grizzled, stoop-shouldered stranger was an old-timer in the cattle business. You could see one or more like him around any chuck wagon. A little bow-legged, stooped and leathery, he had a tobacco-stained gray mustache, worn boots, denim pants and a leather vest as hard-used and greasy as Matt's trail pants. The flat-crowned black hat looked as old as the wearer.

So did the cedar-handled .44, holstered low and tied down. A hard-shelled old-timer, and he could probably use that gun as well as he could burr a horse day and night in any weather.

"You havin' luck, miss?" he asked past a cheek full of tobacco. He turned his head and spat, and stood on spread legs looking Matt over with bright sharp eyes.

"Not much, Tex."

"Lemme ast him." Tex turned his head and spat again. "Look, feller," he began ominously.

The girl said sharply, "Never mind, Tex!"

Tex shrugged, stood frowning at Matt.

She spoke to Matt, holding her temper even. "I have a reason for these questions. I'm sorry Carlos Sedillo is dead. I . . . I've heard of him. He had a good name. I'll guess that the man with the yellow hair killed him. What I want to know is: which way was that man traveling? I'll guess that he's still alive, since you asked about him here in Palomas."

Matt thought that over. "South," he said.

"Toward El Paso?"

Matt grinned then. "Ees hard to tell. He ride fast."

Tex and the girl exchanged a glance. "Big feller?" Tex asked. "Big Mex spurs?"

"*Sí.*"

"One more question," Brenda Scott said. "Did you hear of a Yankee across the border by the name of Brooks?"

"No, *señorita,*" Matt said, and he hadn't.

Brenda looked him over. Her lips curled. "Thank you, whatever your name is supposed to be," she said. "All I wanted was information. The next time you play this game,

161

keep those Yankee blue eyes closed, Matt Davison. You look like a cut-throat and you probably are. But I don't think you killed Carlos Sedillo and I'll give you one piece of advice. Sleep lightly and walk carefully from now on."

Matt said, "Thanks, Miss Scott." He was smiling wryly, and his own dark face was flushing as she walked past him toward the front of the padre's house, without looking at him again.

Tex stared at Matt. "I'll be damned!" he muttered. He spat and swung after her, leaving Matt standing alone, feeling like a damned fool. He swore to himself.

She evidently had been riding through with Tex. Their horses were out front, hers with a side saddle. As they rode off, a buckboard beyond, driven by a younger man, pulled out with them.

The buckboard was lightly loaded under a tied-down tarp. Standing in front of the padre's house, rolling a cigarette, watching them out of town, Matt guessed the three were traveling away from the mountains, toward El Paso.

Matt's wry grin spread. He would soon head for El Paso, too.

III

"DEAL THE DEAD MAN'S HAND"

The next morning Davison, still looking like a *vaquero* on the bum, rode into El Paso on the black horse. Here the mountains pinched into the Rio Grande gate, where the old Mexican town and the new Yankee town faced each other across the river shallows.

The banker, who frowned when the *vaquero* walked into his private office carrying two heavy saddlebags, shook hands with great heartiness when the same *vaquero* departed a little later. "At your service, sir. Call on us at any time."

The pallid and haughty clerk behind the desk at the Eagle Hotel looked at the unshaven Davison, shot his cuffs, said coldly, "No room to rent."

The *vaquero* finished rolling a cigarette and said in perfect English, "I'll just stand here and make sure you don't rent rooms then."

The clerk blinked his eyes, gulped, grinned weakly. "Mistake," he said, turning the register around.

Matt washed first in the big white basin in his second floor room. That got the top coat of trail dirt off. He took one last look at himself in the mirror over the painted pine washstand.

Banker and hotel clerk had seen a *vaquero*. But the Scott girl had seen Matt Davison and called his name, and left him feeling like a fool.

All night as he rode fast across the open country, Matt had thought of her, still half angry with chagrin. After the banker and hotel clerk, he felt a little better about it. Her sharp eyes hadn't been able to read his name. She'd known who he was before he'd come out of the padre's house.

He'd ridden straight across the dry, harsh semi-desert range, and fast, was well ahead of the girl and her two companions, if they were traveling to El Paso, and he believed they were.

Matt hit a barber shop, took a hot bath, then bought new clothes. That afternoon he slept.

When he walked out into El Paso plaza late in the afternoon, he was dressed in black broadcloth, white linen shirt, and string tie. Trousers were down outside fine new black calfskin boots. Black sombrero, new also, was creased through the crown. He was as well dressed as any man in El Paso, even to the good thin cheroot cocked in the corner of his mouth.

He had asked the banker and hotel clerk about a man named Brooks. The banker had said he would inquire. The hotel clerk had shaken his head.

In El Paso a man could find any entertainment he sought. Tonight the dance halls, gambling deadfalls, and saloons would be roaring. Matt had four drinks, walked to the feed barn to see that his black horse was doing well, then strolled back to the plaza. It was then he saw what he'd been waiting to see.

Brenda Scott arrived in El Paso at twilight, still riding side saddle. Matt guessed she'd taken the buckboard seat during the day.

Old Tex, ancient flat-crowned black hat turned up in front, lounged on his sorrel horse as if they were coming into another cow camp. The buckboard followed and Matt followed the buckboard.

He noticed that, tired and dusty as she obviously was, Brenda drew admiring glances from most men. They went to the Boston House, just off the plaza. Matt strolled into the Boston lobby, smoking a fresh cheroot, and watched Brenda Scott engage rooms.

He was sitting in a lobby chair, near enough to hear Tex speaking. "Buck, he c'n bed down near the hosses. Too fancy here, Buck says."

Brenda Scott said, "Buck stays here. You too, Tex. No celebrating."

Tex's laconic, "Yes'm," settled that. Then Tex weakened. "Couple drinks ain't celebratin', ma'am. I'm jist thirsty."

"You be the judge, Tex."

"Yes'm."

Matt almost grinned. Out of the back country to the delights of El Paso, and Buck and Tex were being close-herded. Brenda Scott's glance brushed over Matt as she turned to accompany the clerk up the carpeted stairs to her room. No sign of recognition crossed her face.

She was speaking to the clerk as the two of them started up the stairs. The clerk turned back. She continued on up. The clerk was a pudgy, half-bald man with a florid face. He came to Matt's chair and cleared his throat. He looked uncertain, embarrassed.

"The lady, uh, ordered me to tell you, sir, that . . . ahum . . . that a polecat who changes his stripes is still a polecat. Uh . . . you *are* Mister Davison, aren't you?" The clerk gulped as Matt stood up.

"I am," Matt said. The clerk was backing away. Brenda Scott had disappeared up the stairs. Matt demanded, "Did the lady say polecat or skunk?"

The unhappy clerk gulped again. "Skunk, Mister Davison," the little man said.

"Tell the lady," Matt said grimly, "I'll get down wind from her next time."

The clerk hurried to the stairs again. Matt wondered, as he started out, if his face was as red as it felt. Buck, a broad-faced young man, was bringing in valises from the buckboard. At the doorway old Tex hardly gave Matt a glance.

Matt turned left out of the Boston House doorway. Fifty yards farther on he almost bit through the end of his cheroot. His hand started an instinctive move toward the gun under his new broadcloth coat.

In the doorway of a mercantile store, Hobbs, the yellow hair, stood watching the buckboard. Hobbs's right arm was in a splint and bandages, the whole in a heavy cloth neck sling.

Hobbs had shaved and bought new clothes, a gray broadcloth suit which didn't fit well. Gun belt and gun were under his coat. He scowled as his dark eyes moved over Matt. His glance lingered for an instant, then returned to the buckboard.

Matt strolled on. Not a muscle of his face had moved. But it had been close. The surprise had been complete, even though he'd been looking for Hobbs here in El Paso. The man had made a hard ride with the shattered arm.

Here was trouble if Matt had ever seen it. He had Hobbs's measure now. He'd learned at Black Water Spring what Hobbs could do if it suited Hobbs's purpose.

Back in Palomas, Brenda Scott had wanted to know if Hobbs had been heading toward El Paso. Hobbs had. And Hobbs had either been watching for her arrival or had caught sight of the trio entering town.

They obviously didn't know Hobbs was here. Matt thought of turning back and warning Tex. He would have, probably, but for the message Brenda Scott had sent by the desk clerk. Everything about her was beginning to make Matt bristle. She knew too much about Matt Davison — and he knew nothing at all about her.

She was superior. She must believe she was clever. She was about everything Matt didn't like in a girl. Also, Hobbs was mixed in it now. That made it personal.

The man named Brooks was a missing part of what was beginning to be a nagging puzzle. Brooks, who'd been in northern Mexico. Matt's interest in Brooks increased sharply. And when he walked back to his hotel, he had luck.

The Eagle clerk, respectfully now, handed Matt a sealed envelope. The note inside read:

Sir:
In respect to the man named Brooks, make inquiry at the Longhorn Saloon during the evening.

The note, not signed, was on the letterhead of the Drover's Bank. Lamar, the bearded banker Matt had dealt with, did business with men out of Texas, out of New Mexico territory, and from deep in old Mexico. From some source during the day, as he'd promised, Lamar had obtained the information.

Matt dropped the torn note in a lobby brass spittoon. He wondered if Brenda Scott would be able to locate Brooks so easily.

Again he weighed going to her hotel and telling her. He let it wait until he looked into the matter of Brooks. Hobbs also must be interested in Brooks. Matt, holding an ace now in the whole deal, smiled grimly and applied his thoughts to the matter of a good steak dinner.

El Paso was beginning to stir for a boisterous night when Matt went out to see about the man named Brooks. The Longhorn was a good block from the plaza, toward the river. It was a big establishment, with two golden longhorns painted across the building front, and lighted outside by flickering oil flares.

The place was already filling when Matt walked through the swinging half doors. Men were at the bar. Card games were in progress. A faro bank was just opening toward the back.

The dance floor was to one side, through a wide archway. Girls there were standing in the archway, looking over the newcomers. A piano, a fiddle, and two guitars were playing for a few dancing couples.

It would, Matt guessed, be a large night. He shook his head as a good looking black-haired girl in a low-cut green silk dress started from the archway toward him. She pouted as she turned back to the archway.

Matt walked back along the bar until he was the last man at it. He ordered whiskey, and as bottle and glass were set out he asked the lean, white-aproned bartender, "Brooks in tonight?"

"You mean Colonel Brooks?"

Matt nodded.

"Right over there playin' stud, where he's been most nights for a week," the bartender said.

Matt took his time with the drink, not looking toward the card game. When he finally did stroll over to the game, he was only one of several spectators who came and went with casual interest. He had to wait some minutes before a man with a black, spade-cut beard turned over his hole card and said, "Three treys . . . ! How about it, Colonel?"

"Good enough, sir. Another bad night for me, I see."

The speaker was a rather elegant man with a carefully tended gray mustache, well-turned dark suit, and silver-mounted gun in a blue Mexican sash under his coat.

So that was Brooks! Matt had his chance a little later when one of the players dropped out of the game. He took his place. No one asked his name. No one cared.

Davison was hardly conscious the Longhorn was filling up, getting noisier. Colonel Brooks was a cool player bucking a losing streak which must have been going on for some nights.

It was an honest game, Matt figured. His luck ran well. Chips began to stack up in front of him. Twice Colonel Brooks bought more as the evening wore on. It was cutthroat stud, little talking. Matt was caught up in the game, not caring much for the time being who this Colonel Brooks really was.

Matt's chips stacked high. Brooks continued losing. The dance floor was crowded. Men packed the length of the long bar. Players banked around faro and monte. Matt lit another cheroot. His glance roved toward the front of the long noisy room.

Tobacco smoke was layered in a gray-blue haze under the big brass lamps overhead. The match burned almost to Matt's fingers as he eyed a patch of white up toward the front end of the bar. Men moved out of the way. The white became the bandaged arm of Hobbs, who was drinking with another, smaller man. At the moment Hobbs was looking back toward the stud game.

Matt dropped the match. Face harder, glance colder, he looked at the spade king just dealt him. He pushed in chips, was dealt another king for his last card.

Colonel Brooks had two aces showing. One more ace was up on the table. One more king. Aces against kings. . . .

Brooks, low on chips, lifted his voice, "Is there a buyer here for four hundred head of prime cattle, with this year's increase and a fair remuda?"

The man with the black spade-cut beard tossed in his cards. "You must have your ace in the hole, Colonel. Where's the ranch?"

"I have the papers here," Brooks said. "John Scott,

owner of the JS ranch, west of the Chamorro River, will deliver on request. A bargain for three thousand on the table now."

Matt said, "Make out your bill-of-sale."

It took most of his chips and many of the gold double eagles he'd brought from the bank. In a minute or so he was the owner of the 808 brand in custody of John Scott.

Then Matt played the rest of his chips against Brooks's two aces, gambling that Brooks lacked the third ace down, against the third king Matt had in the hole.

He lost as he deserved. Brooks had the ace. It struck Matt then he'd made a mistake. He tested it as Brooks raked the big pot to that side of the table.

"How about selling you back your cattle now?" Matt inquired.

"I sold, my young friend. I'm not buying," Brooks replied coolly.

Matt's dark face set hard. "The cattle are there?"

Brooks considered him. All friendliness in the game had vanished. Racket off the dance floor was loud across the table. Men watching the game stirred uneasily, sensing trouble building.

"Give your papers to Scott. He'll deliver," Brooks said. "You bought what was offered, friend. No more, no less."

Matt sat motionless. He marked Brooks's fingers. Gambler's hands. Gambler's coldness now in Brooks's stare.

"We'll see about it," Matt said shortly. He stood up and tested the matter further. "Hobbs," he said, "was having a drink a short time ago."

Brooks's eyes flashed fast to the long bar. But he was a good gambler. His quick tensing was barely visible. Then, as the meaning of it went in deeper, he asked

170

with a new note in the demand, "Who are you?"

"Davison," Matt said, and walked over to buy himself a drink.

Hobbs and the smaller man seemed to have gone out. Matt chewed the cigar, thinking hard. He saw Brooks cashing in. The man's eyes were roving around.

Brooks left the stud table. He walked through the archway, skirted the back of the dance floor, turned left through a door. The man was afraid. He might talk now. Matt went after him.

The door led into a dim passage from which small rooms opened off. The dance music, shuffle and stomp of feet came almost as loudly through the closed door. There was another door at the end of the passage.

Matt walked there. His hand was going to the iron handle when gunshots — two of them — smashed somewhere on the other side of the door.

Matt guessed what was happening and he wanted to talk to Brooks. He yanked the door open and went out in a lunging crouch, gun in hand. Out into the pitchy shadows of an alley, where he was blinded for a moment.

He dodged to the left side of the doorway, crouching lower. On to the left he made out light from the street along one side of the Longhorn. Two men on the street were already peering cautiously into the alley. The other way, deeper in the alley blackness, steps scuffed softly on hard-packed dirt. Matt lunged that way.

The steps broke into a run not far ahead. Matt was skirting the building wall. He almost collided with the beer barrels stacked there. He took the middle of the alley, a fool thing to do with the street glow behind him. Then he stumbled over a sprawled body.

171

It might have saved his life. Shots hammered in the blackness ahead. The muzzle flashes made their instant of lurid orange light and Matt fired fast, twice, three times, and ran forward.

IV

"BRAND OF THE 808"

The footsteps ahead were inaudible. The alley grew blacker as Matt advanced, then suddenly a cross alley loomed before him. Matt stopped. He was panting. The stranger could have gone three ways here.

Off to the right and left in the cross alley, dim street glow could be seen. The man might have ducked into a doorway, be running on ahead, or crouching in shadow, gun cocked to kill. Matt shrugged and turned back.

Men poured out the back of the Longhorn, were running into the alley from the street. Matches flared. Voices lifted in excited questions. A bartender brought a lighted lantern out as Matt reached the scene.

Lantern light struck down on the body. It was Colonel Brooks. His hat had fallen off. He'd been shot under the right eye. His gun was still in the blue Mexican sash.

The bartender said, "He never had a chance!" He was the man working the back end of the long bar, the man Matt had asked about Brooks. He looked at Matt.

"Was he robbed?" Matt asked. He stooped to see. When Brooks had cashed in, he'd shoved the money in his coat pockets. They were empty.

Matt looked at the colonel's bloody face and thought of the small man who'd been drinking with Hobbs. The big man with the splinted arm hadn't done this, Matt decided. He tried to get features of the smaller man clear in his mind.

They'd been up toward the front of the barroom, men moving between. But Matt believed he'd know that sharp-nosed, sharp-chinned smaller man if they met again. He became aware of the strained quiet in the men standing close. The lantern light fell full on Matt's face as he stood up.

"Pockets empty," Matt stated briefly.

The man with the black spade-cut beard stood there frowning. "Who shot him, Davison?"

"Don't know. The fellow ran. I followed but he got away."

"How'd you happen to be out here in the alley?"

"Wanted to see where he was going," Matt said shortly. "Had some questions to ask him, too. I was inside the door there when I heard the shots. One missed, I guess."

A man farther back called. "Here comes Marshal Tom Baird!"

Matt had heard of the marshal. Tom Baird was a coldly efficient gun marshal. He'd killed his share of bad ones and still wore the badge. Matt started to reload as the marshal pushed through to the circle of yellow lantern light.

Baird was a spare man with a drooping brown mustache. His guns were in armpit holsters. He got the story in a few words, knelt down, and satisfied himself that the body had been robbed.

While he was kneeling, Baird picked up the three empty cartridges Matt had dropped. He looked at the single bullet hole under Brooks's eye and was juggling the three brass shells in his palm as he stood up and looked Matt over.

"No open quarrel over the cards?" he asked.

The black-bearded man said, "They weren't friendly at the last. But no quarrel."

"You just took a notion to see where he was going?" Tom Baird asked Matt.

"That's right."

Baird continued juggling the three brass shells in his palm. "Mind being searched?"

"Go ahead."

Baird made the search quickly. He turned and looked deeper into the black alley.

"You came back to the body," he mused. "Nuthin' on you." Tom Baird shrugged. "Reckon it's all right. He was a fool to come out in a dark alley like this with his card winnings."

Matt was aware, as he walked slowly from the scene, that men in the crowd had their doubts about the marshal's judgment. Talk like that could spread.

It would have to spread. Matt had no intention of saying who might have killed Brooks. He had no proof against Hobbs or his companion. But bits of the puzzle were fitting together.

Davison walked thoughtfully back to the hotel, knowing he'd made a big mistake in buying the 808. He didn't want four hundred head of cattle and a remuda. He had no land, no intention of settling down. What he'd bought was trouble.

Brooks had wanted to get rid of the cattle. Brooks must have known death waited if he rode to the Chamorro to get his cattle. The look of danger had been on Brooks's face when Matt mentioned Hobbs. Then Brooks had tried to leave safely by the back door. Now Brooks was dead.

The night clerk at the Eagle desk was talkative when Matt got his key. "Your friend find you?" he asked.

"Which one?" Matt countered.

"Short man. Kind of bulgy eyes and narrow chin."

"What time was he asking for me?"

"Came in early in the evening. Wanted to know if you had a room here. Said he'd heard you was in town, Mister Davison. Then he wanted to know where he could find you."

"Did he ask for Davison?"

"Yes, sir."

"He been back?"

"Haven't seen him," the clerk said.

Matt tossed the key back on the desk. "Changed my mind about going up."

He made sure his coat was open freely in front and the Colt easy in the holster before he stepped out again. He walked to the feed barn where he'd left his horse.

The hostler, thin, unshaven, elderly, was tilted back in a wired wooden chair inside the open front of the building. He stood up yawning.

"I'm Davison," Matt said. "Left my black horse in stall eight. Anyone been looking at my horse earlier this evening and asking about me?"

"Just before dark, mister. Short feller with a pointy nose. He walked in, looked around the stalls, an' ast who owned that black'n in eight."

Matt picked the smoky lantern off a spike near the hostler's chair. He walked back into the pungent dimness of the stable. The big black nickered as Matt spoke to him and slapped him on the rump.

"Give him some more corn," Matt told the hostler. "I want a good feed in him."

Matt walked next to the Boston House. From the clerk there he got an envelope, sheet of paper, pen, and ink. The note he wrote was short.

Hobbs in town watching you. Brooks dead behind Longhorn Saloon.

He left it unsigned, addressed the sealed envelope to Brenda Scott, gave it to the clerk to hand to her in the morning. Then he walked back to his hotel.

An hour later Matt was riding out of El Paso. He had left another letter at the Eagle, to be sent to Lamar, the banker. He wore new range clothes, bought along with the broadcloth suit.

The suit and other things were in the new valise he'd also bought, now left behind in care of the hotel. He had enough gold eagles in his money belt for the time being.

El Paso's lights dropped back into the night. Mountains running north from the edge of town piled darkly toward the stars. A coyote yapped off in the distant cactus and yucca. The open night had a clean sweet smell which wiped out the stink of dirty alleys.

Matt had no feeling of running away. There was nothing to be gained by staying in El Paso, dodging a bullet in the back. His business lay north in the Chamorro River country, where he now owned cattle.

He wanted to settle that business quickly. It was Hobbs's country. It was Brenda Scott's range. Carlos Sedillo had come off that range too, and there was unfinished business with Carlos's father and mother. And with Hobbs.

Everything that had to be done was in the Chamorro country. And trouble, too, if Hobbs got back in time.

He made the Chamorro in two and a half days, traveling as the crows would have. He missed Palomas and passed far from Black Water Spring where the dead might still be waiting to be discovered.

A Spanish sheepherder gave him bearings over Big Hat Range, by an old Indian trail, little used now. He passed under the peak the sheepherder had called *Tio Santiago* — Uncle James. He shot a deer by a singing waterfall and cooked fresh venison instead of the hard dark jerky he'd bought at a native hut the first morning out.

He skirted dark cañons and pushed the big black horse fast across high mountain meadows, past the peak the sheepherder had named *Borrachito* — the Little Drunk Man. Then the mountains fell away in front of him, gashed with cañons and rocky hogback ridges.

The final sunrise broke up the valley shadows far below and glinted on water threading the lower range. He rode down toward cattle country that had been Apache country a few short years back — and the first man he met had yellow hair.

Matt heard the rifle shot, then came on the man dressing out a small buck at the edge of a grassy meadow. He was reining over to the spot before he noticed the yellow hair. It was too late then to turn back. This one was a burly young man, hardly twenty.

He had the same high cheekbones and features as Hobbs. Nothing fancy about the patched Levi's tucked in riding boots. He was edging to his black-and-white pinto horse and saddle gun as Matt rode up to him.

His snag-toothed grin was cautious.

His attention was on the black horse as he greeted, "Howdy."

"Any ranches ahead?" Matt Davison inquired.

"Few."

Matt let it go at that and built a cigarette before turning back to the trail. This yellow hair was too young to hold his curiosity. He sidled around, reading the horse brand.

"Chihuahua hoss," the yellow hair said slyly.

Matt lit the cigarette. "Know the brand?"

The snaggy grin spread. "It's old Gen'ral Salazar's brand."

"Been through those parts, I see."

"Oncet."

"Nice country," Matt said, and lifted his hand and reined back to the trail.

It was bad luck. That one would talk. In the middle of the afternoon Matt crossed the clear shallows of the Chamorro and presently saw his first JS cow. A little later he passed several 808 steers. He struck wagon ruts and followed them through some valley roughs and topped a low rise. The JS ranch house, corrals, and outbuildings were there below him. It was a small spread, but there was a kept-up look about what Matt could see. Curtains were at the ranch house windows. Flowers grew in front. A woman's touch.

He was riding down the slope toward the house when a rider came quartering fast over the rise and cut across the slope for a meeting. Matt pulled up and waited.

The first thing he noted was an arm in a black cloth sling. It made him think of Hobbs's arm. Then he marked the angular, loose-knit frame of the man in scarred hide chaps, blue shirt, old vest. Tawny hair, lined face, and pushing fifty, Matt judged.

"I'm looking for John Scott," Matt said as the man rode up.

"I'm Scott."

"Matt Davison." Matt was reaching into his coat. He opened the envelope holding the sale papers. "I bought the 808 brand. Four hundred head and a remuda, and increase on the four hundred tally. Delivery here on your ranch, I was told."

John Scott took the papers with his good hand. He made no move to scan them for the moment. He'd been calmly pleasant. Now all that went away. His gray eyes drilled at Matt intently.

"Who'd you buy from?"

"Colonel Brooks."

"Where?"

"El Paso."

"When?"

"Date's on there," Matt said. "Three days ago."

"You got here fast," John Scott said.

"Good horse," Matt said.

Scott looked at the black horse and nodded. "How long had Brooks been in El Paso?"

"At least a week. That's all I know."

"Brooks coming here?" Scott was frowning; he had the look of a man talking for time while he gathered his thoughts.

"He's dead," Matt said, and told what had happened. "Friend of yours?"

Scott nodded. He was thinking hard. "You want delivery now?"

"Soon as possible."

"Care to sell?" Scott asked. "Take my note?"

179

"I bought at a bargain. I'll sell for what they're worth," Matt said. "Cash, like I paid."

Scott shook his head. "Can't swing it. Where's your trail crew?"

"I'll have them."

"Let's ride down to the house," Scott said heavily. A thought struck him. "My daughter and foreman are in El Paso. Did Brooks speak of them?"

"Not a word," Matt said. "I'll move on. How do I get to Tres Gordos?"

Scott looked surprised, pushed his chin to the west. "About twelve miles. It's a little native settlement. Eight or nine houses."

Matt reached for the papers and left John Scott a frowning, troubled man. Scott looked years older in a few minutes. . . .

V

"RIDING IN CIRCLES"

Carlos Sedillo would not come riding again to his father's house in Tres Gordos. Matt knew the place as if he'd lived there. Around lonely camp fires, and under still stars, Carlos had talked often of home and his kin scattered though this back country.

A little stream came out of the hills and flattened out by cultivated patches. The few adobe houses straggled along both sides of the stream. When Matt dismounted and shook the hand of Ramos Sedillo, Carlos's father, the black horse's brand had already been noted and

Ramos, a chunky, muscular man with graying hair, said, "We have heard from Palomas. *Gracias, señor,* that Carlos was not left like a dog where he died. Our house is your house."

The talk was in Spanish. Carlos's mother, a graying woman, said little as she served strong black coffee in mugs and sweet cookies.

Men of the small native settlement had drifted in. They shook Matt's hand limply, as was their way. Women had come in the back and were crowding in the kitchen doorway as Matt told in Spanish of the fight at Black Water Spring.

"Curt Hobbs!" Ramos Sedillo said with soft savageness. "And those two dogs from old Mexico."

Later, alone with Ramos, Matt broached his business. He needed trail herd riders.

"Hobbs learned my name in El Paso. Not a doubt he knows I bought the 808 beef," Matt said. "Trouble coming fast now."

Ramos nodded. "They hunt together . . . brothers and cousins. Five families of them, *señor.*"

"How many in a fight?"

Ramos calculated. "Fourteen, with Curt Hobbs."

Matt whistled softly. "More than I thought." Matt shook his head. "Might skunk me, after all."

Ramos said, "The sheriff is one hundred forty miles away." Ramos's shrug was eloquent. "A fat man who does not often ride this way, that sheriff. There are not many votes on the Chamorro."

"Nothing's happened . . . yet," Matt said. He drew on his cigarette. "In the Drover's Bank, in El Paso, is three thousand dollars. About half of what Carlos and I brought out of old Mexico. And Carlos had this for his mother."

Ramos took a small gold cross and gold chain from the folded paper Matt handed him. Without shame Ramos wiped a sleeve across his eyes.

"You are a man of honor and a friend, *Señor* Davison."

Ramos carried the cross into the kitchen to his wife. That night Matt slept at Tres Gordos. The next day, at noon, he and Ramos rode to the Scott ranch.

Many of the Sedillo clan and friends worked as top hands. They were men of the mountains and mesas who knew their business. At breakfast Matt learned that yesterday John Scott had sent a man to Tres Gordos and on beyond to hire help for a fast roundup. Scott worked only two hands now, besides Tex and the young man with Brenda. Men from Tres Gordos had left before daybreak for the Scott ranch.

On a flat below the ranch house, brand fires were burning. John Scott was there on foot in the dust, watching a steer being branded. Matt joined them. Scott's JS brand had been vented and the steer was being branded 808.

"I'm not here for your cattle, mister," Matt told him.

John Scott's face looked more lined than it had yesterday. "Part of the 808 stuff has been rustled along with mine," he said curtly. "I'm making up your tally to the last calf."

"That your deal with Brooks?" Matt asked as they walked off to one side.

Scott eyed him. A hard and stubborn bitterness lay in the man's gray eyes.

"Once Brooks saved my life. When I went broke, he loaned me money to start up here. He'd been a gambler and had a notion to settle down, too. That's how he happened to have a brand. But he made the mistake of playing poker with a Hobbs. He won. Pete Hobbs tried to bluff the money back with a gun play. Jack Brooks beat him to the draw."

Matt nodded understanding. "And the rest of the Hobbs clan went gunning for Brooks and he moved across the border?"

"Jack knew, if he stayed here, my daughter and I would be in the trouble too. Told me to look out for his cattle. Didn't say where he was going. Probably didn't know when he left here. That was last year. He wasn't a man to write. First word we had of him, a man rode through and said he'd seen Brooks down Chihuahua way and Jack talked like he meant to go to El Paso." The grimness was still in Scott's tone. "Whatever Jack Brooks sold, I'll deliver."

"I'm not asking it."

"I'm doing it," Scott said curtly and walked back to the fires.

It was late that afternoon when Matt saw two riders on dead-beat horses coming down the long slope to the ranch house: Tex and Brenda Scott.

Brenda had switched to a man's saddle and changed from skirts to riding pants and jacket. John Scott saw them and put his horse into a run from the far side of the rope corral. All three entered the house.

In a few minutes, Tex came out, took both horses back to the corrals, switched his saddle to a fresh animal, and headed for the flat. He seemed part of the horse.

Matt rode to meet him. Tex was the same grizzled, stoop-shouldered old-timer. He looked tireless. His greeting was curt.

"Got your note. We come back. Curt Hobbs headed back too, with a friend. Small feller." Tex spat and shifted his tobacco to the other cheek. "I ain't wishin' you luck. But you'll need it. I'll git this mess straightened out."

Tex rode on.

A half hour later John Scott hauled himself in the saddle with his good hand and rode off. The man had been shot through the shoulder on a dark night by rustlers, Matt had learned.

Matt kept an eye toward the house. When he saw Brenda at the corral, roping out another horse, he pointed the black that way. Shadows lay under the girl's eyes and there was no mistaking her hostility as Matt dismounted and removed his hat.

"You got down wind but the skunk smell was still there," Brenda said coldly. "Before we left El Paso, Tex heard it said you might be the one who shot Brooks."

"Believed it, didn't you?" Matt asked.

Brenda shrugged. "The Matt Davison that Carlos Sedillo wrote home about wouldn't get that low. But you came close to it," Brenda said bitterly, "when you made a sneak ride to find Brooks and buy what you thought he didn't have. Four hundred head and increase, father says."

"So that's how you knew my name?" Matt said. "Carlos's letters!"

"His mother is a friend of mine. She helps me here at the house sometimes. Carlos also wrote you both had seen 808 steers off this ranch that had been sold across the border. Rustled, of course!" Her hostility dug at Matt again.

"None of my business at the time," he told her stiffly. "I was getting pay and bonuses from the haciendas down that way to find who was rustling their own stock. Had to play the busted *vaquero* so none of the natives would get curious. *Gringo* brands we ran across didn't mean much at the time."

"But you bought Brooks's cattle and knew that he couldn't deliver all of them," Brenda insisted angrily.

"Offered to sell them back five minutes later. He wouldn't buy."

Brenda said bitterly, "If you hadn't interfered . . . ! If I could have talked with him!"

"You'd have missed him," Matt said. "Curt Hobbs was in that same saloon. Had a small-built gunman with him. That's the man I think killed Brooks . . . and robbed him."

"Why didn't you warn him?"

"I thought Hobbs was trailing me. But when Brooks wouldn't buy back, I guessed he didn't want to get back here in Hobbs's territory. I told him Hobbs had been in the saloon. Brooks cashed out of the game and tried to leave by the alley. I think they outguessed him."

"Curt Hobbs heard he might be in El Paso and went after him, like I did," Brenda said. "I guess this finishes us."

"How?"

"We've been rustled too! After father delivers your herd, there won't be enough left to pull through with."

"Told him I didn't want any of his cattle. He sulked up and got stubborn about it."

Brenda flared, "He offered to buy from you on his note!"

They faced each other between the horses, Brenda fair and slender, Matt weathered leather-dark, taller, hard muscled.

"Brooks sawed off a hunk of trouble on me, and knew

it," Matt told her. "All I want is to move on and get my cash money back."

"Why did you buy?" Brenda was getting angrier. "I was trying to find Brooks. We could have settled things."

Matt stood watching her flushed anger. Pretty, he thought. Fair and pretty, in a way different from any girl he'd known. Stubborn, full of temper.

"Why?" he said, and was angry enough to tell the truth which he'd hardly admitted to himself. "Did it to get down wind on you! And bought myself the devil and trouble, like any fool who lets a pretty face get on his mind."

Brenda gulped, "Why . . . why. . . ."

"Tied my money up! Put myself where Hobbs has a strangle hold on me now. I didn't know how many there were of them."

"You'll know now, Davison."

"I'll know a lot of things when I'm through with this deal."

"Yes, you will," Brenda assured hotly. "I warned you in Palomas! And I saw Curt Hobbs before we left El Paso. He knows you're the one who shot him. Now he has you cornered. And we want no more trouble with them because of you. What you bought will be tallied off down there on the flat. The rest is up to you."

Brenda mounted the sorrel mare, slashed with the rein ends, left with a rush. Matt watched her line out in a long run in the direction John Scott had gone. Shaking his head, he walked the black horse slowly back to the branding fires. Once he grinned wryly as he thought of her.

The hurried roundup was Scott's business. Ramos had sent to a cousin's small ranch for an old chuck wagon.

Matt rode back to Tres Gordos that night with Ramos. A silver moon pushed up behind them.

"I see you talk with Miss Scott," Ramos said carefully.

Matt grunted.

Ramos mused, "That picture you and Carlos had made in Mexico, where you look like yourself. Miss Scott see it. She thinks you are very handsome young man. All time after that asking about you."

Matt snorted.

They rode in silence.

"Asking about me?" Matt finally said.

"Oh, *sí*," Ramos said, smiling faintly. "My wife, she dig the elbow in me. 'If *Señor* Davison come here,' my wife say, 'look out.' Now you come, you go. Where you go with these cattle?"

"Haven't decided. Anywhere I can sell 'em."

"Why you not stay? Nice cattle country."

"The Scotts want me to trail out fast, before they have trouble with the Hobbs bunch over me. Which I meant to do anyway."

"The yellow hairs will still be here. There will still be trouble for all of us, *señor*. It gets worse."

"I knew Hobbs was a rustler when he recognized General Salazar's brand at Black Water Spring," Matt said flatly. "They've about ruined Scott. They'll keep at it."

"*Sí*," Ramos agreed

Matt looked off into the silver-dusted night. "Nice country," he admitted. "If a man had land, he could build up a real ranch back in here."

"There is land, *señor*, if a man has cattle."

Matt rolled a cigarette, lighted it, and they rode in silence. After a time Matt asked, "Who heads this Hobbs bunch?"

"Curt Hobbs and his brother, Sam Hobbs," Ramos said. "And their cousins, Jim Hobbs and Lew. Kill them and you kill the head of the snake. Many of the rest are young. With the head they are dangerous. Without, they are all tail."

"Can't kill men until they start trouble."

"No," Ramos agreed.

The next day, back on the Scott ranch, Matt spoke of it again. With Ramos he was inspecting remuda horses corralled behind ropes for the 808 tally. Good horses.

"Have to wait until they start something," Matt muttered

Ramos looked at him silently.

"Fourteen, an' maybe that gunman from El Paso," Matt mused. He looked at Ramos. "How about the men I hired?"

Ramos shrugged. "You go, they go."

Matt reined away from the horses. "Step down over here and draw me some more map."

Down on a knee, with the nose of a .45 cartridge, Ramos drew his map on the hard hoof-marked dirt.

VI

"CLOSING THE CIRCLE"

"South . . . three ways," Ramos said. "Los Palos Cañon here. Or by Las Mesas to Rabbit Lake. Or by the Pole Springs Road. East . . . by the valley. West . . . you follow the Chamorro, and the road over Cap Rock to the Gila country. North . . . this way, by Crazy Woman

Mountain. Not too good road up Crazy Woman Creek."

Ramos punched dots south of the line that was the Chamorro. "Hobbses live these places. You pass near them at Crazy Creek."

"There's a cañon on Crazy Woman Creek, you said yesterday," Matt pointed, indicating the spot.

"Sí."

Matt studied the lines in the dirt. "Two weeks' grub in the chuck wagon and the driver has picked up the bedrolls?"

"Sí."

"The men got plenty cartridges?"

"Sí."

Matt looked at the halfway afternoon sun. "Moon tonight." He reached for the reins. "Let's count what Scott has got ready."

All day John Scott had shown little friendliness. Three times Brenda had passed near Matt and ignored him. Now Matt found father and daughter some two miles from the brand fires, watching a gather of about forty head pass toward the flat.

Scott was ordering some of the bunch cut back. Not the best ones either. He was a stubborn man, bent on delivering exactly what had been bought. Matt held back until it was finished. Then he joined them.

"Two hundred eighty-three head ready," Matt stated briefly. "It's good enough for me."

"Not for me," Scott retorted.

"I'm pulling out tonight," Matt told him. "Here's the sale papers."

Scott waved them back. "You'll get what you bought."

Matt tore up the papers and dropped the pieces. "Got all I need." He looked at them, dark-tanned, hard, in-

189

different now to emotion.

"Scott, you're an honest man. On my way out, I'll do what I can about your rustlin' worries."

"You?" Scott asked.

"Me."

They looked at him. Brenda asked, "How many men are you taking?"

"Six, the cook, myself. Call it seven."

"You won't have a chance," Brenda snapped.

Matt's thin grin had an edge. "You warned me at Palomas, didn't you? Ought to be a lesson for me, oughtn't it?"

"You'll be killed."

Matt sneered at them. "What of it? I won't be plucked like a crippled turkey, one feather at a time. I won't be ducking across the border to keep my skin safe. They want me. They know how to find me. Let 'em come get me."

Brenda said, her voice shaking with temper, "We're not border-jumping gunmen, not caring who is killed!"

"Enough, Brenda!" her father said angrily. "Davison, I can't stop you. I wash my hands of it."

"You never had your hands in it," Matt informed him. "Curt Hobbs started this with me at Black Water Spring. A range is no good to me that's run by a thieving bunch of bushwhackers who've been let run wild."

Brenda pointed at her father's arm in the black cloth sling. "Does that look . . . ?"

"Enough, Brenda!" John Scott roared.

"Why don't you talk that way to them yellow-haired Hobbses?" Matt sneered, and swung his horse back toward the flat. And when he was a short distance away, he grinned to himself. John Scott had been a defeated

190

man. Now anger was piled on Scott's proud stubbornness. When a man is angry, he isn't defeated.

It was a small trail herd when it lined out. A poormouth outfit with a rickety chuck wagon, a small remuda, and a native crew that had rifles and side arms, and might fight and might not. Probably not. They were helping a friend of the Sedillos'. But helping and dying were different matters.

Ramos Sedillo meant to go also. Matt was close to anger in his refusal.

"Carlos was enough," he said, and meant it.

Ramos's dark face was expressionless. "Because of Carlos, I must, *señor.*"

"I'll shoot your horse and put you afoot," Matt said with such hard warning that Ramos bowed his head in acceptance.

" *'Con Dios* . . . with God," Ramos said, shaking hands.

The sun was still half an hour above the blue rise of the peaks to the west when the point man led off after the remuda and chuck wagon. The branding fires had been kicked out, and John Scott watched from his saddle in moody silence. Scott had the look of a man uncertain and angrily dissatisfied with what was happening.

The ranch house was well back out of sight when Brenda and Tex rode up through the dust of the drag. Tex went on to the point. Brenda fell in with Matt. The sun was below sight, but a riot of red on the cloud bunches overhead strewed color in her tawny, windtossed hair. Her anger was controlled.

"This is foolish, Matt Davison. Tex agrees, you haven't a chance. He knows. Several of the men have sighted Hobbs riders today. They know what's happening, of course."

"Yesterday," Matt reminded, "it wasn't foolish. You told me to get going quick, and worry about it myself."

Brenda bit her lip. "We were quarreling. We always seem to quarrel when we start talking. But . . . this is today."

"I'm thinking about tomorrow," Matt said.

"They'll kill you. Do you have to be so hard headed?"

"Looks that way," Matt said mildly. "I never got anything by waiting for it or running away."

"Then tomorrow we'll bury you!" Brenda cried. She wrenched her horse around and galloped back toward the ranch house.

Matt brought his big black horse around to a halt and sat watching her until she disappeared over a rise. The drags were plodding by when he rode on, and Tex was dropping back to meet him, chomping leisurely on his tobacco.

"I slung my tarp roll in your wagon afore it started," Tex said. "You still aimin' to head up Crazy Woman Creek?"

Matt noticed that Tex had brought his saddle gun.

"This your idea?" Matt asked

"Uh-huh." Tex turned his head, spat, wiped the back of his wrist over his brown-stained mustache. "I been gettin' tired of them yaller-haired Hobbs," Tex said calmly. "They're dark-of-the-moon men. If they ride out tonight, there'll be a moon." Tex turned his head again and spat. "An' they will," he promised calmly. "They been gettin' by with so much in these parts, they won't let you bluff 'em."

Matt said gently, "Tex, I don't bluff."

Tex looked at the small strung-out herd and the native riders.

"If this ain't a bluff," Tex said sourly, "I never seen one. Them Hobbses will snap you, bite you, chew you up, spit you out, an' be worse than ever. You won't git past Crazy Woman Mountain."

"Turn back," Matt suggested lazily. "Still time, Tex."

"Hell, I know what time it is," Tex said gruffly. He slapped at his hard-used, greasy leather vest and pulled out tobacco sack and papers, and then stared at Matt. "But I can't figger you, mister. You made one hell of a buy from Brooks, all things added up. You know you're boxed in here on the Chamorro, same as if you was backed up in a pocket cañon. You can slip out alone easy. But you won't get these cattle out. You know it. I know it. Ever' man in these parts knows it, includin' Curt Hobbs an' all his yaller-haired kin."

Tex sounded aggrieved, insulted, hard-used by the inescapable facts. "But you go bullin' ahead," Tex said, and swept a match along his leg and pulled cigarette smoke fiercely to the roots of his lungs, shaking his head afterwards.

Matt grinned. "Tex, I can't figure you either. Bullheaded like me . . . and no reason for it."

Tex rode in sour silence for a moment. "I'm gittin' old," Tex admitted finally. "This Chamorro stretch is where I aimed to hunker down an' stay. Scott's a good man. But he's goin' busted from rustlin'. Them damn yaller hairs are gettin' bolder all the time. I been gittin' enough of them fast. When they travel clean to El Paso to coldgun a man, an' rob him too, I've had a bull's bellyful. I ain't a young fiddlefoot caught in a squeeze an' stubborn about it. I got a stake on this range."

Tex sucked smoke deep again. "I took a notion to fight for it," Tex said sourly. "You got any objections?"

"Help yourself, you cantankerous old fool," Matt said without emotion. "But get this through your head. I'm not dodging the Hobbs bunch now. If I tried chasing that lot of skunks through the timber an' brush, I'd only get stink an' bad luck. This way I'm baiting 'em out in the open."

Tex snorted. "One man talkin' big, and fifteen of them, countin' that gunman Curt Hobbs scrabbled up in El Paso. Fifteen!" Tex said explosively, and shook his head.

"Night coming," Matt reminded. "A good moon. I've got a chuck wagon, a remuda, and near three hundred head along with me."

"To worry about," Tex said.

"They'll wait until I'm far up Crazy Woman an' boxed in, because they haven't made a move so far," Matt estimated. "They'll have to wait for the moon so they can pick me out. Curt Hobbs will sweat blood to have me killed. The moon will catch us about in Crazy Woman Creek Cañon, which is about where I want them to jump me," Matt said.

"An' what'll you do when they jump?" Tex asked sarcastically.

"Jump too," Matt said, and chuckled for the first time. "How long a gut do you tuck under that holster belt?"

"Long enough, sonny," Tex drawled.

Matt grinned again. "Then here's what ought to happen before we're killed. . . ."

Tex listened. He grunted frequently. When Matt finished, Tex spat. "I've wondered how big a fool I was," Tex said wonderingly. "Now I know. Come sunrise we'll be hunkered in hell, talkin' it over. I think you're crazy!"

"Got a better idea?"

"One way of gettin' killed is as good as another," Tex said sourly.

Crazy Woman Creek came brawling out of a cañon that was more like a stubby arm of the valley, wide at the mouth, and narrowing in fast. Light still touched the high head of Crazy Woman as night came stalking along the creek bottoms. Matt at that time was trailing the drive with Tex. They had dropped well back and were riding with rifles across their laps, keeping a sharp watch.

"Not a skunk back there," Matt commented as the full night came clotting in blackly over the strung-out drive.

Tex still sounded sour. "I'd hate to bet how many has been watchin' from behind high ground. Laughin' at us."

"Try laughing too," Matt advised.

When the full night was down on them, Matt said, "Might as well get ready."

He jogged the black horse through the drag dust and conferred with the two riders who were hazing the cattle along. He rode, then, up the off-side of the strung-out herd and talked with the wing man, then went to the point man. This was Eliseo Sedillo, the best man, and Eliseo protested, "*Señor, this I do not understand.*"

"Do it!" Matt ordered, and dropped back to the other wing man, then rode on ahead to the wrangler and skimpy remuda, and then still farther on.

The rickety chuck wagon, by Matt's orders, led the drive. Four horses were in the rope-patched harness. A black-and-white pinto horse and a sorrel, without saddles, trailed the wagon on lead ropes, making an extra team if the wagon got into hard going.

The cook, old Francisco Abeyta, had driven off the Scott land and through the last of daylight, hunched over and silent, hardly moving, his old black hat pulled far over his wrinkled face. He was driving that way now when Matt rode alongside in the dark and ordered a halt.

"Seen or heard anything?" Matt inquired.

"No, *señor*."

Matt gave orders in a low tone. Francisco took his saddle from the wagon without argument and cinched it on the sorrel horse. Matt, at the same time, transferred his own saddle and bridle from the big black to the black-and-white pinto. Francisco rode the sorrel back into the night, leading the black by a neck rope. Matt dropped the reins over the pommel on the paint horse, took his rifle to the chuck wagon seat, and drove on.

The night wind was in his face. Boxed cartridges were under the wagon seat. Matt stuffed extra shells in his coat pocket.

The cañon was still wide. It would swing west soon, into a bottleneck. The creek would rush out of a knife cañon on the right, and the road would climb on to its high point and descend over wide mesas.

Matt hunched on the seat, driving as old Francisco Abeyta would drive. The slope contracting in on the left bristled with pines, and across the creek sheer rock lifted blackly. Moonlight flooded the narrowing way into which the wagon advanced, and Matt looked back. The remuda was coming, and the strung-out herd was close behind.

One of the chuck wagon horses nickered. A breathless moment later two shots echoed along the cañon, back by the cattle.

Matt stopped the wagon and set the brake. He heard the pound of running horses ahead. Bunched riders took form in the moonlight, rushing at him, and Matt laughed softly at the sight.

This was what he wanted. He had them in the open now, starting trouble. He stepped back under the old patched wagon sheet and knelt in the dubious protection between two bedrolls, with his rifle. The drumming rush reached the wagon, riders yelling loudly and firing in the air. The wagon horses plunged uneasily, and Matt caught the reins off the seat and steadied them.

He counted seven riders racing by on the left, close-bunched, firing their guns. One shot the wagon team's nigh leader. Others drove bullets through the wagon's board sides. Not trying for a target, just throwing lead.

The rush swept by toward the remuda. Seven of them, and one had an arm in a sling. The others would be scattered up the slope in the pines, where the first two signal shots had been fired. The wounded horse was kicking in the road, and the other three surged in the patched harness. Matt wasted seconds running ahead and finishing off the horse, before he ducked to the back of the wagon.

The black-and-white paint horse was still on the lead rope, nervous but unhurt. Matt jammed rifle in saddle scabbard, swung up, and followed Curt Hobbs and his kin. This promised to be good even if he didn't have a chance.

He was behind them now, where harmless old Francisco Abeyta should have been. What was going to happen would be bloody and violent, and probably the end of Matt Davison. But the Hobbs tribe wouldn't be the same after it was over.

The wrangler, point man, and the rest of the crew had orders to ride for home at the first gunshot. They hadn't understood why, and had protested. But with them out of the way every man ahead was a Hobbs. Every gun that flashed was a Hobbs gun. Couldn't make a mistake. But the Hobbs bunch would have a time keeping track of each other. Matt grinned again over it as he raked the pinto into a hard run.

One of the seven riders had been forking another black-and-white pinto. He'd be the young one who had been dressing out a deer when Matt came from El Paso. Matt had selected the pinto under him on the chance the Hobbs pinto would also be in the mêlée, adding to the confusion.

The Hobbs men continued to fire as they scattered out and turned the remuda back into the lined-out herd. The night was filled with dust and wild confusion as horses and cattle milled back from the yelling, shooting men.

Guns up in the pines were firing also. Muzzle bursts licked in the shadows up there like over-size and vicious fireflies. Matt rode hard into the dust and confusion and became part of it without being noticed. This was what he'd planned.

A broad-shouldered man with a close yellow beard wrenched his horse close, smoking gun in hand, and yelled, "Where's that damned Davison?"

Matt pointed. The man looked. The short savage arc of Matt's gun barrel caught him behind an ear. The soggy feel of steel on bone traveled into Matt's arm as he reined away.

Men were spurring back and forth in the thick dust, shouting, yelling. A few remuda horses were plunging up through the brush on the steep slope, and on up into the pines. A few of the steers, too. But the main body of the drive was milling back. The riderless horse of the big Hobbs man bolted over in front of Matt. Another man on the left saw it and wheeled over to Matt, gun in hand also.

"What happened?" he yelled, peering. "My God, you ain't . . . !"

It was quicker recognition than Matt hoped for. He shot faster than the Hobbs man, a tearing double burst, close up and square into the middle. The man arched, kicking his feet up in the stirrups, then folded over in the middle, grabbing the saddle horn. And the fast double shot drew another rider over through the dust.

Perhaps this one had sighted the riderless horse. He saw also the dying man's sidewise topple and wrenched in close to catch the man. He missed and hard bitted his horse toward Matt.

All these Hobbses seemed big men. The full untrimmed yellow mustache was visible in the moonlight as he shouted, "That you, Pete? What happened to Sam?"

Matt roweled in close and answered harshly, "I killed him! I'm Davison!"

This one was fast with a gun. He fired as Matt's bullet slammed into his chest. A slug seared Matt's side, twisting him as he fired again. But when he saw that one drop gun and reel, Matt pulled back, reloading swiftly.

Now there were four in the road, two well ahead at the heels of the remuda. The horse under him quivered to the soggy slap of a bullet. A gun up the slope had done that. A second bullet shrilled close as Matt dropped off the wavering pinto. He hit the ground, staggering for several steps — without his rifle.

The roan horse of the man he'd just shot swerved near him. Matt's diving run headed it. He grabbed pommel as the roan shied, made a running drag up into the saddle leather — and caught the tied reins out of the roan's mane.

"Four in the road now — and about seven up the slope among the trees."

The paint horse of the younger Hobbs was over near the creek bank, to the left. Up ahead was the big figure of Curt Hobbs, arm in a sling. Siding Curt Hobbs was the slight-built El Paso gunman. Still farther over to the right, up in the first brush, was the fourth man.

Lead whipped through Matt's hat crown. He drove the roan up the slope into the brush, riding higher on the slope than the fourth man, who was a little ahead of him. The snap and crash of breaking brush, and the low trampling thunder of the herd on the road filled the night as Matt put the roan back down the slope. He burst through crackling brush and quartered hard into the Hobbs horse and rider.

"Look out you crazy fool!" the man yelled.

The savage swipe of Matt's gun barrel caught him on the bridge of the nose. The man's horse, knocked away, bucked in sliding leaps toward the road, its rider barely hanging on.

Hobbs was looking back. He saw the barely conscious rider appear in the road. Hobbs's voice lifted. "Somethin's wrong! Where's the others?"

The injured man lost a stirrup, then his saddle seat, and fell heavily close to Curt Hobbs's back-wheeling horse.

"Outa the road, everyone!" Hobbs bawled. "Who's up there in the brush?"

A rifle somewhere among the trees drove a bullet through Matt's right arm. He managed to snatch his gun with the left hand, then raked the roan, quartering up the slope again to shelter among the trees. The rifle reached for him again. And then again.

The hidden man was yelling as he shot, "Curt! It's Davison!"

"Get him!" Curt Hobbs roared.

Matt made a running drop off the horse, and the animal blundered on up through the trees. Here the moon's light was cut off. Shadows bunched thickly again. Matt stood still as the man behind the rifle shouted, "He's hidin' up the mountain. Better watch your step!"

The rifle reached again after the roan horse. Matt stood motionless, gritting against pain in his arm. He couldn't use the arm, but what the hell was the use of kicking. Curt Hobbs had ridden away from Black Water Spring with an arm as bad. The rifle fired after the roan horse again, blind-shooting at the diminishing sound. Matt eased across the spongy pine duff, gun cocked in his left hand.

Curt Hobbs and three companions were riding noisily up through the brush as Matt made out the crouching shadow he was stalking. He thought he saw the man look toward him. He shot twice and ran in for the third shot and found his target twisting on the ground, moaning. Matt's foot stubbed against the rifle.

He hooked the boot toe under the barrel and kicked the weapon away. Then he made out a hand groping toward side holster. Matt stamped down hard on the arm and chopped the gun barrel roughly to the man's head.

But Curt Hobbs and the gunman from El Paso were bursting up through the brush, Hobbs calling, "That you, Jack? Where is he?"

Matt waited, gun cocked. The riders pulled up, not

fifty yards away, all three of them. Beyond them in the thick shadows old Tex's cold drawl invited, "Right here, you yaller-haired thieves!"

Hobbs yelled, "Get him, Slinger!"

Tex must have opened up with a gun in either hand, so fast his shots pounded. Matt went flat by the unconscious man, wincing at the wrench his shoulder took. Lead slapped the tree beside them. He heard a horse flounder down. The rider stumbled on foot toward Matt, and Matt came up in a running crouch to meet the ducking shadow.

The gunfire broke off as suddenly as Tex had started it. One rider, one only, was taking his horse in frantic haste up the slope.

It was Curt Hobbs who called close to Matt, "Slinger? Get him?"

Curt Hobbs stiffened and held it as Matt's gun barrel punched against his spine.

"Let's wait and see," Matt said softly. "Drop it an' kneel down!"

Voices were calling urgently along the slope. "Curt! Curt! Where are you, Curt?"

Tex's sour undertone reached through the dark. "In hell, I hope. Here's one of the snakes won't rustle no more."

Matt said, "Hold it, Tex! Hobbs wants to talk!"

Tex was silent a moment. His disgusted, "You'll git shot talkin' out like that," reached him.

Hobbs's remark was a mushy groan. "You ain't shootin' a man in the back, are you?"

Tex materialized out of the blackness and heard that.

"Shoot him front or back, but shoot the dirty thief," Tex said, and he was beside them a moment later.

The shouting for Curt Hobbs died into an uneasy silence.

Matt said in a low voice, "Here's your chance, Hobbs. Tell 'em to drop guns, walk in, and save your hide for you."

Curt Hobbs obeyed, thick desperation in the shout he sent through the timber.

"Davison's got a gun in my back! Walk over here, boys, without your guns, an' give up! Don't try tricks!"

The answer when it came was mounted men bursting down through the brush into the road, and quirting, spurring after the stampede. They went by in a strung-out line, six or seven of them, bending low as they rode for safety.

Still kneeling, Hobbs said in thick desperation, "I knowed they wouldn't come in. But I told 'em."

Tex said dryly, "They'll learn."

Matt said, "Hobbs, you killed Jack Brooks, didn't you?"

"Not me. It was Slinger did it."

"If you mean that rabbity-size hard case you brought from El Paso, he's cold turkey over there," Tex said. "You gonna shoot this one?"

"Where's Brooks's money?" Matt demanded.

Curt Hobbs had a sort of mushy despair. "It's in Slinger's money belt, I reckon. He kep' it all."

"See if it is, Tex."

Tex vanished. He was back in a few moments. "Plenty gold in it," he said.

"Give it to Scott," Matt said. "He's got more right to it than anyone." Matt tilted his head intently as the distant roll of gunfire echoed up the cañon. "What's that? The rest of our men? Somebody's raisin' a lot of hell!"

Tex chortled under his breath. "An' some others," he

said, his voice taking a rich drawling satisfaction. "John Scott an' his men, an' most of the natives up the valley, under Ramos Sedillo, tagged away back of us, in case these damn Hobbses started trouble. Reckon they waited for the stampede to clear, an' them Hobbses rode right into them." All Tex's sourness was dispelled. "I reckon this crops them yaller hairs to the head bone. Who's gonna shoot this one? A damn' sidewinder like him ain't got no right to live!"

"Take him down to the road for John Scott," Matt ordered. "I need some bandaging in the moonlight somewhere down there."

Matt had coat and shirt off in the road. Curt Hobbs was kneeling again, back toward them, and Tex, an eye on him, was helping with the wounded arm when the mass of yelling horsemen came sweeping up. Quickly the road was clogged with horses, and men were moving over the scene of the fight.

John Scott, his lined face hard now in the moonlight, said, "They rode right into us. I'm sorry we laid back too far, Davison. We'll get your drive rounded up tomorrow and you can move on, if that arm will let you. But it looks bad to me."

"Not moving on," Matt said. "Didn't mean to when I started. This was to bait the Hobbs bunch out and settle 'em before they got me in the back, like they did Brooks. Had to do it so I could stay in peace."

"I guess I don't understand," John Scott said uncertainly. "I guess there's a lot of things I don't savvy. I'm just startin' to get clear on things."

"I'm like Tex," Matt told him calmly. "Got a stake on the Chamorro now, and it looked like time to fight for it. Turn my cattle back. I'll work out the details when

I get my arm fixed."

Ramos Sedillo, there also in the moonlight, was the only one who understood. He spoke with warm satisfaction and some sly humor, which made sense only to Matt.

"My wife, she is one smart woman," Ramos said. "She dig the elbow an' say, 'If *Señor* Davison come to the Chamorro, look out.' You come, you look, you stay. *Bueno*. The women, they understand better than a lot of men."

All Matt could think of was the same word. That was the way he felt, thinking of Brenda Scott, back there on the Chamorro. *"Bueno,"* Matt agreed, his smile broadening.

In his Western stories T.T. Flynn never had series characters the way he did in his race track stories or his crime fiction. There is only one exception to this. Following publication of "The Rawhide Kid," readers of *Dime Western* wrote to the editor asking that the author please continue the saga of Holy Joe Moran and Laramie Scott. On August 18, 1935 Flynn completed "Bandit of the Brindlebar" which was bought for *Star Western* where it appeared in the January, 1936 issue under the title "Last Of The Wild Shotwells." He turned next to the sequel editor Rogers Terrill had requested and wanted titled "The Return of the Rawhide Kid." Of course, calling the first story "The Rawhide Kid" had been Terrill's idea. The appellation is not to be found anywhere in the story itself. Flynn complied, but he altered the proposed title slightly, and Terrill ran it under Flynn's title in the April, 1936 issue of *Dime Western*. Rawhide was often called Mexican iron by the *vaqueros* because, among other things, it wore like that metal. In retrospect, the Kid was well named.

THE RAWHIDE KID RETURNS

I

"NORTH OF THE BORDER"

Laramie Scott sighted carefully along the barrel of his rifle until the front sight was squarely on the silver *concho* breast button of the first rider. The bright midday sun of old Mexico glinted on the polished surface of that metal button. A bullet smashing into the chest there would knock the big, gaudily-dressed man out of the saddle, killing him instantly. Then the other five men — those five scantily-dressed peons, barefoot and shabbily outfitted except for their rifles and bandoleers of cartridges — would probably turn back when their leader fell.

Lying there, behind two big boulders on the ledge up the cañon's side, Laramie was an unbelievable figure to be in this wasteland south of the border. Small, thin, shabby, his patched and ragged Levi's at least three sizes too big for him, he looked like a wizened scarecrow. He was not more than sixteen. Only a Yankee kid, from north of the border.

Laramie's finger began to squeeze the trigger. He moved the rifle barrel gradually to keep up with the slow advance of the target. Then Laramie slowly took his finger off the trigger. His thin, freckled face screwed up in a frown.

The six armed men riding down there in the cañon were puzzling out the trail of a single horse. Half a mile up the cañon those tracks struck a narrow, steep trail and came out on bare rocks at the top, and vanished. At least for all practical purposes they vanished. A Yankee from north of the border could not follow them. A cross-breed peon, with veins running full of Indian blood, eyes uncannily sharp, trail sense acute, might be able to puzzle out where the tracks of that shod horse had passed two days before. A scratch here, a chip there — it could be done, perhaps.

Slowly, carefully, Laramie drew his rifle down out of sight and lay quietly, motionlessly while the clatter of hoofs on stones and the occasional murmur of voices passed on up the cañon. When the six were out of sight around the next turn, Laramie wriggled to his feet, clapped his big flop-brimmed hat on his head, and tilted it jauntily over toward one eye. He was perspiring and panting when he reached the top of the cleft.

Whipping his hat off again, he took half a dozen steps to the shelter of a great rock which balanced on two smaller rocks. Peering around the rock he watched the six men ride up out of the cañon, half a mile away. They stopped and looked around. There the weather of ten thousand years had scoured and worked the barren rock into fantastic slopes and ledges, into gloomy *barrancas* with sides deep and sheer.

Laramie grinned faintly as he saw the futile efforts of those six men to find the trail. The waving arms of their gaudily-dressed *caballero* leader scattered them out.

They searched on foot like eagerly questing hound dogs. For an hour their search widened; finally they drew together again and talked. Then they rode slowly back down into the cañon. Laramie walked to the cañon edge, wriggled close on his belly, and looked down at them as they passed out of sight the way they had come.

Half an hour's brisk pace brought Laramie to the edge of another cañon, deeper, wider than the one he had left. No trail led down into this cañon. A ten minute search along the edge brought Laramie to a spot where a rider might get down, by angling his mount along the side and picking a careful way. Descending, Laramie followed the cañon down until it widened suddenly into a great bowl-shaped space between the rocky walls.

Here, for a hundred yards on each side of the rocky bed, dirt, carried down from the higher lands to the east, had lodged. Grass had taken root. A saddle, a pack saddle, a small pile of gear lay in the grass. Further down the cañon two horses lay dead, where they had been struck by a small rock slide.

Laramie turned to the saddle, the pack saddle, the small pile of gear on the grass. He carried them, an article at a time, to the nearest rocks. He could barely lift the two heavy leather sacks which had been lashed to the pack saddle. Opening the rawhide thongs which closed the tops, he dumped half the contents of each sack on the ground.

Since the first human foot had trod the ageless rock of this deep *barranca*, no man's eye had ever beheld a more astounding sight than the bright yellow streams of gold Laramie poured out of those ancient leather sacks. Gold coins of Mexico, they were stamped: "Maximilian — 1866."

Laramie lugged the two half-empty sacks to the rocks, cleared a space, dug into the soil as deeply as he could with his hands, and dumped there the remainder of the gold in the sacks. Going back, he scooped the first pile of coins into the now empty sacks and carried them over with the others. When Laramie finished, no eye could have told that human hands had shifted the rocks to cover the articles beneath. He surveyed the spot critically, picked up his rifle, smoothed over his foot marks as best he could, and started back up the cañon.

Laramie plodded after the trail which the six men had taken. When night came, he munched some jerked meat he took from a pocket, laid down, and slept. Toward morning the bitter cold brought him up shivering.

Sunrise found him emerging from the cañon into a low, bleak valley. Late in the afternoon he came to low hills, trees, stretches of grassland. And before nightfall he struck a trail, and followed it, and came to a small hut, built of upright poles chinked with dried mud.

A man stepped out as Laramie came up. Short, stocky, part Indian, he spoke with the grave courtesy of his kind.

"You are lost, *señor?*"

Laramie answered in Spanish not too fluent. "I look for the village of Tres Angeles."

"It is the ride of half a day, *señor*. At night it is not good for a stranger to walk. The way is crooked and hard. But this house is your house, *señor*. Enter and eat with us. It is little . . . but you are welcome."

When you were starved, giddy from hunger, it was hard to eat slowly. Laramie forced himself to do so, and stopped eating before he had enough. There was not much food, and the man, his wife, and five black-eyed little ones also had to eat.

"You have a horse to sell perhaps?" Laramie asked casually in Spanish at the finish of the meal.

Regretfully the man shook his head. "No, *señor*. But four days ago another man, a *viejo* . . . an old man . . . tall as a mountain tree, with his beard long and white, rode by on a horse that limped, and offered gold for horses. We have no horses, only goats. But in Tres Angeles you will find. . . ." The man waved a hand, implying that in Tres Angeles one could find anything.

"Did the *viejo* go to Tres Angeles?"

The man shrugged. "*¿Quien sabe?*" He hesitated, cast a surreptitious look at his wife. Something was on his mind. "He did not return past here, at least."

"You have not heard of him?"

Again that uneasy look between husband and wife. The man stared at Laramie. "The *viejo* was a friend?"

"He is from my country . . . *uno paisano* . . . a countryman . . . I would see him."

The man nodded understandingly. He picked up a fragment of tortilla. "I think it is not good for him in Tres Angeles, *señor*," he said slowly.

"Manuel," the woman warned sharply.

He ignored her. "But yesterday," he said to Laramie, "*Señor* Don Antonio Ibarra rode this way from Tres Angeles, asking for news of this *viejo's* passing."

Laramie's face remained blank. "You told him?"

"*Si,*" the man assented, spreading his hands palms up. "It is not good, *señor*, for a poor man to bite his tongue when Don Antonio Ibarra, a *rico grande* and the *jefe* of Tres Angeles as well, asks questions."

"What did this Don Antonio Ibarra want with the *viejo?*" Laramie asked.

213

A shrug, another, then *"¿Quien sabe?"* was the answer to that.

Laramie stood up. He was tired, wanted to sleep. He was welcome here, he knew, but it occurred to him that this man, who could not expect favors from Laramie Scott, might value the good will of Don Antonio Ibarra.

"Please have the goodness to show me the way to Tres Angeles," Laramie requested politely.

He left a silver coin for his food. A few minutes later, he was following a rough trail.

The night was dark, moonless. An hour Laramie walked, then turned off the road, found a level spot, lay down, and slept again. Only this time, with a full stomach, he felt better. When the false dawn gave light to the trail, Laramie walked on.

Twice more Laramie sighted adobe huts near the trail, tried to buy horses, and had no success. But he asked no more about the *viejo* — the old man, tall as a mountain tree, with a white beard long and wild.

The old man was Holy Joe Moran who had left Laramie behind in that forbidding landscape of rocks and deep *barrancas*. When the rock slide had killed two of their horses, lamed the third and last, Holy Joe Moran had said: "I'll ride over towards Tres Angeles an' try to pick up some hosses. Stick here with the gold, kid. You got food. You'll be all right. If I don't show up in three or four days, you better mosey on north to the border."

Laramie had waited, casually, then anxiously. Holy Joe Moran knew this northern Mexico as only a man could who had wandered the length and breadth of it for over forty years. But Holy Joe had been wounded when men had died over those old leather sacks of Maximilian's gold.

Holy Joe had not returned. A *caballero* called Don Antonio Ibarra from Tres Angeles had come back along Holy Joe's trail with armed men.

News of Holy Joe, then, must be in Tres Angeles. So Laramie trudged on toward Tres Angeles, lugging the heavy rifle. It didn't occur to him that he would be safer by following Holy Joe's advice and heading north toward the border.

Around noon Laramie stopped at a small stream, ate the last scrap of jerked meat in his pocket, and rested. He was smoking a cigarette when four uniformed riders galloped up the valley. Guns were slung on their backs.

The riders were almost abreast before one of them sighted Laramie. He called, pointed; the four reined up.

"Buenas dias," Laramie greeted them politely. The man who had pointed was a young officer. His colonel's uniform was new, smart; he rode a fine black gelding; his silver-trimmed saddle and handsome leather boots were elaborate, expensive.

The officer ignored Laramie's polite greeting. "By the holy Virgin, what is it?" he sneered in Spanish, looking down disdainfully.

Laramie flipped his cigarette end away and started to roll another.

"This is the trail to Tres Angeles, *mi Coronel?"* he asked politely.

The officer ignored the question. "What rascal are you?" he demanded sharply.

Laramie's thin face remained expressionless as he lighted the cigarette. *"Señor* Laramie Scott," he replied calmly. "And you, my colonel?"

The colonel laughed. "This boy calls himself a man!"

"*Señor*, I *am* a man."

Before Laramie could dodge, he was answered by a slash from the colonel's quirt. The hard leather lash stung like the brand of a sizzling iron. Laramie staggered back, clapping a hand to his cheek.

A stain of blood came away on Laramie's fingers. The men sat there on their horses, laughing. The colonel was smiling around at his men.

Laramie drew out a dirty handkerchief and wiped his cheek in silence. His eyes stayed on the officer's face. He would know this man if they met again.

"Where are you going, *cabron*?" the officer demanded.

Laramie's jaw muscles tightened. A brother officer would have killed the man for using that term. But an attempt at it now would only mean suicide, and somewhere Holy Joe Moran needed help.

"To Tres Angeles," Laramie answered woodenly. "Perhaps there is work there."

The nearest soldier said something in a low tone. The officer stopped smiling, looked at Laramie sharply.

"Tell me," he asked curtly, "have you crossed the trail of an old man with a white beard?"

"What does this *viejo* look like?" Laramie asked.

The officer swore at him. "An old man, a *Yanqui viejo!* He rode a horse that limped."

"I have no horse, *mi Coronel*. A *Yanqui viejo* would have helped me get one."

The officer reined his black horse around, swearing under his breath. Water splashed as he galloped across the small stream. His men followed, and they took the trail toward Tres Angeles.

Laramie's thin, freckled face was stony as he watched them go. Slowly he wiped the bleeding mark on his cheek again, then picked up the rifle, and trudged on toward Tres Angeles.

II

"TO SAVE A PARTNER"

The afternoon was waning when Laramie came to a wide, lush valley and looked down the slope at Tres Angeles below. There was a mine, just north of town, ringed by the scattered adobe houses of the miners. Dirt roads angled out across the valley. In the center of town a church raised two tall spires crowned with crosses. The town itself was a sprawling clutter of adobe houses with a plaza in the center, before the church.

Dogs yapped; children called shrilly; people stared curiously as Laramie walked toward the plaza. He had hidden his rifle outside of town. In the plaza were big ore wagons, sleepy burros, several two-wheeled carts drawn by oxen, and saddle horses. In a *cantina* a man was playing a guitar and singing.

Laramie saw a small place to eat, went in, and ate chili beans, meat and tortillas. Feeling better, he grinned at the dark-eyed young girl who had waited on him, paid her, and walked out onto the plaza again.

For an hour Laramie moved about Tres Angeles. Several times he asked men if there was work to be had and received no encouragement. At the mines, perhaps, when times were better, but the work was hard. The man who said that looked askance at Laramie's thin, bony build.

The massive-walled barracks interested Laramie. A force of soldiers was stationed here, headed by a Colonel Juan Ramiriz. From a distance Laramie saw the dapper, handsome colonel emerge from the fort-like barracks, cross a corner of the plaza, big-roweled spurs jingling, and enter the nearest *cantina*.

Don Antonio Ibarra, Laramie found, was the *jefe*, the owner of the mine, many houses, a *cantina*, and several stores. Ibarra lived in a style almost feudal in a big adobe palace-like structure on high ground beyond the plaza. A wall surmounted with fragments of sharp glass surrounded the place. An armed guard stood at the gate.

Twilight was falling when Laramie walked past the end of the barracks building for the third time. The windows in this end were fitted with iron bars. It was the *carcel*, the jail for civil and military prisoners alike. Armed sentries were on duty on the flat roof.

Laramie had passed the fifth barred window from the end when a hoarse — "By the old jumpin' Judas tree! What you doin' here, kid?" — stopped him in his tracks.

Behind the bars of that fifth window were visible the vast white beard, the fiercely hooked nose, the glinting eyes under bushy brows which could belong to no one else but Holy Joe Moran.

Laramie backed over against the wall and began to roll a cigarette with shaking fingers. "What happened to you, Holy Joe?" he asked huskily.

"Huh!" Holy Joe snorted. "What didn't happen? I come into Tres Angeles here lookin' fer hosses, kid, an' played the gosh awful damn' fool! Had me a drink of tequila to wash the dust outa my throat, an' had a couple more fer luck, an' wound up with a couple bottles an' a fight. I had to lick half a dozen Mexes . . . an' by that time half the town was hot to get me. They called out the soldiers. I tried to lick the army too, but couldn't quite make it. A little *soldado* got me behind the ear with a rifle butt . . . an' here I was."

"Ought to be able to fix that. How much'll your fine be?"

Holy Joe looked almost embarrassed. "Never you mind about the fine, kid. Best thing for you to do is hit the trail north for the border, *pronto*. Don't worry about me."

Laramie was standing with his back to the wall, apparently paying no attention to the barred window. "I ain't leavin' till you git out an' come along."

Holy Joe Moran held his voice low, but it was fierce. "I'm tellin' you to git out! The *jefe* here is a bad *hombre*. You'll be in trouble before you know it!"

"Him? I seen Don Antonio Ibarra followin' your back trail up the cañon with five armed men lookin' for the gold. They lost your sign up at the top on rocks an' came back."

Holy Joe swore. "I figured somethin' like that was goin' on. You git out now! I'll come along as soon as I get outa this an' meet you in Tucson. We'll git ourselves all fixed up an' sneak back an' get that gold, if it's still there."

"It'll be there. I hid it."

"What's that slash mark acrost your face?"

"Colonel Ramiriz cut me with his quirt. I met him an' three of his men out a ways. They was lookin' for your back trail too."

Holy Joe was silent for a moment. "So Ramiriz is greedy for gold too?" he muttered. "I might 'a' knowed it. It's wuss'n I thought, kid. Get the hell away from this window an' make tracks outa town! With Ramiriz an' Ibarra after that gold, you won't have a chance if they find you know anything about it."

"I ain't talkin'."

"They got ways of makin' you talk. They'd take your skin off in patches if they thought they'd find gold underneath. Start travelin', kid."

A sharp voice spoke overhead. One of the guards up there on the roof had looked over and seen Laramie standing below.

"*¡Vamos!*" the guard called roughly in Spanish. "What do you do down there?"

Laramie spoke under his breath to Holy Joe as he walked off. "I'm stickin'."

From behind the bars Holy Joe's hoarse whisper followed him: "Damn you, kid! See Panchita at the Holy Ghost!"

Darkness was falling fast. The air was fragrant with the smell of cedar smoke from cooking fires. A small knot of soldiers stood in front of the barracks arguing loudly. Laramie paused to let a string of half a dozen patient burros file past with their towering loads of cut wood.

He hardly saw the burros. Something was wrong, far more wrong than having Holy Joe behind bars. Laramie couldn't decide what it was, but Holy Joe had been too anxious to get him out of town.

Why see Panchita? Who was *she?* What was the Holy Ghost?

Laramie stopped a man in the plaza, spoke in Spanish. "Where's the Holy Ghost?"

The man pointed to the south side of the plaza, where

the windows and doorway of a *cantina* already were glowing with light. That part of the riddle was simple enough at any rate. The *Cantina* of the Holy Ghost had seven or eight customers drinking at the bar when Laramie entered and looked about curiously.

The place was larger than it looked from outside. The room in front ran off to the right and left in the back in a T-shaped extension. The center and left wing of the T was a dance floor. Curtained booths were placed around the walls of the left wing. In the right wing were gambling tables, deserted at this early hour of the evening.

The bartender looked at the ragged stranger, frowned, and spoke impatiently. "What is it?"

"Beer."

The bartender drew a foaming glass and slid it along the bar. Laramie slid a silver peso back. He had only three more silver pesos and several smaller coins.

A money belt next to his skin — a belt which he had taken off a dead man after the fight for Maximilian's gold — was fat with gold. But that wealth was no help now. Worse, it was dangerous. Gold coins stamped with the name of Maximilian were a passport to death in Tres Angeles.

As a customer, paying with good silver, Laramie ceased to be regarded with suspicion. But curiosity remained. The bartender wiped the top of the bar with a damp towel and asked abruptly: "Where do you come from, *señor?*" The bartender was short, thick-set, and fat under his dirty white shirt rolled up at the sleeves.

The other men were staring as Laramie wiped foam off his lips with the back of his hand.

"I'm a wild horse breaker," Laramie said. "Have you

any horses to ride?"

That made them laugh. The bartender slapped his wet towel on the bar and wheezed, "¡Dios! A breaker of wild horses, eh? I think maybe you're a wild horse yourself." He chuckled as he looked at Laramie's freckled face under the huge, old hat.

Laramie grinned. "Who knows? I ain't so tame."

The customers began to drift out. It was time to eat again. Laramie returned to the place where he had eaten once already and ordered food again.

All the tables in the low, dim-lit room were filled. Two girls were serving food. The same girl who had waited on Laramie earlier tossed him a flashing smile of remembrance. She was young and pretty, in a dark-skinned, sultry way.

Laramie lingered over his food. As some of the tables began to empty, he found a chance to talk to the girl. "The Holy Ghost is the best *cantina?*" he asked her.

She agreed that it was.

"Who is Panchita?"

The saucy little waitress tossed her head. "That Panchita!" she said scornfully. "Bah!" She threw a forefinger across her throat to show what should be done to Panchita. "All the men are monkeys when she smiles."

"Must be some woman," Laramie grinned.

Fingers snapped contemptuously. "If it were not for Don Antonio and Colonel Ramiriz, Panchita would be a common woman."

"Colonel Ramiriz's girl, huh?"

"Don Antonio would not like to hear that. She works for Don Antonio, who owns the *Cantina* of the Holy Ghost."

Laramie cleaned up the gravy in his plate with a piece

of tortilla. "Don Antonio an' Colonel Ramiriz are rivals?"

The little waitress lowered her eyes and spoke with sudden caution. "Who am I to know what Don Antonio and Colonel Ramiriz are? They are the *gente fina* . . . the fine people. I am only a poor one. Their business is not my business." The little waitress flounced off.

Laramie paid for his meal, wandered outside. He wondered if he'd understood Holy Joe right. What good would it do him to see a girl whose suitors were Ibarra and Ramiriz? It looked like quick trouble.

Full dark had come now. Laramie drifted by the end of the barracks building, stopping under the fifth window, felt around on the ground for pebbles, and tossed them through the bars. Nothing happened. He did it again. Holy Joe's hoarse whisper did not answer.

Slowly Laramie moved off into the night. Holy Joe wasn't in that cell. A long life with danger ever at his elbow had made Holy Joe Moran as wary as a wild creature. The sound of those pebbles striking the floor would have brought him out of a sound sleep.

Laramie loitered about the dim-lit plaza, and then he walked toward the *Cantina* of the Holy Ghost. Inside all was different now. The bar was crowded. He ordered a beer. The booths in the back were beginning to fill. Gambling had started at the tables. A man was playing the piano, and in a few minutes four more men with guitars joined him and started to play. Couples began to dance.

Presently the music stopped. The dancers drifted off the floor, smiling, talking, looking toward the back as if expecting something. Laramie saw a door back there open. A girl stepped in. The people began to clap and call: "Panchita! Panchita!"

Laramie stood rooted to the floor at the end of the bar. Perhaps it was the two steins of beer he had drunk; perhaps it was the fact that he was worried over Holy Joe — and Holy Joe had told him to see this girl. Whatever it was, Laramie was struck dumb with admiration.

Panchita was small, slender, young. She couldn't be over eighteen, probably was younger. Her hair was piled high on her head and held a huge Spanish comb set with brilliants that threw back the light in little glancing glints as she bowed to the applause.

She wore a long, fringed white silk shawl. As the orchestra struck an opening chord, Panchita flirted the shawl from her shoulders and walked forward slowly. The orchestra started to play and Panchita began to dance.

Every eye was on her. But Laramie didn't know that. He stood alone with his thoughts, watching the slender grace of that black-haired little beauty. Laramie had seen dancers, many of them, and girls galore. But none had ever held him spellbound as this Panchita did. As he watched, Laramie had a queer feeling about her. Panchita didn't look Mexican despite her dark hair and Mexican costume. Her skin was blonde, her features too Anglo-Saxon; once, when she whirled near him in the dance, Laramie could have sworn her eyes were blue.

Another thing. Panchita seemed to be smiling, gay, happy — but, after watching her face for a few minutes, Laramie could have sworn she was not happy at all. Behind her laughing face he could see or sense a taut strain, very close to tears. Then he remembered her. Once before he had seen her, in Agua Fría, the same night he had first met Holy Joe Moran.

When the music stopped, Panchita bowed, laughing,

and ran off the floor to the orchestra. Amidst wild applause and shouts, Laramie came out of the spell and realized he was acting like a fool.

What did that girl have to be sad about? She was a favorite here. There she was at the piano holding a small impromptu court. One *caballero* in tight-fitting trousers, a silver-buttoned jacket, and sleek black hair brought her a glass of wine and presented it with an elaborate bow. Panchita took the glass, thanked the man with a laugh, touched her lips to the edge and returned the glass.

The *caballero* bowed, laughed, and ostentatiously turned the glass rim and drank from the spot Panchita's lips had touched. When he had drained the wine, he smashed the glass on the floor against the wall and said something. Panchita hesitated, then stepped forward into his arms and danced away with him.

"So that's how it is," Laramie muttered to himself. "You git a dance if you act pretty. Reckon that's how I'll have to see you, lady."

III

"HONKATONK GIRL"

Laramie hung his old hat on a wall peg and edged forward. When the music ended, Panchita left the young dandy, laughing, shaking her head as he begged for the next one. She was returning to the piano. The music was starting up again. Laramie pushed past several couples and reached her side while she was yet alone.

"I'd shore like to have the next dance, lady."

Panchita cast a startled look at his thin, freckled face, his ragged old clothes. Laramie knew he wasn't much to look at, but he hadn't counted on the emotion that flashed over her face as she looked at him.

"You recognize me, don't you?" she asked hurriedly in English — perfect English. "Don't look so flabbergasted. We met at Dandy Gonzalez's *cantina* in Agua Fría."

"I know," Laramie gulped. "Holy Joe Moran told me to see you. That's why I'm here."

"Quick!" she urged under her breath. "We'll dance. Come!"

She was breathing rapidly. A small pulse was pounding in her smooth white neck. Her eyes *were* blue — and in Laramie's arms she was light as a bit of thistledown floating on the wind.

Panchita smiled at someone she knew; but her voice wasn't smiling when she spoke to Laramie, for his ears alone. *"What are you doing here?"*

"I'm Holy Joe Moran's partner."

"You're . . . you're only a boy!"

"I'm a man," Laramie said with the stubborn insistence of one who had to say it a lot.

Panchita did not argue. "Holy Joe did not tell me about you being here."

"No reason why he should, I reckon. He didn't want anyone to know he had anyone with him. I came here after Holy Joe tonight."

"After him," Panchita repeated with a choked laugh, and shifted into Spanish with the ease of one who used it as a second mother tongue. *"¡Madre de Dios!* You come after him *now!"*

226

"What's wrong about that?"

"You should have come before he got drunk. Now it's too late. He . . . he is going to be shot!"

Laramie forgot he was dancing, stumbled, and almost fell. He wasn't conscious of the eyes that were watching them, did not know that more than one person had been smiling at the sight of Panchita, who could have had her pick of any man on the floor, dancing with this ragged kid.

"Goin' to be shot!" Laramie gulped. A knot had balled up in his middle. He felt sick at the thought of it. Strangely he didn't doubt Panchita. Holy Joe — gigantic, loud-talking, wise old Holy Joe Moran — going to be shot. Laramie hadn't realized until this moment how much the old man really meant to him.

"Who's gonna shoot him?" Laramie swallowed awkwardly. "What for?"

"He started a fight. Before they could stop him, a man was killed. Holy Joe didn't fire the shot . . . but in Tres Angeles that doesn't matter. Don Antonio has decided Holy Joe is guilty and will be shot. Don Antonio is the *jefe*."

Casting about for some hope, Laramie asked hoarsely: "Ain't this Don Antonio your sweetie? Can't you do somethin' about it?"

Panchita laughed. It was a despairing laugh, almost hysterical. "Perhaps I could do something," she said, and her voice quavered near to tears. "I've been on my knees in the church all afternoon praying to the good God to show me the way. Don Antonio will listen to me . . . but he has his price."

"What's that?"

"I go to live at his house."

"You mean marry him?"

"He has daughters older than I am," said Panchita. "His wife is living . . . but not in Tres Angeles."

Laramie's thin-corded arm tightened about her small shoulders. Sometimes a girl was up against worse than powder and lead.

Panchita went on talking in a voice that had gone dead and flat. "I spoke with Holy Joe before he got drunk. He promised to help me get north, over the border."

"What're you doin' here anyway? You don't have to stay."

"My mother was Mexican," said Panchita. "I was raised in California. I came to Mexico as a dancer. Our show went broke. I went to work for Dandy Gonzalez at his *cantina*. When he was killed, I was offered good money to dance here in the Holy Ghost *cantina*. It had sounded good. I came. And then Don Antonio decided he wanted me to stay. His word is law here in Tres Angeles. I can't leave. Don Antonio is like a cat playing with a mouse . . . waiting . . . !"

"Won't Colonel Ramiriz help you?"

She shivered in Laramie's arm. "You've been listening to them talk! They are laying bets on who wins me. Ramiriz is as bad as Don Antonio. They're both waiting, hating each other, demanding that I make my choice."

"You pore kid!" said Laramie, and tightened his arm again. "I'll help you."

"What can *you* do?"

"I don't know," Laramie confessed. "I'll think of somethin'. Where you stayin'?"

"With the sister of the priest, in the little house behind the church. I am safe with her for a time. But not even the priest can go against the anger of Don Antonio or

228

Colonel Ramiriz for too long."

"I've got a little account to settle with this Ramiriz," Laramie muttered.

"You've met him?"

"Look at my cheek."

Panchita looked, and in her blue eyes quick pity glowed. "Ramiriz *would* do something like that. He's cruel."

"I got a cure for that feelin'," Laramie promised. "I aim to cure him before I leave."

The music stopped. Laramie spoke very rapidly under his breath. "I seen Holy Joe in his cell just before dark. He ain't in it now. They've moved him. What do you reckon that means?"

"I don't know," said Panchita hopelessly. "Perhaps he is dead now."

Sudden fright leaped into her eyes. She gave Laramie's arm a push. A hand now slapped his other shoulder and spun him around.

Colonel Ramiriz was standing there, red with anger.

"¡Pelon!" Ramiriz said furiously. "You dare to put your dirty hands on her. For a *centavo* I would have you shot. Get out!" A fist knocked Laramie staggering into another couple. Laughter burst out as the man shoved Laramie aside. Ramiriz stood glowering with a hand near the gun he still wore.

Laramie straightened. One hand was in the pocket of his Levi's. The raw furrow on his cheek was flaming with blood. Panchita had caught Ramiriz's arm and begged him to come away. Ramiriz pushed her back.

"Get out!" he ordered Laramie angrily.

Laramie gulped. His shoulders were slumped. The hand came out of his pocket. He walked off the floor, staring right straight ahead. As he took his old hat from the hook and walked out of the Holy Ghost, laughter followed him. The music had started again. When he turned and looked around, Ramiriz was holding Panchita's slender figure close and they were dancing.

The night air cooled Laramie's hot face as he walked blindly to the middle of the plaza. Everything was a tangled mess. Holy Joe was going to be shot. Panchita was smiling to hide despair. In Tres Angeles no one but Laramie could help and he didn't even have a revolver. Laramie knew he was a man. He was ready to fight to prove it — but right now it took a fierce effort to keep a lump out of his throat. After all, he was alone, the border was a long way north, and the odds were heavy. He didn't even know where Holy Joe Moran was.

IV

"AT DON ANTONIO'S"

Laramie was smoking a second cigarette when a slender figure in a dark cloak came hurrying under the plaza trees toward him. Panchita had his arm and was speaking before he recognized her.

"Quick! Over here it is darker! I ran out the back way. I have to get back quickly."

Panchita had taken off her gay shawl, her big comb, had thrown a black shawl over her head and put on a dark coat. She spoke rapidly as they walked in the darker shadows near the middle of the plaza, with the huge old trees towering over them.

230

"Don Antonio has taken your Holy Joe to the big house on the hill. Just before dark Don Antonio sent for him. Colonel Ramiriz could not refuse, but he is furious. Never have I seen Ramiriz in such a rage. It is a wonder he didn't shoot you. He wants to hurt something . . . anything. Even me," said Panchita desperately.

"What's the *jefe* want with Holy Joe up at his house?"

"I don't know. I think Ramiriz knows, but he won't tell me. But Ramiriz says in the morning Holy Joe will be shot . . . and his men will do the shooting. I think Ramiriz would like to kill Don Antonio too."

"He ain't the only one," Laramie retorted bitterly. "I got a pretty good idea what it's all about. Holy Joe come to town with some gold money. Don Antonio an' Ramiriz figger there's a heap more where it came from. They're tryin' to find out. Both want a whack at the gold, an' neither one's havin' any luck, an' each one's scared the other'll beat him to it. Each one's about ready to kill Holy Joe to keep the other'n from havin' any luck with him. I reckon your Don Antonio's havin' the last whack at Holy Joe tonight to see if he'll talk. Holy Joe won't last to get shot by Ramiriz."

"Not *my* Antonio!" Panchita protested fiercely. "I hate him . . . hate them both! And at Don Antonio's house you can do nothing. Armed men guard it day and night. Don Antonio knows many men would like to kill him."

"I'll look around," Laramie said.

"I think," said Panchita unsteadily, "that tonight you are going to die too. *Pobrecito* . . . poor little boy!"

"I'm a man!" said Laramie gruffly. "Watch yourself. You'll be cryin' in a minute. Just like a girl. Go on back an' keep the burrs outa your hair."

"Good bye," said Panchita. She said it in the manner

231

of one bidding farewell for good.

Before Laramie knew what was happening, Panchita stood on her toes, threw her arms around him, kissed him fully on the mouth. A fierce, moist, warm kiss.

"Good bye!" she said again. "I will always remember you, so young, so brave!"

She slipped off through the night.

Slowly Laramie lifted a hand and then rubbed his mouth. "Gosh!" he said gruffly. "What'd she go an' do that for . . . the little fool!" But Laramie's eyes were smarting, and down inside he didn't feel as gruff as he sounded.

Ten minutes later Laramie trudged up the steep grade which led to the residence of Don Antonio Ibarra. The gate in the high adobe wall was open. Through it he could see light in the big windows of the house and an armed sentry who stood before it.

Laramie did not try to hide his approach. As he advanced, he could see the man peering toward him, holding the rifle at ready.

In Spanish the guard called sharply: *"¿Quien es?"*

Laramie continued on, said meekly, "I want to see Don Antonio Ibarra, with your permission."

Laramie stepped into the lantern light, and the guard's vigilance relaxed somewhat as he saw what manner of person he was dealing with.

"I have a surprise for Don Antonio," Laramie said.

The guard, staring from narrowed eyes, said: *"¡Yanqui!"* He held his rifle so that the bayonet was at the ready. He had also a .45 revolver holstered at his waist.

"Sí," Laramie agreed. "I am a *Yanqui.* Where is Don Antonio?"

The guard showed bad teeth in a smile. "Don Antonio

232

is busy with another *Yanqui*. He has no time for you now. *Vamos*."

"*Bueno*," Laramie assented obediently.

He started to turn away. Grinning, the guard had lowered his rifle — and Laramie whirled back. His hand came out of his pocket. A blade flashed in the dim light. Before the guard knew what was happening, he was back against the wall with the blade at his throat.

"Inside!" Laramie ordered.

The guard backed through the gateway. Laramie followed, keeping the knife edge hard against the throat, guiding the man inside the wall, where the lantern light did not reach.

In the darkness there the quiet pressed heavily. Laramie could hear the man's breath hissing softly through his clenched teeth. The throat muscles quivered under the knife blade. Laramie's whisper was hoarse with the strain of it. "Where's the *Yanqui*?"

Stiff lips answered. "In the house, *señor*."

Aloud Laramie muttered in English, "I oughta slit your gullet . . . but I reckon that wouldn't help."

Laramie released his grip on the man's sleeve, felt for the revolver in the side holster, got it, and struck with the barrel. The guard collapsed on his rifle and stayed there.

Laramie took the revolver, gun belt, rifle, and left the man. Don Antonio's house was easily the largest in Tres Angeles. Inside the adobe wall, behind the main house, were some smaller buildings. Lighted windows in the big house suggested life within but, when Laramie stepped close to the windows, he heard no voices inside.

He walked to the side of the house, caught the smell of a stable, saw a lighted window or so in the smaller buildings, heard a woman crooning a song, a man laugh. But that was back in the darkness. Laramie drifted close to the main house.

Holy Joe was inside. Servants and armed men would be in there also. How much chance did one man have against all that?

Behind him a door opened, letting out a square of dim light. A man stepped out, closed the door and turned toward Laramie, who had plastered himself up against the side of the house.

The man's padding steps were almost inaudible. He drew abreast of Laramie — and stopped suddenly as the revolver muzzle jabbed hard into his back. One startled gasp, and the man froze.

"Where is the *Yanqui?*" Laramie's voice was gritting.

"In the house, *señor. ¡Por Dios* . . . have mercy!"

"Take me to the *viejo.*"

The man edged carefully around and started back to the door. He was shaking as he opened the door and stepped inside. A lamp in a wall bracket shed light along a low-ceilinged passageway. Near the end of the passageway they came to a heavy door. Before the door the man hesitated, still trembling.

"*Señor,*" he gulped, "I cannot! Don Antonio does not wish to be disturbed."

Laramie cocked the revolver. Words would not have carried the threat that the sharp click conveyed. The prisoner opened the door and advanced like a man going to his execution.

They descended a flight of steps that went down, down deep under the house. Laramie grew wary of a trap; he was more wary when he saw the gloomy, low passage into which they came. A damp stone wall rose on their right. On the left was a row of barred cells.

Here under his house Don Antonio had his own private *carcel*, his own jail. One single lantern hanging from a hook in the wall shed faint light.

"Where's Ibarra?" Laramie whispered.

"Here, *señor*."

Another thick door closed the end of the passage. A thread of light was visible under it. Laramie's prisoner stopped again, seemed to nerve himself, opened the door soundlessly. There was the whistling stroke of a rawhide whip, the dull, sodden impact of the lash on flesh covered their entrance. A voice ordered lazily, "Stop for a little, Pedro."

V

"THREE HORSES ARE READY"

The room was longer than it was wide, and low-ceilinged as was the passageway. A lamp on a wooden table and two wall lamps lighted it brightly. At the table a man sat with his back to the door. A revolver lay by his hand. A whiskey bottle and a glass stood near it.

Against the wall Holy Joe Moran stood stripped to the waist, lashed to a wooden framework with his back to the table. The peon who had been plying the whip was breathing heavily.

On Holy Joe's naked back long red weals glistened with fresh blood. The whip wielder stood stolidly watching Holy Joe's back. He did not turn his head as the man at the table put his cigarette down, reached for the whiskey bottle, and spoke politely.

"Perhaps, my friend, your memory improves?"

Holy Joe answered without turning his head. "My memory's all right. I said, 'To hell with you, Ibarra.' I'm still sayin' it."

Ibarra drank the whiskey he had just poured, smacked his lips, and drew deeply on the cigarette. Through the blue smoke he spoke sadly.

"If the whip does not kill you, you will be stood against a wall and shot. That would desolate me. Speak about the gold, and I will fill your pockets and give you an escort north of the border. On my honor as a gentleman, I swear it."

"You wouldn't know a gentleman if you saw one, Ibarra."

The *jefe* settled himself comfortably in the chair. "It is sad to see a man so stubborn," he sighed. "Pedro, ten lashes this time, lower, where the skin is not so much cut."

Pedro lifted the whip.

"Never mind, Pedro. Sit still, *chivo!*"

The last Laramie snapped at Ibarra who, with an oath, whirled quickly in the chair, grabbing for the revolver on the table. Ibarra saw Laramie's gun covering him from one side of the trembling servant. He snatched his pudgy hand back from the weapon on the table.

Twisted half around in the chair, he blustered, "Carlos, what is this?" His voice was not too steady.

Laramie's prisoner wailed, "*Patrón*, this *Yanqui* would have killed me!"

"Shut up!" Laramie ordered. "Get away from that table, Ibarra! Tell your *mozo* to free the *viejo!*"

Holy Joe had turned his head; he spoke now violently.

"You damn' fool, kid! I told you to get outa town! You've jabbed your head into a trap now."

"I ain't in any hurry to leave," Laramie said. "Move fast, Ibarra. I'm itchin' to see if a *jefe* dies like a *mozo*."

Biting his lip with impotent anger, Ibarra lurched away from the table. His voice shook as he ordered the man with the whip to free Holy Joe.

Holy Joe staggered as he stepped back from the wooden framework. His wrists were swollen where the cords had cut deeply. He had to massage his hand for a moment before he could pick Ibarra's gun off the table. With the gun in his hand, Holy Joe seemed to swell, to tower and grow more huge as he turned, with the white beard sweeping down over his naked chest.

Ibarra dropped his eyes from the terrible look Holy Joe fastened on him. But when Holy Joe spoke, his words were as soft and polite as Ibarra's voice had been.

"You will be pleased to try it yourself." Holy Joe gestured with the gun. "Tie him up," he said.

"Wait a minute," Laramie was saying. "There's hosses in a stable out back. Make him order three of 'em saddled an' held at the gate."

"Three?" said Holy Joe.

"I seen Panchita."

Holy Joe grunted approvingly. "Three it is, Ibarra. Open the door a little and order three horses at the gate."

Holy Joe gripped Ibarra's coat collar from the back and held the *jefe* while Ibarra's shouts through the slightly opened door brought a man running down from above.

Ibarra gave the order for the horses and, when the servant had left, Holy Joe spun the *jefe* over to the wooden rack and closed the door.

"Tie him up, strip his back, and use the whip," Holy Joe ordered grimly.

Ibarra did not struggle. He feared death more than the whip. And his servants feared Holy Joe Moran's terrible quietness more than they did their master. Ibarra stood three strokes of the lash, then began to whimper, groan, struggle.

Holy Joe gulped a stiff drink, pulled his shirt on over his bleeding back, donned his coat on top of that, and stood watching grimly. Ibarra suddenly went limp and hung by his wrists.

"Enough," Holy Joe ordered. "I want him to live and remember."

A knock sounded on the door. "*Patrón*, the horses are ready!"

Holy Joe opened the door a little, keeping behind it. "Come in," he said mildly.

But the man retreated from the door. "Don Antonio!" he called.

Swearing, Holy Joe opened the door wide. The servant was already bolting down the passage, shouting an alarm. Holy Joe fired twice, cursed, and called over his shoulder.

"Come on, kid! I plugged him, but he got up the steps. We'll have to shoot our way out now."

They left two servants there with Don Antonio Ibarra and ran along the passage. The man Holy Joe had shot lay sprawled at the top of the steps, half way through the open door. Holy Joe burst out past him with white beard flying and gun cocked. The two female servants who had ventured into the hall screamed and ran. Men shouting, feet running.

"They'll have the hull damn' army out again!" Holy Joe

rasped as he ran out into the night. "Which way's to them hosses, kid?"

Laramie took the lead in the darkness, skirting the house to the front, where the horses should be.

"The hull damn' place's like a hornet's nest!" Holy Joe panted and raced past Laramie.

They reached the front of the house, saw the gate still standing open in the dim glow of the lantern outside. Saddled horses were standing inside, the gate held by two men. The uproar in the house was audible out here. The man at the horses had evidently been uncertain what to do. Laramie ran out, snapping a shot at the nearest Mexican. The man took one look and tried to stampede the horses by slashing them across the faces with the rein ends before he ran. The other man closed in with a drawn knife.

Holy Joe's long arm lashed out. His other hand scooped at the reins. Holy Joe was still struggling when Laramie's revolver jammed in the face of Holy Joe's assailant. The man dropped the knife and turned to run. At that moment the frantic voice of Don Antonio Ibarra rose in the night.

"Kill them! Kill the *Yanquis!*"

Soldiers and Don Antonio's men came running from the front of the house.

VI

"THE RAWHIDE KID FIGHTS BACK"

Holy Joe mumbled disgustedly, "I mighta knowed he'd get loose in a hurry. I should 'a' kilt him an' had done with it. That other hoss got away! Dust your leather! Here they come!"

Back in the night beside the house a gun barked. Other guns joined in as they swung up into the saddles and pounded through the gate and down the steep road toward the houses of Tres Angeles.

Holy Joe swore in his beard. "We'll never get into the Holy Ghost an' get Panchita outa that crowd! She was a cute kid, too, an' I promised her to help."

Out of the houses people were running also. Laramie swung his horse into the dark street at the left.

"Maybe she's home," he called, and rode hard.

The little one-storied house where the priest lived was not difficult to find. Snuggled back of the larger mass of the church, it was dark and quiet.

"She ain't here!" Laramie gulped as Holy Joe stopped beside him.

"Have to leave her then! I hate to do it, but if we go in the plaza, we're goners."

"You ride on," said Laramie desperately. "I'll wait here. Maybe she'll savvy what the trouble is an' start home."

Laramie climbed down off his horse.

"I reckon I've lived long enough anyway," Holy Joe said with resignation. "Gimme them reins! That horse'll bolt if a shadow moves."

"You don't have to stay."

"Shut up!" Holy Joe snapped.

The high warning cry of a girl came from inside the house. "Look out! Ramiriz is . . . !"

Panchita's warning was cut short by the crashing report of a gun in the doorway. Other shots followed. Laramie felt the first bullet slap through the crown of his old hat. But only that one. The red licking flashes from the gun were erratic. Each following shot came from a different position, as if the gunman were struggling with someone.

Laramie had snatched his gun and cocked it at the first shot. Then the truth hit him. He couldn't stop his shot, but he managed to twist the muzzle aside and down, throwing the bullet to one side of the doorway, then he dropped the gun and plunged forward, reaching into his pocket.

The fifth shot was delayed an instant. Two struggling figures were barely visible in the doorway. In his ears Laramie heard a voice swearing wildly in Spanish.

Panchita had caught Ramiriz's arm as he opened fire, was struggling with him. Any shot intended for Ramiriz might hit her. Laramie moved so fast he was entering the doorway as his hand came out of his pocket. His thumb pressed a button in the knife handle and the sharp blade flicked out.

Panchita cried out with pain and stumbled back. Ramiriz's gun was invisible — but Laramie knew what was coming. He dodged as best he could, entering the hallway in a twisting plunge. And the sixth shot, the last shot in Ramiriz's gun, blasted almost in his face.

Powder particles burnt the skin. Laramie felt the shock

of the bullet in the muscles of his left shoulder. Blinded by the flash, he lunged against the gun muzzle. Swearing, Ramiriz stumbled back, clubbing the gun, striking down. The blow fouled on the high crown and broad brim of Laramie's old hat, and ended on his shoulder, not too hard. Ramiriz caught him by the throat, squeezing wildly.

Helpless, Laramie knew Ramiriz would brain him in another moment. He plunged the knife high into Ramiriz's throat. Ramiriz fell heavily, and he never spoke again after that.

Panchita was sobbing. Holy Joe charged into the doorway, shouting: "Did he get you, kid?"

"I'm all right."

Holy Joe saw Ramiriz's body. "My God! You used that knife! Makes me cold every time you take it out an' start practicin'! Is the girl here?"

"I've got my arm around her," said Laramie in the darkness. "Can't you hear her cryin'?"

"Great red-eyed rattlers!" Holy Joe exploded. "Git your arm away from her! Toss her on a hoss! Them shots was heard all over town!"

Panchita gulped, "Ramiriz followed me. Father Martínez and his sister are away for the night. He . . . he wouldn't leave, not even when he heard the trouble. I was s-scratching his face when you came."

"Never mind about that! Here we go!"

Panchita clung tightly to Laramie's hand as they ran outside. She wasn't the little beauty of the Holy Ghost *cantina* now. She was only a girl, shaken and terrified by blood and violence.

The horses stood where Holy Joe had left them. Laramie swung into the saddle. Holy Joe gave Panchita a quick boost up, and then swung on his own horse. From both ends of the street men were shouting.

"This way!" Holy Joe yelled, yanking his horse around away from the plaza.

In the lead, kicking his horse into a wild gallop, Holy Joe gave a shrill cowboy yell. Across the saddle, in front of Laramie, Panchita clung tightly as they followed Holy Joe. Ahead of them the tumult grew. Holy Joe's fierce yell cut the night again. His gun blasted and they rode furiously through an angry crowd scattering on both sides.

Bending low over Panchita, Laramie raced after Holy Joe. They turned sharply down a darker street, rode between houses where lighted doorways showed watching figures. But no one tried to stop them. No shots followed them down this dark street. Only dogs barked and were left behind. And in a few minutes Tres Angeles was behind and they were riding through the open night, following a dirt road off which Holy Joe soon turned.

They rode half a mile off the road, stopped, listened, and presently heard pursuit drumming along the road off which they had turned. No one swung over toward them. Holy Joe made sure of that, grunted with satisfaction, and rode on toward the first slopes of the hills to the east.

"We'll stay off the roads an' be outa their district by morning," Holy Joe said. "It'll take more riders than Tres Angeles has to pick us up by then. How's the girl?"

Panchita was still clinging to Laramie. Slender, soft, warm, she was not so tense now.

"I . . . I think I'm all right," Panchita said. "But I am still afraid."

Holy Joe snorted. "You needn't be, with that young

wildcat carrying you! Tres Angeles'll be talkin' about him when the babies has grandchildren." Holy Joe chuckled. "Ain't he some kid?"

"I ain't a kid," Laramie said stubbornly.

From the crook of his arm, Panchita helped him. "He is a man, Mister Holy Joe. I didn't think so when I first saw him . . . but I know now."

Holy Joe chuckled. "Shore, I know it, but I gotta be reminded of it. He fools me same as he does everyone else. Laramie, you sure that gold is hid good?"

"Plenty."

"We'll leave it lay for a little an' get Panchita acrost the border." Holy Joe chuckled again. "We hit these parts with a mule load o' gold . . . an' we're going out with a pretty gal. It shore is a joke on someone."

"I'd rather be taking her out th-than the gold," Laramie stammered.

"Shucks," said Holy Joe. "Takes a man to talk like that. I reckon you are a man at that. Hold her tight, kid. We got some hard ridin' ahead."

Laramie continued to hold on tightly.

THE END

ABOUT THE AUTHOR

T. T. Flynn was born Thomas Theodore Flynn, Jr., in Indianapolis, Indiana. He was the author of over a hundred Western short novels for such leading pulp magazines as Street and Smith's *Western Story Magazine*, Popular Publications's *Dime Western*, and Dell's *Zane Grey's Western Magazine*. His short novel "Hell's Half Acre" appeared in the issue that launched Star Western in 1933.

He moved to New Mexico with his wife Helen and spent much of his time living in a trailer while on the road exploring the vast terrain of the American West. His descriptions of the land are always detailed, but he used them not only for local color but also to reflect the heightening of emotional distress among the characters within a story.

Following the Second World War, Flynn turned his attention to the book-length Western novel and in this form also produced work that has proven imperishable. Five of these novels first appeared as original paperbacks, most notably *The Man From Laramie*, which was featured as a serial in *The Saturday Evening Post* and subsequently made into a memorable motion picture directed by Anthony Mann and starring James Stewart. *Two Faces West*, which deals with the problems of identity and reality, served as the basis for a television series.

Flynn was highly innovative and inventive and in later novels, such as *Riding High*, concentrated on deeper psychological issues as the source for conflict, rather than more elemental motives like greed. He was so meticulous about his research that he once spent days to determine the exact year that blue-(as opposed to red-) checked tablecloths were introduced. All anachronism was anathema to him. Flynn is at his best in stories that combine mystery—not surprisingly, he also wrote detective fiction—suspense, and action in an artful balance. The world where his characters live is often a comedy of errors in which the first step in any direction frequently can, and does, lead to ever deepening complications.

NIGHT
OF THE
COMANCHE
MOON

T. T. FLYNN

Ann Carruthers has no idea what searching for her brother in the wild New Mexico Territory will mean. But what else can a girl, even an English girl not much past twenty, do when her brother vanishes? How can she know that bandits, Indians, and violence are things people in the territory live with every day? Ann doesn't realize how much danger she is in until the son of a Comanche chief offers one hundred horses for her. To save herself she has to pretend to belong to John Hardisty. Sure, he is a loner and a hardcase, but he can ride, shoot, and fight. And he is her one chance of survival in the lawless wilderness.

___4689-X $4.50 US/$5.50 CAN

Dorchester Publishing Co., Inc.
P.O. Box 6640
Wayne, PA 19087-8640

Please add $1.75 for shipping and handling for the first book and $.50 for each book thereafter. NY, NYC, and PA residents, please add appropriate sales tax. No cash, stamps, or C.O.D.s. All orders shipped within 6 weeks via postal service book rate. Canadian orders require $2.00 extra postage and must be paid in U.S. dollars through a U.S. banking facility.

Name_____
Address_____
City_____ State_____ Zip_____
I have enclosed $ _____ in payment for the checked book(s).
Payment <u>must</u> accompany all orders. ❏ Please send a free catalog.

RATTLESNAKE

T. V. OLSEN

The Apache wars took almost everything from Indian Jim
Izancho. Now Senator Warrender wants the one thing he has
left—his land—and Warrender's Indian-hating son soon
begins a reign of terror against the Izancho family. The only
man who will try to save Jim is his boyhood friend, Sheriff
Frank Tenney. Only Tenney can stop a deadly feud between
a white man—who happens to be his father-in-law—and the
Apache who once saved his life, a man who has been pushed
too far and is now hell-bent on vengeance, a man as
dangerous as a cornered rattlesnake.

___4620-2 $4.50 US/$5.50 CAN

Dorchester Publishing Co., Inc.
P.O. Box 6640
Wayne, PA 19087-8640

Please add $1.75 for shipping and handling for the first book and
$.50 for each book thereafter. NY, NYC, and PA residents,
please add appropriate sales tax. No cash, stamps, or C.O.D.s. All
orders shipped within 6 weeks via postal service book rate.
Canadian orders require $2.00 extra postage and must be paid in
U.S. dollars through a U.S. banking facility.

Name_____

Address_____

City_____ State_____ Zip_____

I have enclosed $_____ in payment for the checked book(s).
Payment <u>must</u> accompany all orders. ❑ Please send a free catalog.
CHECK OUT OUR WEBSITE! www.dorchesterpub.com

A KILLER IS WAITING

T. V. OLSEN

Will Parry lost an arm in the Civil War, but he finds the strength to carry on with his life, to build a future for himself and his family on a ranch in the Wyoming Rockies. But that bright future starts to turn dark when a shadowy gunman begins shooting at Parry's house. It isn't long before Parry learns the identity of an enemy he never knew he had, a man with a bitter grudge still festering from the war. A man with the cunning of an animal—and the cold-blooded patience of an executioner. Parry knows he'll die if he has to in order to protect his family, and when he looks out into the black night he also knows a killer is waiting.

___4549-4 $4.50 US/$5.50 CAN

Dorchester Publishing Co., Inc.
P.O. Box 6640
Wayne, PA 19087-8640

Please add $1.75 for shipping and handling for the first book and $.50 for each book thereafter. NY, NYC, and PA residents, please add appropriate sales tax. No cash, stamps, or C.O.D.s. All orders shipped within 6 weeks via postal service book rate. Canadian orders require $2.00 extra postage and must be paid in U.S. dollars through a U.S. banking facility.

Name_____
Address_____
City_____ State_____ Zip_____
I have enclosed $_____ in payment for the checked book(s).
Payment <u>must</u> accompany all orders. ❑ Please send a free catalog.
CHECK OUT OUR WEBSITE! www.dorchesterpub.com

BLOOD RAGE

T. V. OLSEN

Mike Rhiannon's Irish temper rarely slips, but when it does, Alec Dragoman—Rhiannon's oldest enemy—is almost always the cause. Now Comanches have kidnapped Dragoman's daughter, and he will go to any lengths to get Melissa back, even if that means forcing Rhiannon to help him. Against his will—and his better judgment—Rhiannon leads a ragged band against the Comanches to rescue young Melissa. But will Dragoman keep his end of the bargain?

__4500-1 $3.99 US/$4.99 CAN

Dorchester Publishing Co., Inc.
P.O. Box 6640
Wayne, PA 19087-8640

Please add $1.75 for shipping and handling for the first book and $.50 for each book thereafter. NY, NYC, and PA residents, please add appropriate sales tax. No cash, stamps, or C.O.D.s. All orders shipped within 6 weeks via postal service book rate. Canadian orders require $2.00 extra postage and must be paid in U.S. dollars through a U.S. banking facility.

Name_____
Address_____
City_____ State_____ Zip_____
I have enclosed $_____ in payment for the checked book(s).
Payment <u>must</u> accompany all orders. ❑ Please send a free catalog.
     CHECK OUT OUR WEBSITE! www.dorchesterpub.com

DEADLY
PURSUIT

T. V. OLSEN

Silas Pine is about to turn fifty. What he wants more than
anything is one last chance to make peace with his son, who
is marshal in the isolated town of Grafton, Wyoming. But
arriving in the middle of a bank robbery isn't quite the way
Silas has pictured the reunion. Neither is leading a posse in
a pursuit more deadly than bullets.

___4463-3 $4.50 US/$5.50 CAN

Dorchester Publishing Co., Inc.
P.O. Box 6640
Wayne, PA 19087-8640

Please add $1.75 for shipping and handling for the first book and
$.50 for each book thereafter. NY, NYC, and PA residents,
please add appropriate sales tax. No cash, stamps, or C.O.D.s. All
orders shipped within 6 weeks via postal service book rate.
Canadian orders require $2.00 extra postage and must be paid in
U.S. dollars through a U.S. banking facility.

Name_____
Address_____
City_____State_____Zip_____
I have enclosed $_____ in payment for the checked book(s).
Payment <u>must</u> accompany all orders. ☐ Please send a free catalog.

MEN BEYOND THE LAW

These three short novels showcase Max Brand doing what he does best: exploring the wild, often dangerous life beyond the constraints of cities, beyond the reach of civilization . . . beyond the law. Whether he's a desperate man fleeing the tragic results of a gunfight, an innocent young man who stumbles onto the loot from a bank robbery, or the gentle giant named Bull Hunter—one of Brand's most famous characters—each protagonist is out on his own, facing two unknown frontiers: the Wild West . .. and his own future.

___4873-6 $4.50 US/$5.50 CAN

Dorchester Publishing Co., Inc.
P.O. Box 6640
Wayne, PA 19087-8640

Please add $2.50 for shipping and handling for the first book and $.75 for each book thereafter. NY, NYC, and PA residents, please add appropriate sales tax. No cash, stamps, or C.O.D.s. All orders shipped within 6 weeks via postal service book rate.
Canadian orders require $2.50 extra postage and must be paid in U.S. dollars through a U.S. banking facility.

Name_____
Address_____
City_____ State_____ Zip_____
I have enclosed $_____ in payment for the checked book(s).
Payment <u>must</u> accompany all orders. ❑ Please send a free catalog.
        CHECK OUT OUR WEBSITE! www.dorchesterpub.com

MAX BRAND

RONICKY DOONE

First Time In Paperback!

"Brand is a topnotcher!"
—*New York Times*

Doone's name is famous throughout the Old West. From Tombstone to Sonora he's won the respect of every law-abiding citizen—and the hatred of every bushwhacking bandit. But Bill Gregg isn't one to let a living legend get in his way, and he'll shoot Doone dead as soon as look at him. What nobody tells Gregg is that Doone doesn't enjoy living his hard-riding, rip-roaring life unless he takes a chance on losing it once in a while.

_3738-6 $3.99 US/$4.99 CAN

Dorchester Publishing Co., Inc.
P.O. Box 6640
Wayne, PA 19087-8640

Please add $1.75 for shipping and handling for the first book and $.50 for each book thereafter. NY, NYC, and PA residents, please add appropriate sales tax. No cash, stamps, or C.O.D.s. All orders shipped within 6 weeks via postal service book rate. Canadian orders require $2.00 extra postage and must be paid in U.S. dollars through a U.S. banking facility.

Name_____
Address_____
City_____ State_____ Zip_____
I have enclosed $_____ in payment for the checked book(s).
Payment <u>must</u> accompany all orders. ☐ Please send a free catalog.

THE MOUNTAIN FUGITIVE

First Time In Paperback!

"Brand is a topnotcher!"
—New York Times

A wild youth, Lee Porfilo is always in trouble. If he isn't knocking someone down, he is ready to battle any cowpoke who comes along. But a penniless brawler can't stand up to the power of rich ranchers, and the Chase brothers will do whatever it takes to defeat Lee—even frame him for murder.

Porfilo has to choose between the hangman's noose and a desperate bid to prove his innocence. His every move dogged by lawmen and bounty hunters, he flees into the wilderness. But a man can't run forever, and Lee Profilo would rather die facing his enemies head on than live as an outlaw and coward.

__3574-X $3.99 US/$4.99 CAN

Dorchester Publishing Co., Inc.
P.O. Box 6640
Wayne, PA 19087-8640

Please add $1.75 for shipping and handling for the first book and $.50 for each book thereafter. NY, NYC, and PA residents, please add appropriate sales tax. No cash, stamps, or C.O.D.s. All orders shipped within 6 weeks via postal service book rate. Canadian orders require $2.00 extra postage and must be paid in U.S. dollars through a U.S. banking facility.

Name_____
Address_____
City_____State_____Zip_____
I have enclosed $_____ in payment for the checked book(s).
Payment <u>must</u> accompany all orders. ❑ Please send a free catalog.

MAX BRAND

THE WHISPERING OUTLAW

FIRST TIME IN PAPERBACK!

"Brand is a topnotcher!"
—New York Times

He is a mystery among frontier bandits—a masked gunman who never shows his true face or speaks in his honest voice. A loner by design, The Whisperer holds that it is above all foolishness for a man to have a partner in crime if he hopes to ride free. But a gent who plays a lone hand will never make a big killing.

So The Whisperer decides to do something either wildly desperate or extremely clever. He plans a spree of daring robberies that will make him a legend, and for a gang, he recruits a passel of ornery outlaws. All The Whisperer wants is one chance to strike it rich—all it will take to bring him down is one man who gets too greedy.

_3678-9 $3.99 US/$4.99 CAN

Dorchester Publishing Co., Inc.
65 Commerce Road
Stamford, CT 06902

Please add $1.75 for shipping and handling for the first book and $.50 for each book thereafter. NY, NYC, PA and CT residents, please add appropriate sales tax. No cash, stamps, or C.O.D.s. All orders shipped within 6 weeks via postal service book rate. Canadian orders require $2.00 extra postage and must be paid in U.S. dollars through a U.S. banking facility.

Name_____
Address_____
City _____ State_____Zip_____
I have enclosed $_____in payment for the checked book(s).
Payment <u>must</u> accompany all orders.□ Please send a free catalog.

ATTENTION BOOK LOVERS!

CAN'T GET ENOUGH
OF YOUR FAVORITE WESTERNS?

CALL 1-800-481-9191 TO:

- ORDER BOOKS,
- RECEIVE A **FREE** CATALOG,
- JOIN OUR BOOK CLUBS TO **SAVE 20%**!

OPEN MON.-FRI. 10 AM-9 PM EST

VISIT
WWW.DORCHESTERPUB.COM
FOR SPECIAL OFFERS AND INSIDE
INFORMATION ON THE AUTHORS
YOU LOVE.

 LEISURE BOOKS

We accept Visa, MasterCard or Discover®.